C000062973

Near Death

Near Death

By

Richard C Hale

This book is a work of fiction. Names, characters, places and incidents are either the product of the author's imagination or are used fictitiously. Any resemblance to actual persons, living or dead, or to actual events or locales is entirely coincidental.

Copyright © 2011 Richard C Hale. All rights reserved, including the right to reproduce this book, or portions thereof, in any form. No part of the text may be reproduced, transmitted, downloaded, decompiled, reverse engineered, or stored in or introduced into any information storage and retrieval system, in any form or by any means, whether electronic or mechanical without the express written permission of the author. The scanning, uploading, and distribution of this book via the Internet or via any other means without the permission of the publisher is illegal and punishable by law. Please purchase only authorized electronic editions, and do not participate in or encourage electronic piracy of copyrighted material.

Cover Designed by: Richard C. Hale; Jacksonville skyline courtesy of Devon Bradford.

Copyright ©Richard C Hale 2011

ISBN: 098477890X
ISBN-13: 978-0-9847789-0-4

For Mom, I know you would have loved this

Please Visit the Author's Website at:

http://www.richardchaleauthor.com

Richard always answers e-mails. Drop by the website and say 'Hello!'

ACKNOWLEDGMENTS

First, I'd like to thank my wonderful wife and family for putting up with me during this period of discovery. If not for their support, I may never have had the courage to see this through.

Thanks to my friend and mentor, Chuck Barrett, for his encouragement when I needed it and his constructive criticism. The tale would never have been told if he hadn't lit the fire in me.

Thank you to my readers: Kin Daniels, Chris Klein, Amanda Hale, Liesl Powers, Tony Villereal, Bruce Kessler, Dianne Hale, Tanya Christensen, Matthew Shafer, Gary Weaver, Emily Hale, Paula Hale, Nancy Beggs, Lynn Hale, Ann Hale, and Mark Brown. Your wisdom and insight helped shape the story and keep me on the path.

Thanks to Devon Bradford for the fantastic picture of the Jacksonville skyline at night.

Many believe Near Death Experiences to be real and to those who have lived through them, very powerful. If you would like more information and to read thousands of actual testimonials, please visit the Near Death Experience Research Foundation at their website, http://www.nderf.org/

Part 1

Richard C Hale

PROLOGUE

Jake Townsend turned to his pregnant wife of two years and said, "Sorry it's so late. I can't believe I kept you out this long. Do you hate me?"

Beth smiled, touched his face and said, "No, silly, I was having fun too. Karen and Vito always throw a good party." She rubbed her slightly distended belly. "I don't think she sleeps anyway."

Jake was annoyed with himself for losing track of time and keeping his wife out past 2:00 a.m. He knew better. Their unborn child was not getting its proper rest and this was his fault. Beth seemed to somehow sense his distress and grabbed his hand, placing it on her rounded stomach. She then moved it a little to the left. He felt a little burble under his fingertips as their child shifted inside her.

His angst melted away and he smiled. "He's practicing his field goal kicks again."

Jake signaled and maneuvered the old Toyota Land Cruiser off of A1A in Callahan, Florida, and headed south on U.S. 1 toward home in Orange Park. The vehicle was the only one on the road at this late hour.

"You mean *her* cheerleading kicks?" Beth said.

Jake laughed.

The baby continued to press softly against his palm. He still couldn't believe he was going to be a father in just four short months. He was excited and terrified all at the same time.

Jake's cell phone rang and it startled him. He couldn't figure who would be calling him this late. He glanced down at the LCD on the phone and shook his head as he smiled.

He said to Beth, "Tony."

She nodded and smiled. "He probably wants you to hang out tomorrow. He still tries to take you away from me."

Jake laughed. He pressed a button on the phone and said, "Yo! What's up man?"

An obviously drunk and angry Tony said, "I left the bitch, that's what's up! I can't stand her! She's ruining my life."

"Whoa!—calm down buddy. What happened?"

Beth asked "What's wrong?! What happened?!" and Jake couldn't hear what Tony was saying.

"Hold on honey, give me just a sec...no, not you Tony, go ahead."

Beth gasped and Jake looked up to see a huge deer standing in the road. He jammed on the brakes, swerved to miss it, but the top heavy Land Cruiser never had a chance and as the vehicle began flipping, Beth started screaming.

It was the most violent thing Jake had ever experienced. He was tossed from side to side like a ragdoll and before the Land Cruiser came to rest on its passenger side, Jake's head slammed into the door frame and everything went blank.

Total darkness. The sound of dripping and hissing. His head pounded and he could feel something wet and sticky on his face. Jake was hanging almost upside down, tangled in his seatbelt, filled with shock and fear.

He called out "Beth!" but all that escaped his lips was a whispered croak.

He coughed, spat blood and then yelled louder. "Beth!"

He searched frantically around the inside of the car and could see nothing. He was beginning to panic now as he struggled with his seatbelt, blood running into his left eye hampering his vision. He kept calling her name, but could hear no answer.

The seat belt finally let go and he suddenly thumped face down against the pavement, but still in the car, the passenger window shattered, and the cold asphalt digging into his skin.

Kicking and wrestling his legs under him he finally stood with his head popping up through the driver's window. His right shoulder protesting as he tried to clamber up and out of the window, he slammed back into the SUV.

Struggling and clawing up and out, Jake fell onto the pavement beside the car, crying out. Shaking, he stood, looking around, trying to find Beth. The moonless night and the eerie glow of his taillights were all he could see at first. He thought he could make out a vague shape lying on the road back there.

Calling Beth's name, terrified, he came upon her motionless body and sank to his knees beside her.

"Beth! Oh God. Beth! Can you hear me?! Are you all right?!"

Forcibly getting a grip on himself, he could see and feel her breathing ever so shallowly. *She was alive!*

Looking and feeling for injuries, he was hampered by the low light and the blood in his eyes. Headlights appeared over the horizon, and as the distant car approached, more light bathed the scene and his wife.

Massive amounts of blood were around her head and pooled around her upper body. As the light brightened he could see a pulsing gush of blood flowing from a large gash on her neck.

Jake moaned. He knew it was bad.

He slapped his hand over the gash but blood still oozed and leaked from around his fingers. He knew she would need immediate attention to survive. There was no one to give it out here.

"Oh God, Beth, no…hang in there! Come on!"

He ripped his shirt sleeve and used it like a bandage, pressing firmly on her neck and the flow seemed to subside a little.

As the car approached and slowed, Beth woke and turned onto her back. She immediately coughed up blood and her breathing sounded harsh and ragged. When she stopped coughing, small bubbles of blood formed on her lips and burst silently as she struggled to breathe. The wound in her neck now had air escaping through it and was making a wet rattling sound. She was drowning.

"Beth! I'm going to roll you on your side so you can breathe. It's all right! I'm here."

The approaching car stopped and Jake could hear footsteps rapidly coming toward them as a voice called, "Oh, man! Is she all right?!"

Jake yelled, "Call nine one one! Hurry! My wife!"

The stranger yelled back toward his idling car, "Sammy! Use the cell! Call nine one one! Now!"

Beth was trying to speak, but Jake couldn't hear her.

"Don't talk," Jake said. "You need to save your strength." But she continued to say things he couldn't hear.

"Hey man. Can you turn your engine off?" Jake said to the man kneeling beside him. "She's trying to tell me something and I can't hear her."

"Sure—yeah—sure. I got it!" The man jumped up and ran off.

As the engine died, he leaned close and heard Beth say, "Jake, I'm so cold. And I can't see you. Where are you?"

"I'm right here, Baby. Right here. I've got you. Just stay still. You're hurt and you couldn't breathe on your back, so stay on your side and lie still. I'm here and everything is going to be all right."

She coughed hard, her whole body wracked with spasms. More blood trickled from her mouth. She looked pale and ashen and seemed so frail and weak. Jake was scared she was slipping away

"Jake, I'm feeling better now. Not cold anymore, but I can't see you. It's so bright here. Where am I? Where are you? I can hear you, but I can't see you. It's so bright! Jake?"

The man came back to Jake's side and said, "They're coming. What can I do?"

"Can you turn off the headlights, she keeps saying they're too bright?"

"Sure, anything."

The man got back up and ran to the car, extinguishing the headlights.

"There Baby, is that better?" Jake asked Beth.

"Is what better, Jake? I feel ok, just tired. So tired. I still can't see you and its getting so bright. It feels good. The light. Mom? Where did you come from? Where's Jake?"

Jake knew Beth's mother had passed away when she was young. He couldn't understand what she was talking about.

"Beth, I'm right here. I love you! Everything will be ok."

"Oh—there you are Jake," Beth said smiling weakly. "You're so far away though—ok Mom. Jake—Mom's here with me now. I'm ok. I'm not cold anymore and I don't hurt. I love you! Be good to Madison and Lucas."

This last part so faint, Jake wasn't sure what he'd heard. He carefully cradled her in his arms trying to hear.

"Beth, what? Stay with me! I've got you! I've got you!"

"Madison and Lucas—Ter…" Beth said, faintly. "Love you…"

She went limp in his arms and the blood stopped flowing from her wound.

He pulled her tight to him and cried, "No! Beth! No! Stay with me! I can't lose you. No! Beth! Please!"

Sobbing into her still breast, a pain erupting from within him so great he thought he would burst, he wailed in anguish, and felt her slip away.

* * *

Dawn broke over Kandahar Airbase and Qayum Omar rose from his hiding place in the rock outcropping and peered over the boulder at the airfield. He smiled.

He glanced down at the weapon on the ground and waited for the Marines to assemble in the mess hall for breakfast.

The morning was cool and clear. Only a slight breeze was coming through the pass just to the north of his position. The wind would have negligible impact on his plans. The conditions were almost perfect.

He watched as the men filed into the open double doors, chatting and slapping each other on the back as they waited in line. Even from this distance, the smell of food was drifting up toward him from below.

It was time.

He crouched and began assembling the weapon.

He held what many believed to be an expensive toy. A radio controlled aircraft which he had purchased over the internet and modified for his needs. In his testing, it worked with deadly precision.

Turning on first the transmitter and then the electrical components of the aircraft, he armed the detonator and prepared to launch the plane into the morning air.

To him, the quiet whirring of the propeller as he tested it seemed very loud but he was confident the noise would be minimal and would not draw attention until it was too late.

Slipping the helmet on, he activated the virtual reality goggles and the screens in front of his eyes came to life. The helmet assembly displayed the view from a camera mounted to a gimbal system on the Styrofoam aircraft. He turned his head left and right testing the camera's ability to track his head movements.

Everything worked flawlessly.

As he pushed the left stick on the transmitter all the way forward, he heard the propeller spool up to full power and could feel the aircraft vibrating in his hand, waiting to be liberated. Pointing the nose up at about 45 degrees, he tossed the aircraft up and away from him, setting the weapon free.

The virtual reality goggles caused him to panic briefly as the world spun crazily, then the aircraft stabilized and climbed steadily above the desert floor. He leveled it off and pointed the nose directly at the mess hall doorway and watched it grow larger in his vision as the craft rapidly approached the base.

He dropped the aircraft's altitude until it was about head high above the desert scrub and remained there until the twenty foot fence loomed large before it. A little gust of wind buffeted the aircraft and he had to correct quickly to keep it from crashing into the dust.

Climbing again to clear the fence, he caught brief glimpses of faces manning the guard towers and watched as one saw the aircraft and pointed. It would not matter.

The doorway was very close and they would not be able to stop what was about to happen.

The line of men waiting to dine had thinned with most already inside sitting at their tables eating. The staccato of small arms fire drifted over the mile distance and reached the terrorist's ears, but soon stopped because the Marines would not risk hitting their own as the weapon flew closer to the mess hall.

He smiled and held his finger against the detonator switch. A few seconds more.

The doorway bloomed, filling the view completely as the aircraft flew through the opening. Flipping the detonator switch, he reflexively ducked as the screen flashed and then went blank.

The explosive shock wave reached him in his hiding place a second later. It was very strange to be so disassociated from the destruction, yet be right on top of it as viewed through the camera.

The last thing that Omar saw before the screen went blank was the shocked look of disbelief on the face of one of the Marines as he turned toward what must have been the whirring of the motor. The vision remained frozen in his mind as the craft struck the Marine and then exploded.

The terrorist packed his things quickly and fled into the mountains.

1

January 8, 2010 8:32 am

Two Years Later

Orange Park, Florida

Frank Lucas sat in the confessional and waited.

Soon he heard footsteps and watched as the vague shape of the priest entered the adjoining booth. He started to sweat.

"You may begin."

"Forgive me, Father, I cannot remember how long it has been since my last confession."

Only silence greeted this revelation and Frank waited, expecting some reaction he did not get.

"I'm not quite sure what to do next Father. Like I said, it's been a long time."

The priest sighed. "Tell me your sins and then the Act of Contrition. Do you remember the Act of Contrition prayer?"

"Not the whole prayer, Father. I'm sorry."

"It's printed on a plaque to your left and you may refer to it as needed. You may begin."

Frank took a large breath.

"This afternoon I lied to my wife about where I was going. She thinks I'm playing golf with my friends. Yesterday I..."

The priest interrupted him and said with some humor in his voice, "My son, if it truly has been as long as I think since your last confession we'll be here for the next month if you continue with these small, venial sins. It may be best for you to start with your mortal sins and we'll go from there."

"Yes, Father," Frank said, pausing. "I have killed a man."

Frank could see the silhouette of the priest react and heard him take a sharp, quick, breath.

He waited and finally the priest said, "Tell me, when did this happen?"

"Over thirty five years ago, Father."

"Now, tell me how this happened."

Frank told him.

As Frank spoke, an uncomfortable pressure started to spread across his chest. A pain, like a live wire electrifying his skin, raced up his arm and spread into his neck.

"I had no choice," Frank said, "he would have killed..."

Frank's voice faltered. He was having a hard time breathing. A high pitched whistling noise invaded the confessional and it took Frank a moment before he realized it was coming from his own lungs. His throat was clamping shut and he was unable to speak.

As the pain intensified, he thought, *I'm going to throw-up!*

He trembled and shook violently, then finally lost his balance as he fell from his bench and crashed through the confessional door onto the floor of the church.

The pain was overwhelming. Frank had never felt such anguish. It was a searing, tearing pain that seemed to permeate his whole body. He was blacking out.

He could see the priest over him yelling into a cell phone for an ambulance and then there was a final ripping pain along with a tearing sound.

Then the pain stopped.

He found himself moving up and away from the floor and thought the priest was helping him to stand, but then realized that he could see the priest and his own body below him. He was floating and felt surprisingly calm at this revelation.

Suddenly, his long dead father was next to him. He looked nothing like he remembered, but he instinctively knew it was his dad, only in a much younger body. He smiled at Frank and reached out to grasp his hand. As their fingers touched, two things happened simultaneously.

Frank heard a wonderful sound. It was the most glorious musical chord he had ever heard. Such a wondrous sound no human could ever imagine creating. Made up of impossible tones, it had such depth and color he wasn't sure if he was hearing the music, feeling it, or both. It washed over him and through him, making him feel so peaceful he never wanted it to end.

Along with the music came visions flying by on his left and right. It was his whole life. Everything that had ever happened to him. The good on the right, and the bad on the left, but no joy or sorrow accompanied the sights, only a feeling of complete amazement. A final tale of his life and all he had accomplished and all he had failed to do.

There was no judgment in the visions, only a sense of energy. A sense that his whole life had fueled something greater than himself and he felt proud and honored that it had some purpose he now understood.

As his dad held his hand and the music and visions surrounded them both, a glowing orb of light appeared over their heads; a golden radiance which pulsed and grew in beauty and brightness. He saw the parade of visions flow into the light, and he felt inexplicably drawn to it.

There was comfort and peace there. A peace he had never felt before. He moved toward it, his father smiling beside him.

Frank glanced down and realized the priest and the newly arrived paramedics were frantically working on his dying body. The scene was distant and fuzzy. He couldn't hear what was being said and his gaze kept wandering toward the light.

As the paramedics used a defibrillator on Frank, a huge sucking sound invaded the beautiful music and he heard his father say, "It's not time Frank. Soon."

The golden light began to fade and the sucking sound grew louder. Frank lost his grip on his father's hand and fell back toward his body.

Blackness followed and he awoke some time later in a hospital room filled with noises and smells from which he wished he could escape. A pang of sorrow and loss swept through him as he realized he was still alive. Then the smiling face of his wife, Eve, came into view and the world was good again.

Frank cried.

2

January 9, 2010 8:32 am

Orange Park, Florida

Jake Townsend entered his laboratory and found Peter Vargas hooked up to the machine.

His assistant, Teri Newton, was connecting leads to Peter's arms and legs. He frowned. He didn't like Peter Vargas.

Jake signaled Teri over as he walked in. She sighed and met him behind the console that housed all the computer components of the system.

"Why is he here?" Jake whispered.

"Rachael canceled," Teri said. "Her aunt is sick and she had to fly to Denver. He was the only one I could get on such short notice."

"All right. Nothing we can do about it, I guess. I was just thinking this morning that we shouldn't have brought him into the program. It's as if the machine doesn't like him."

The machine Jake was talking about was his own invention. NDEEE was her official name, but he called her Andee for short. The acronym stood for Neurologic Demand Encephalon Electrical Enhancer.

"Personally, I don't think Andee likes anyone," Teri said.

"She likes me," Jake said and grinned.

"She should. You spend enough time with her."

"She needs my attention. Until she finds what we're looking for, I need to baby her."

Teri rolled her eyes.

Jake knew she took some of Andee's failures personally.

In the simplest terms, Andee essentially read minds.

Since there was nothing else out there like it, Jake used the term EEG loosely to describe her, giving him something simple to associate her with so the normal every day layman could grasp a basic concept of her without having to get into all the technical jargon. In reality, she incorporated many different technologies including EEG, CAT, MRI and computer AI, or Artificial Intelligence.

Andee represented a huge leap in advanced electrical studies of the brain. Not only did she read the electrical activity, she could see a subatomic energy source in the body which had previously been undiscovered. She then attempted to interpret this activity and present it in a visual form. A video.

In the initial visit to the lab, Peter had been measured for what was essentially a mold that encompassed his whole body. This mold was how Andee was able to read the subatomic energy the body emitted during the session.

Other leads were connected to his head, arms, legs and torso which not only measured his vital signs, but also brain waves and other electrical activity. There were over one hundred wires attached to Peter, threaded through the body mold and then connected to various electrical components which led away into the ceiling where they fed information to Andee.

"How's Andee doing this morning?" Jake asked.

"She's a finicky bitch," Teri said and smiled. "But, I think she'll hold together."

Jake grinned back. Teri had a knack for speaking her mind. Andee was giving them problems.

Jake helped Teri finish connecting Peter to the system and they chatted about the lab, Encephalographic Systems, and anything else Peter wanted to talk about. He seemed nervous this morning.

Peter squirmed a bit and Jake asked what was wrong.

"Something's digging into my lower back. I think it's a wire."

Teri reached under Peter's back, and slid one of the wire leads out from under his body.

"Better?" She asked.

"Much. Thanks."

Jake walked over to the computer terminal and typed in a command.

A humming noise began from behind the rear wall as the equipment prepared itself for the task at hand. The machine used enormous amounts of energy and a majority of the room space was taken up by cooling equipment used to disperse the heat created from the system.

The computer which ran Andee was the next level of processing beyond the famous CRAY C90 and T90 computer systems of the nineties. Since Jake had been involved in the development of this new computer, he was allowed the use of one at a reduced cost. His work in the electrical properties of the brain and the algorithms developed from this work had proven invaluable to the software engineers at CRAY. Artificial intelligence was the next big thing on the horizon.

"A question?" Peter asked. "How much radiation are you guys pumping into me?"

"None," Teri said. "The system's connections to you are only listening devices. All the high voltage and radioactive components of the machine are shielded from us by the protective material in the walls and ceiling. Jake and I would be growing third arms or large warts on our bodies if these shields were not in place. You can relax. It's all good."

Peter seemed satisfied with this answer.

He took a deep breath and sighed. He appeared to be relaxing, his heart rate and breathing showing this. They were ready to begin.

When Jake had begun testing with Andee, he had started with normal subjects, people without Near Death Experiences. The program had grown rapidly during the first year, but then stagnated when progress slowed and glitches in the system hampered further developments. His sponsors were expecting more and he had struggled trying to give them what they wanted: Unlimited access to the human mind.

Then Beth had died and everything shut down.

He couldn't go on. At least until he discovered Andee may be able to help his grief. She might be able see into a place no one had ever gone before.

And Jake needed to find a way to that place.

3

April, 2009

9 Months Earlier

Orange Park, Florida

Jake would never have considered putting someone with a Near Death Experience into the machine had it not been for the death of his wife.

While he held her in his arms, the life running out of her onto the cold, black asphalt, she said things that still haunted him. Things which didn't make sense at the time. And as his life stagnated and he floundered, trying to make some sense of her words, he became aware of others with similar experiences.

After meeting a man one day whose daughter died in his arms, uttering startlingly similar things as Jake's wife Beth, the man told him there were people who had survived their brush with death and carried what he called Near Death Experiences around with them for the rest of their lives. Experiences which seemed to share certain traits and characteristics.

Jake went online, searching out people with these unusual encounters, hoping to find some answers to his questions, but no one he contacted provided any clarity on the matter and his wife's confusing last words remained a mystery to him. Most of the people didn't want to talk about what happened.

Desperately searching for any clue, he decided he would seek and find test subjects with these unique experiences, and by looking into these people's minds, hopefully begin to understand, and perhaps, even find what was missing in his life. His wife.

* * *

The first subject with a Near Death Experience came to the lab almost a year ago.

It was spring in north Florida and everything was blooming. The days were warming up into the eighties and the nights were cool and sometimes chilly. Pollen counts were high and the hay fever sufferers were miserable.

Sara McClaughlin was horribly congested and watery eyed as she entered the lab for the first time. As she shook Jake and Teri's hands, she sneezed and apologized, then blew her nose in a pink handkerchief. Jake thought, *This should be good.*

Before any experiments were conducted, Jake and Teri interviewed the subjects and had them tell their story. Jake wanted to hear details of the NDE before any interaction with Andee took place.

With this first subject, he believed he would watch Sara's experience unfold on the computer monitors, but this was, as yet, an untested system with this type of activity and he wanted a preview of what had happened to Sara. She also needed to be measured for the body mold and necessary leads for the experiment.

Sara enthusiastically told them how she had drowned in a pond behind her house when she was eleven and had seen her own body from above as paramedics worked on her. Her grandma, who had passed away the previous year, was there with her, along with her cousin Jenny, who had died three years earlier.

Her story was typical, in that she saw a bright light and visions of her life flashed by her into the light. 'A happy song was playing,' as she put it, and everything was peaceful. She was drawn to the luminous area and yet reluctant to go to it. Her grandma and cousin were gently guiding her that way when a great thump was heard and felt on her chest.

Sara's attention was ripped from the beckoning glow and became focused on the scene below her as the paramedic raised his fist and brought it down hard on the middle of her chest. The precordial thump he performed was heard louder this time and even caused Sara to gasp as she felt her chest rocked from the blow.

As she plummeted back to her body, she heard her grandma say, 'Charlotte and Madison,' and she knew these would be the names of her two daughters. Then Grandma and Jenny were gone, the light, extinguished, and darkness invaded her world until she awoke three days later in the children's ICU at Baptist Medical Center.

The first two words out of her mouth were the names of her unborn daughters.

Sara had been given a glimpse into her future.

When Sara returned the following week, after the mold had been fabricated and the computer programmed for her electrical leads, she was still having problems with her hay fever. As they talked and chatted while preparing her for the session, she would periodically sneeze or blow her nose. This wreaked havoc on the sensors and Jake thought they would have to postpone the experiment. She offered to take some Sudafed but Jake said no. He didn't want any type of drug in her system which might encourage skepticism later as to the effects it may have had on the outcome. They would just see how things went.

As the experiment began, Sara was asked to think about her Near Death Experience, her NDE.

The scene unfolded in front of them with sparkling clarity. The video Andee produced was nothing less than spectacular. It was almost film-like in its quality. The detail and subtle nuances were leaps and bounds above the interpretations of the normal test subjects and Jake's awe and excitement was tangible. He couldn't stop grinning.

Originally, Jake and Teri considered hypnotizing their subjects for the memory to be fully recalled, but as he watched Sara's experience unfold, he realized that was unnecessary. Her memory of the experience was phenomenal and the clarity profound.

Then, the first anomaly showed up.

Andee had the ability to produce an audio track along with the visual representation the computer drew. When Sara's NDE started, the sound seemed normal, but then suddenly changed. A loud distorted screeching noise came blaring out of the speaker system and he cringed.

At first, Jake thought it a minor glitch in the system, a hiccup in the power. The machine was using about seventy percent of its available resources, which was way above anything they had yet seen, and this concerned him.

Jake reached to turn the volume down as Sara said, "What's happening?! Is everything ok?"

With the loss of concentration on her part, the visualization changed on the monitors and the screeching sound stopped.

"Yes," Jake said. "We were getting some kind of distortion of the audio during your recall and we're not sure what it is. We've never had that happen before. Were there any strange sounds going on at that point in your experience?"

"No. Not really." Sara said. "Except, maybe the music, but I wouldn't call it strange. It was beautiful and happy."

Jake thought about this and asked, "Was this music something you recognized? Like your favorite song?"

"No." Sara said. "I'd never heard it before. It was so beautiful and full though, it felt like it had presence. Not just sound. It was all around and inside me too. A part of me."

"All right," Jake said. "Do you think you can continue?"

"Yes, for a little while longer anyway. This contraption over me is making it hard to breathe and I'm feeling a little confined at the moment."

Just then, Sara sneezed. A warning light lit up on the console indicating a loss of communication in a section of the sub atomic energy collector. The body mold.

Jake swore under his breath. "Great. Now what?"

"Her sneeze probably blew some particles on to the sensing fabric," Teri said. "I should be able to bypass that section, but we'll be losing data from that part over the face."

"Do it. We'll have to make some modifications to the body mold later."

As Teri typed commands into the computer, Jake stepped around the console and stood next to Sara.

"Your sneeze may have affected some of the sensors in the body mold and Teri is working on a fix to compensate for this. Are you hanging in there?"

"Yes."

"Give us a couple of minutes and we'll start over again. If you think you need to sneeze again, try turning your head to the side. That will prevent saliva droplets from spraying over the section of the mold above your face. Do you have room to do that? Try it."

"I think so—yes, I can turn a little but my nose bangs into the side of the mold."

"All right, do the best you can." He returned to the other side of the computer console.

Teri nodded and said, "Got it."

"Good, let's try again. Sara? Can you start at the beginning? I'd like to see if this sound anomaly shows up in the same place, if at all."

Sara said, "Of course."

The horrible, screeching distortion started up again at the same place and Jake made an entry, attenuating the sound so it didn't overwhelm them. He let the scene continue to play out and as he watched, a section of the video began to distort. Jake frowned as he saw this. Teri pointed to it and Jake nodded his head as if to say, 'Yes, I see it.' Another distorted area showed up next to the first and at this point it was obvious what they were.

Pointing to the distortions Teri said, "Is this Grandma and cousin Jenny? Is this what we're seeing?"

Jake nodded slowly. "I think so. Let's see what develops. Maybe Andee can sort it out as she learns."

A bigger distorted area had begun to form at the far right of the screen and it grew as they watched. Suddenly, the whole screen began to stutter and freeze, repeatedly. Finally the scene changed and was replaced with a dark view of the inside of the body mold.

Sara had lost her concentration.

"Get me out of here!" Sara yelled. "I can't breathe!"

Jake could hear the panic in her voice as she flailed her arms, pulling on the leads. He thought she would yank them right out of the ceiling. Teri rushed over and began unhooking wires and electrodes as fast as she could, trying to calm Sara down.

"It's ok Sara," Teri said. "Try to slow your breathing down. We're right here. Take deep breaths and close your eyes. Try to visualize yourself in a huge open meadow with a gentle breeze blowing and wild flowers swaying all around you, sunlight on your face and the scent of the flowers in the air."

Sara sneezed.

"That's right. You can smell the flowers."

Sara showed signs of relaxing and Teri was able to disconnect enough of the leads so she could lift the body mold up and away from over her.

Sara seemed instantly better.

"Oh God! I'm so sorry! I feel so foolish! I just lost it."

Jake came over and said, "It's ok. I should apologize to you. We didn't think about how closed in you would be in this set up. Of course you would feel claustrophobic. We'll have to make some modifications to the mold."

"Yes, please! I don't think I could get in there again the way it is. I think if my face was open, it would probably be ok."

"We could cut that section out," Teri said. "I've already bypassed it in the computer program and since we have this session recorded, we could compare it to future sessions with the modified body mold and see if we're losing any important data."

"Ok," Jake said. "Sounds like the best option at the moment. Sara, I think we're done here today. We'll get you cleaned up and scheduled for the next session. That is, if you're willing to continue."

"As long as I can breathe under that thing, I'll come back as much as you like. Can I see some of the recorded video?"

"Not just yet. We need to analyze it and see what we actually have first. We'll want you to corroborate the video with your actual memory of the event, of course, but we'll do that in a future session. Ok?"

Sara nodded.

Jake could see her disappointment.

"May I bring my daughter next time?" Sara asked. "It would mean so much for her to understand what I went through. She's heard the story all her life. To see it with her own eyes would be special for her. And me."

"She may not get to see much of anything at this point. We're having issues with the video. Part of the sequence is distorted and the audio is malfunctioning. That's the main reason I'm not ready for you to see the recording yet. I don't think so."

"Oh please, Dr. Townsend. Just this once? She has so many questions about all of this. It would go a long way in answering them." She paused and a sad look crossed her face. "She doesn't believe me."

Jake looked at Teri.

Teri shrugged.

Jake shook his head but said, "Ok. Just this once."

He hoped he wasn't making a big mistake.

When Sara arrived the following week, a striking young woman with long red hair and startling green eyes walked in with her. Thin and tall, she carried herself with sadness and a burden that seemed to detract from her beauty ever so slightly. She did not smile and had a skeptical look in her eye as Jake and Teri greeted them.

"Dr. Townsend, Miss Newton," Sara said. "This is my daughter, Madison. Madison, this is Dr. Townsend and his assistant, Teri Newton."

Jake looked at Teri who bore the same expression that was probably plastered on his face. A look which conveyed surprise and recognition all at the same time. The same look you have when you already knew something, but were surprised to hear it anyway. This was the Madison of Sara's NDE.

Madison extended her hand and said, "Hello. Mother's talked nonstop about you."

Flustered for a second, Jake hesitated, then took Madison's hand in his own and said, "Hello. Very nice to meet you. Please, call me Jake."

She only nodded, and then proceeded to shake Teri's hand as she said "Miss Newton."

"Please, call me Teri."

As Teri took Sara over to the chair to prep her for the experiment, Jake gave Madison a brief tour and explained what they would be doing today and what she would be seeing. She seemed interested, but skeptical and said very little, only nodding here and there.

Jake told her to sit on a stool behind where he and Teri would be working. She should be able to see the monitors and remain clear of the work area.

Sara lay fully reclined with the new body mold in place above her and seemed relaxed and comfortable.

"This is much better," she said. "I can see and breathe!"

"I'm glad," Jake said. "We'll see if we lose any functionality with the adjustment to the sensors and the mold. How is the hay fever?"

"Practically gone. I've been feeling better since Friday."

"Good. Then let's begin."

As the system loaded and the cooling components spooled up, Madison perked up and actually looked a little worried. Jake reassured her that it was normal and everything was working properly.

"Sara?" said Jake. "Humor us a bit while I show your daughter what Andee can do. I want you to think of a large, red, beach ball in a white, square room."

Sara laughed and said, "Ok."

On the monitors, a large, red, beach ball appeared resting on the floor of a white surface. Madison looked slightly amused, but unimpressed.

"Now, Sara? Think of the ball bouncing up and down."

The ball began bouncing in place in the white room.

"Now, make the ball any color you want, but don't tell us what it is."

The ball turned purple, and then changed to yellow with purple spots. Jake chuckled and Teri laughed.

"What color did you make the ball Sara?"

"First purple, then I changed my mind to yellow with purple spots. Is that ok?"

"Yes. Perfect!" Jake said.

Madison's mouth hung open and she seemed to be paying full attention.

Jake asked, "Can you think of something for her to picture in her mind? Something personal that only you and she would know. It could be a piece of jewelry, or a favorite book, or even a favorite song. Andee does sound too." Jake grinned. He was showing off now.

Madison thought for a moment and then said, "Mom? Think of our favorite restaurant in our favorite vacation town and the music that is always playing while we wait for a table."

She looked ashamed of herself, but Jake grinned.

The yellow ball with purple spots disappeared and in its place a vision of a beachside themed restaurant with umbrellas, tiki torches, and ceiling fans filled the screen. The wall had a mural painted with a scene of cows dancing and frolicking in the Florida sun. Across the top of the wall was painted *The Island Cow*. Through the speakers of the workstation came the unmistakable sound of The Beach Boys, <u>Surfin' Safari</u>. Madison smiled, her face glowing.

"That is amazing!" she said.

Jake turned and said, "I know you were having a hard time with this, Madison. I wanted you to see we're not trying to take advantage of your mother or trick her in any way. We are conducting serious research in this lab with life changing possibilities and though this little exercise was a fun example of what Andee can do, the potential of this machine should be apparent to you now."

Madison became serious and nodded, saying "I never would have believed…" and trailed off in thought.

"Ok Sara, let's get to work. As before, let yourself relax and begin visualizing your experience as best you can remember."

Just before the screen changed scenes from *The Island Cow Restaurant* to the beginning of Sara's NDE, a picture of a young man appeared. He was in his mid twenties, blond with blue eyes, and a goatee. He was smiling and standing in the stern of a fishing boat holding a large Mahi Mahi he had apparently just caught. The picture then disappeared and Sara's NDE began.

Jake noticed but paid no real attention to the brief vision as he had seen this kind of thing before with the normal test subjects.

People's minds did not always work in an ordered, cohesive pattern. Random thoughts and images often penetrated normal thinking patterns. This is what he thought this was; some random thought that had popped into Sara's mind before she concentrated on the task at hand.

Madison's reaction behind him made Jake rethink this.

It was as if she had been slapped in the face. She turned white as a ghost, swayed slightly in the stool, swooning, and then got control of herself, placing a steadying hand on the desk next to her. She glanced over at her mother in a jumble of wires and machinery and shook her head as a tear trickled down one cheek.

Jake was unsure how to react. He felt like he was interrupting a private moment and quickly turned away.

Sara's Near Death Experience began as her first session had and as the monitors displayed her memories of it, Madison watched, enthralled. When the first anomaly showed up in the same spot as before, Jake was ready and adjusted the sound accordingly, applying some filter element in an attempt to clean up the audio.

The adjustment had little effect on what they heard so Jake left it alone and would see what he could accomplish with the computer later. He didn't want anything interrupting Sara this time.

The video artifact showed up right where they expected it, but it looked clearer. The shapes were more human-like, with blurry eyes, noses, mouths and heads. One shape was clearly an adult, the other a child. If they were saying anything, it was indistinguishable from the noise that seemed to dominate the audio portion. Jake turned slightly and could see Madison's intense concentration as she stared at the images. Her knuckles were turning white from the grip she had on the armrests of the stool.

Jake watched intently as they approached the area in Sara's vision where she'd had the claustrophobic attack and the experiment had been terminated. A larger distorted area began forming on the screen, only this time it was gaining brightness as it grew.

Then, an amazing thing happened.

Slideshow-like images appeared rapidly from nowhere and whizzed past eleven year old Sara with increasing speed. They seemed to head straight for the glowing area of lighted distortion and meld into it, causing it to grow.

The images flew by so rapidly it was nearly impossible to distinguish one from the other. Jake could just catch flashes of blurry faces and objects racing across the screen, nothing distinct, and then they were gone.

Eleven year old Sara and the two shapes beside her began moving slowly toward the growing and brightening distorted area. Sara's face was so happy and peaceful. Suddenly, breaking through the audio distortion, a loud booming thump shook the room. Madison gasped and Teri flinched. The large, bright, distorted area on the screen wavered and shrank a little.

Eleven year old Sara turned back toward the scene below her and watched a paramedic raise his fist, bringing it down hard onto her sternum.

"Whump!"

Even though the volume was turned down on the speakers, the sound blasted out of them and shook everything that was loose in the lab. Jake felt the pressure wave and took a deep breath. He watched Teri and Madison do the same, like a shuddering collective gasp.

Jake hadn't noticed it before, but the hum of the cooling system had increased and as he realized this, he glanced at the gauges and was surprised to see them in the yellow, rapidly approaching the red area.

He was about to terminate the experiment when it ended on its own, but not without a dramatic conclusion. Just as Sara had described, as she rejoined the real world, her grandmother spoke two words as clearly and distinctly as if she were standing there in the lab.

"Charlotte and Madison."

As the cooling machinery spooled down and silence enveloped the lab, Jake turned to Sara's daughter and found her with tears streaming down her face, sobbing.

"I never believed her. I never believed her. I'm sorry Mom, I never believed you."

* * *

As all of them sat behind the console and watched the recorded session, Madison asked, "Mom. Why?"

"Ryan?" Sara asked.

Madison nodded.

"I guess I wanted to make sure you were thinking of him through all of this. I know what awaits me at the end of this life and I wanted you to know what was waiting for you—Ryan."

"I think about him every waking minute of every day, Mom. That's all I do." She paused. "Will he really be there?" Madison asked, pleading as fresh tears sprang from her shining green eyes.

Sara nodded, smiling.

Not wanting to intrude on the moment, but unable to help himself, Jake asked, "Who is Ryan? Wait! Was that the young man we saw in Sara's mind just before the NDE began?"

Regaining some composure, Madison nodded and said, "Yes. He was my fiancé."

"What happened?" Teri blurted. Then, "Sorry—I mean if you don't mind telling us."

"I'll try," Madison said. "It's still difficult for me." She took a big breath and began. "Ryan and I were to be married last fall. We had been planning the wedding for over a year and I was so excited. The ceremony was to take place on Jekyll Island, our favorite place. The place he proposed to me. But he was killed in a car accident three weeks before." Her voice cracked as more tears spilled from her eyes. "He was coming home from fishing with his friends. He was talking to me on his cell phone, so excited about the big Mahi he had caught and I guess he wasn't paying attention. The highway patrol said a logging truck drifted over too far into the oncoming lane and he didn't react in time. He was thrown from his truck as it flipped. I could hear everything over the cell phone. Sounds I'll never forget— and then the silence." Sobbing now, she said, "If only he hadn't been on his phone talking to me. I distracted him. I killed him."

"Honey," Sara said, gently, "we've been through this. It's not your fault. It's a tragedy it happened, and it must have been horrible being on the phone with him, but the driver of the truck is to blame. He was the one driving drunk."

"No, Mom. If he hadn't been talking to me he would have seen the truck coming and been able to get out of its way. I'll never be able to forgive myself and I miss him so much."

"Madison," Jake said, "you will see Ryan again. Just like I will see my wife. I won't rest until we are able to see and talk with them again."

Jake watched Sara turn away, frowning.

* * *

Teri sat at her desk, worried.

She wasn't sure what had happened today and the more her mind tried to wrap itself around the events, the more it created excuses for what she had heard and felt. She knew Jake's mind worked in its own way and most people could not even compete with him on his level, but what she saw today was way beyond anything even he could conceive. She glanced over at him and frowned.

Jake was at his desk, working like a crazed lunatic. She could see he was spooled up. Teri knew he hadn't been like this since the subatomic cellular discovery and it bothered her. He must have felt her eyes on him because he looked up.

"Everything ok, Teri? I thought things went well, considering."

Teri nodded her head but didn't reply.

"The anomalies seemed better, except for the sound," Jake continued. "And Madison sure was convinced. I know we can help her. She seemed so distraught."

"Jake, what are we doing? Have you even been paying attention today?"

"Of course. What do you mean?"

"I mean that earth shattering thud during the session. The one that blew my eardrums out even with the volume turned down. The one that shook objects on the desk and rattled the teeth in my head. The one that scared the shit out of me! You did notice that, right?" Teri stood and paced. "Oh, and how about the temperature of the cooling system? What kind of energy causes that much heat? We've never seen that kind of consumption. I was worried the system was

27

going to overload. And did you notice that neither one of those things occurred during the playback of the session? Energy levels and sound levels were normal and definitely not felt. What was going on?"

She watched Jake study her.

"I hear you. I don't have an explanation for those things yet, but I think we should keep working on it until we understand it better. Don't you?"

"I'm not so sure. I know you're excited about what happened but I'm a little scared. You're so reckless when you're like this. Maybe we should slow down a bit, take a step back, and see where we want to take this."

"I know where I want to take this. We're getting closer and this is such a big breakthrough. I can't slow down now, you know that. Beth wouldn't want me to."

Teri couldn't argue with him when he brought Beth up. She knew his dead wife was the sole reason this obsession consumed him. Not for the first time since she knew Jake, Teri wished he had never met Beth.

4

January 9, 2010 – 9:14 a.m.

Present Day

Orange Park, Florida

In the lab, Peter was hooked up to Andee and ready to go. This was his third session with the machine and he seemed a little apprehensive and anxious.

"Uh—guys? I need to go to the bathroom," Peter said.

Jake and Teri looked at each other and then Teri said, "Mr. Vargas, are you sure? You just went before we hooked you up. I mean, if you gotta go, you gotta go, but it will take ten minutes to disconnect you and another twenty to hook you back up. You know this."

Peter hesitated, then said, sighing, "All right, I'll be ok I guess. How long will I have to stay in here?"

"For the length of your NDE and then ten minutes to unhook you," Jake said. "It should be about thirty minutes total according to your last session."

"All right," Peter said.

Jake busied himself prepping the computer while Teri checked over the connections and Peter's leads.

Everything looked good to Jake so he said, "All right Peter, are you ready to start?"

"Yes."

"Try and relax. Take a few deep breaths and then take us back to your experience."

Andee's video screens showed a view of wide open desert with billowing black smoke in the distance. A battle was taking place and Jake knew this to be Iraq in the first days of Desert Storm.

As the scene panned around, battle scarred buildings came into view. Mortar fire could be heard in the distance with the staccato of small arms fire punctuating the 'whump' of exploding munitions. Shouts and curses, along with radio static could be heard during lapses of intense firing. Wounded and dead Iraqi soldiers lay strewn across the area.

The scene was intense, but to Jake it seemed less detailed and not as vivid as most of the other Near Death Experiences they had viewed and recorded. This is what bothered Jake the most about Peter Vargas. His anomalies weren't like the others which showed up in the prior NDE's. His were more like inconsistencies.

Teri interrupted his train of thought. "Here, this is what I was talking about. See—this is different than the two previous recordings we have of Peter's NDE. There was a tank right here. I remember because it was hit with some kind of bomb and it exploded."

"You're right," Jake said, looking over her shoulder at the monitor. "I remember that. Why does his memory of it change? Could his injuries have affected his recall?"

"Not just his lapses in memory, Jake, but during his sessions, we haven't seen any of the anomalies we've come to associate with an NDE. No video gaps or artifact, nothing in the way of sound distortion or static. Zip."

Jake thought hard about this, and as he realized what the issue was, he grew angry.

"Dammit! I should have seen it. He's faking it! He's never had an NDE. He's been making it up this whole time. We're being conned."

Teri, looking dumbfounded, shrugged her shoulders. "Why would anyone fake an NDE?"

"Let's find out."

Jake punched the abort button, shutting the machine down and ending the session. He walked over, raised the body mold up and began disconnecting Peter's leads.

Peter looked confused. "What happened? Is everything all right? Were you getting a bad signal or something?"

"You tell us, Peter," Jake said. "Why?"

"Why what?"

"Why are you here? Why are you wasting our time?"

"How am I wasting your time? I thought you needed subjects for your experiments. I'm here to let you test me and hopefully get some answers. What's wrong?"

"What's wrong is your so called NDE has holes in it. Inconsistencies galore. Every session is a different version. The one confirming aspect of all the other NDE's we've recorded is the accuracy and consistency of the visions they have. Their memory of it is exact and the detail, phenomenal. With you, it's like a lie. You tell it, and then when asked over and over again to explain the story, it grows bigger because it's not the truth. Things change because you can't remember what you made up. You had us fooled for a while, I'll give you that, but you had to have known we would catch on. Now, I'll ask you again. Why are you here?"

Peter's whole demeanor suddenly changed. One minute he was weird, insecure, Peter Vargas, the next, he was something completely opposite. Peter rose up slowly and arrogantly.

He glared first at Jake, then Teri. "General Breckenridge will have to explain everything to you. I suggest you contact him. Be prepared to answer some hard questions."

He ripped the remaining leads off his body and without another word, stood and strode purposefully out of the lab.

5

January 9, 2010 2:30 pm

Orange Park, Florida

Four hours later, General Thomas Breckenridge marched stoically into Jake's lab.

Tall and solidly built, he stood well over Jake's head. His hair was cropped short and graying over his ice blue eyes, and the uniform, impeccably neat. Jake could not find a single wrinkle in the fabric. Numerous awards and medals adorned the upper left breast of the dress coat and the two stars on his shoulder boards glinted in the harsh florescent light of the lab. He was followed by a Lt. Colonel Jake did not know, presumably his assistant. In his right hand, the General carried a large manila envelope.

The man looked angry. But so was Jake, and he wasn't about to let this pompous ass push him around. He wanted answers and according to Peter Vargas, the General had them.

Jake and Teri had both been shocked at the mention of General Breckenridge's name. The military's involvement in Jake's work was not widely known and some aspects of it were actually classified. So, when Peter threw out the General's name, Jake had a pretty good idea who and what Peter was and what had been going on. It did not make him feel any less angry. Actually, it angered him even more.

"Dr. Townsend," the General got right to the point. "I understand we have an acquaintance in common and you have some concerns about him."

"An acquaintance? Concerns? General, you sent a spy into my lab, injecting false data into the system and possibly disrupting months of work. I want to know why?"

"Agent Smith, or Peter Vargas as you know him, was a necessary evil. The reports my department were receiving regarding your progress here were creating concerns that you might be getting off track."

"Off track? What does that mean? I consider this lab and this project very much on track. Andee is, and always will be, a work in progress, but she is learning in leaps and bounds and is way ahead of anything else out there. How can she be 'off track' as you say?"

"This research using subjects of Near Death Experiences and the application of it is of little or no value to the U.S. Military. We're providing funding for applications in your development of equipment which allows for access to the human mind. We are not interested in your ventures into the 'afterlife' and frankly, we find it somewhat questionable behavior for a scientist of your training and stature."

Jake felt his face flush. "I don't care what you question, General. You have no idea what is applicable or not in my research and I find it offensive for you to even suggest my behavior is anything other than professional. If I feel studying the feeding habits of gerbils to be beneficial to the outcome of this project, then I will study them. You are paying me to give you results, and I will arrive at those results in the manner in which I see fit. Do I make myself clear?"

"You just stated the obvious," the General said. "We are paying you to give us results, and we are not seeing results. All I get is reports of loud noises and video artifact which can't be explained. Then there are the reports of you suggesting to these subjects that they will be able to see and communicate with their loved ones who are dead. Are you a psychic, Doctor, or a scientist? What relevance do these things have to the work we are paying you to do?"

"They are the most relevant aspect of the study that I have. These people are extraordinary. Something has happened to them which makes them special." Jake paused. "I believe they are the key to unlocking the mind so that the tool you seek will be plausible. Right now, all Andee can do is see whatever the test subject is thinking, and this makes Andee easy to fool. You and I both know that if you have information in your mind you don't want shown to Andee, you just think of something else. But by studying these NDE's, and finding what makes them unique, I should be able to pull information from any human mind like I'm accessing a computer. All of their memories, dreams, thoughts, and feelings will be exposed and readily accessible at the push of a button."

The General considered this for a moment, looked Jake hard in the eye and said, "All right, Doctor. I'll take your word at face value and go along with your thinking for now, but I still believe you're keeping something from me. Some of your actions and those of your staff reported to me by agent Smith are somewhat suspect and the US Government is not in the business of supporting the supernatural. I'll be watching you closely, and if I don't like what I see, I'll pull the plug on your funding and you'll be out of business."

"You're one of many interested sponsors, General. Threatening my funding will have little impact on how I conduct my research. I have other investors."

"Not anymore."

He handed Jake the manila envelope he had been carrying, turned, and with his aide scurrying close behind, left the building just as he had entered it.

6

January 9, 2010 3:00 pm

Orange Park, Florida

"How did he get these?" Teri asked, holding the contents of the manila envelope in her hands.

"Who knows?" Jake said. "I'm sure he has resources beyond what we can imagine. What bothers me the most is the fact he somehow influenced their decisions."

"I can't believe *First Coast Diagnostics* and *Out of Sight, Out of Mind Software* just backed out like that," she said, staring at the letters again. "Now, our only source of income is the U.S. Government."

"I'm pretty sure that's exactly what General Breckenridge wanted. He needs to control the whole show and doesn't want any other outside influences delaying our work, or as he put it, getting us 'off track.' I need to speak with Bill over at First Coast Diagnostics. Let's see what he says. Can you find me the number?"

As Teri looked it up, Jake read the letters again, shaking his head in disgust. They were almost identical, basically terminating their relationship with the company and pulling any future funding they would have received. Their reasoning, though somewhat vague, was clear in its outcome. They felt that he and the lab were moving in a direction which did not support the company's goals and needs.

"The direction in which your research is moving is not conducive to the productivity needs of our organization, therefore, we will no longer be providing funding for further studies on our behalf."

Blah, blah, blah. The letters rambled on. Jake felt sick.

Unless he could convince their private investors to change their minds, they were at the mercy of whatever the military wanted. They could quit of course, but that word didn't exist in Jake's vocabulary.

Teri had the number and after dialing, handed the phone to Jake.

"Bill, Jake Townsend here."

"Jake, hello. How are you?" Jake thought he could hear some tension in his voice.

"Not good, Bill. Not good at all. Why have you decided to pull your funding? I thought we had an agreement here."

"You got that already, huh?" Bill asked.

"Let's just say I got a heads up on what was coming. I called right away and wanted to hear it from you. What's the problem?"

"The board members and I feel the path you are taking, is—uh, well—not the path we originally hoped for."

"And what path were you hoping for? When you signed on, you knew exactly what we were doing here. What's changed?"

"Let's say you have some persuasive friends, and leave it at that. Jake, I'm really sorry it's come to this, but my hands are tied. The board is in total agreement and they will not change their minds. You have some powerful friends—or enemies, whichever way you want to look at it."

"I thought you, of all people, could see the vision of this project. I am very disappointed."

"Jake," Bill said, "I am too. I tried everything. Somebody put a lot of pressure on my people. You need to be careful. Good luck." And he hung up without waiting for a reply.

Jake shook his head as he pressed end on the phone.

Teri looked at him expectantly.

"It's just as I suspected. Somebody from the General's office put some pressure on them. Apparently they were quite convincing. The board was unanimous. We don't stand a chance getting them back. And Bill sounded frightened. He actually told me to be careful. Shit, this sucks!"

"I agree, but it's not the end of the world. We knew the military was going to be a tough one to satisfy, but we agreed we needed their support. Now, we're stuck with it. You don't want out do you?"

"No. It's all we have now. I just don't like losing control."

"I don't either, but it's sure better than packing it in and going home. Reading these letters gives me a sick feeling in the pit of my stomach, but losing all of our funding makes me feel even worse."

Jake couldn't decide if he was angrier at the General for getting the best of him, or at himself for jeopardizing all his work.

In reality, the General had been mostly right. Jake was off track. He was using all his resources with Andee in the hope he would be able to discover the secret which would enable him to see Beth again.

Jake was stringing the General along, making him believe he could produce something which he was no closer to producing than he had been five years ago. He hoped the General could be put off a little longer. Either that or some major breakthrough needed to happen soon.

Jake knew time was not on his side.

7

January 9, 2010 4:00 pm

Mandarin, Florida

Peter sat fuming in his low rent apartment.

He'd never failed a mission this badly before and was ashamed of what had transpired. He was sure the General was pissed at him. He would probably be sent back to Afghanistan, or Pakistan, or some other hell hole in the world as his punishment.

His secure cell phone went off.

"Yes."

"Smith? Breckenridge. I know your cover was blown in the Townsend thing, but I need some additional work from you on the case. Are you still in the vicinity?"

"Yes, General. What do you need?"

"We have equipment planted in the lab and his office, correct?"

"Yes."

"Good. I need those monitored and additional equipment placed at his house and cell phone. Any problems with that?"

"None what so ever, sir."

"Oh—and reserve some resources for the assistant, too. I know she's very involved in his day to day operations. They probably talk a lot."

"Consider it done, General. Anything else?"

"Negative. I'll expect weekly reports. If anything urgent should arise, contact me through the usual channel, immediately."

"Yes sir," Smith said, but the line was already dead.

Apparently he was still on the case and he smiled.

8

January 10, 2010 3:30 a.m.

Orange Park, Florida

Jake slept horribly that night with his recurring nightmare making its usual appearance.

He was at the accident scene, holding his wife Beth in his arms as the life bled out of her onto the cold black pavement. The strange light fluctuated, and at times, seemed palpable. Then the gloom would wane and become penetrable, like it was breathing.

Beth's ashen face, taut with pain, conveyed the seriousness of the injury as her black blood flowed out from her wound in such copious amounts it covered the entire area, spreading out away from her in an ever widening circle of death.

Her head was turned to the side, facing away from him and she was muttering nonsense as he tried to console her. In the nightmare, he struggled to hear what she was saying, but could never make it out.

The same despair he felt the night of her death was amplified a thousand fold as he relived it again in his dream.

Tonight's nightmare started like it always did, but finished much differently.

As he was leaning down trying to hear Beth's muttered words, a loud thump shook the air around them and Jake, startled, looked all around the dream world trying to find where it came from.

"Whump!"

Another louder thump shook the air and rattled his teeth.

He noticed Beth had stopped muttering and looked down upon her. She stared right up at him, eyes wide open, ringed red against her pale skin. The color had drained completely out of her face, except for her red lips, and her corpse-like mouth was drawn into either a grin or a snarl. Jake could not tell.

She said simply, "Stop!"

Jake awoke with a scream on his lips and his body drenched in a cold sweat, gasping, the loud thumps chasing him into his room.

9

January 10, 2010 - 8:30 a.m.

Orange Park, Florida

Teri said, "What happened to you?" as Jake walked into the lab the following morning. "You look like crap."

"Didn't sleep well," he said, and sat at the computer console cradling the cup of coffee he had bought on the way into the lab. He knew he looked a wreck. In the mirror at the coffee shop, he had seen his hair sticking up in clumps, and his eyes, bright red with drooping lids, felt on fire. His lab coat looked like it had been slept in.

"Worried?" she said, misinterpreting the cause of his appearance.

Jake started to open his mouth, thought better of it, and nodded.

"These were on the floor when I got here this morning. They must have slipped them through the mail slot in the door after we left yesterday." Teri handed him two plain white envelopes.

Jake and Teri had closed up shop early after the incident with Peter, the General, and then the disappointing call to Bill at First Coast Diagnostics. They rarely left the lab early, but decided yesterday was as good a day as any.

Jake opened the envelopes, slipped the single sheet of letterhead out of each, glanced at them, and then tossed them on the desk.

"Official notice," he said, and went back to studying his coffee.

She picked them up, looked at both and sighed.

"Ok," Jake said, "what have we got today?"

"Nothing," Teri said. "Peter Vargas—or whatever his name is, was supposed to be our subject today."

"When does Rachael Swanson get back?"

"I'm not sure. She didn't know. Her aunt is sick, and she didn't have a definite return time. Do you want me to try and call her? See if she's back?"

"No—no, I know she'll contact us when she's ready to get back to it. I guess we'll review her tapes and see if we can find anything we missed."

The front door buzzer sounded. Teri pressed the intercom button and said, "May I help you?"

"Yes, this is Madison McClaughlin. I'd like to see Dr. Townsend if he's in."

Teri looked at Jake questioningly and he shrugged his shoulders.

She pressed the intercom button again and said, "Ok Miss McClaughlin, come right in." She buzzed her through.

Madison walked in, smiling. She was dressed casually in jeans and a sweater, but looked radiant. She was one of those stunning redheads who could make anything look good, and as Jake watched her approach, he couldn't figure out why he hadn't noticed how beautiful she was when they met ten months ago. She noticed Jake's rough appearance and looked concerned, as if she had interrupted something.

"Have you guys been working all night? I hope I'm not disturbing you," she said.

"No, no, Miss McClaughlin," Jake said. "Please come in and have a seat. We just got here ourselves."

"Please, call me Madison," she said, taking the nearest stool and propping herself up on it.

Teri asked, "Can I get you some coffee, or a soda?"

"Yes, a cup of coffee would be great—uh, sugar if you have it."

Teri went to get the coffee, and Jake asked, "How is your mother?"

"She's good," Madison said. "Busy, but good."

Jake nodded, thoughtfully, thinking of Sara's face the last time she had been in the lab.

"She hasn't returned our calls and I'm worried I might have done something to offend her. Is she upset about something I've done?"

Madison looked uncomfortable, nervously twirling a lock of her hair.

After a pause she said, "Well, she loves you to death, just so you know, but she thinks your desire to actually bring back your wife is unhealthy."

Jake raised an eyebrow.

"But the thing she's most worried about," Madison said, "is the fact you might actually succeed and disrupt some natural order or something. Change the balance of the universe and wreak havoc on the world. Crazy, huh?"

Jake laughed a little too quickly and it felt unnatural and tense.

"She doesn't have to worry right now. We've had somewhat of a set-back and we're trying to get things back on track. It seems so distant at the moment. I'm feeling a little discouraged."

Teri returned with the coffee and Madison said, "Thank you. What kind of set-back? Is everything all right?"

"We've discovered an imposter in the study, and we're in the process of seeing how much damage he's done to the database. He could've affected the way Andee has been interpreting some of the experiences. We'll see soon enough. We're also having some sponsorship and funding issues, but that's mainly business."

Madison looked thoughtful, but remained silent, sipping her coffee.

After an uncomfortable moment Jake asked, "So, what brings you back to our little hole in the wall?"

She looked uneasy, the hand wandering back to the lock of hair, twirling it again, nervously.

"I'm not quite sure how to start," she said. "I feel kind of stupid, now that I'm here…"

"Nonsense," Jake said. "Tell us what's bothering you."

"I had a dream."

"What kind of dream?" Teri asked.

"A nightmare, actually. It was kind of scary. It involved Ryan."

Jake squirmed. "Your fiancé who was killed?"

Madison nodded. "Yes. I sometimes have this recurring dream about the accident. I haven't had it in a while. At least not until last night."

"What happens in it and why do we need to know?" Teri asked, seeming suddenly impatient.

Jake looked at Teri hard, but said to Madison, "Tell us about it."

She hesitated and then began. "I'm on the phone with him as he's driving. He's telling me about the fish he caught, and then the accident happens and I'm hearing all the horrible noises from the crash again. After I stop screaming, I hear him saying something faintly through the phone, but I can never understand what it is. I press the phone so hard against my ear it hurts but it does no good. It's just gibberish. It's definitely his voice, I just can't understand him. Last night was different. He said something in the dream I could hear. It was very loud and booming, like it was coming from somewhere other than the cell phone." She stopped, clearly upset. "He said, 'Jake.' And then I woke up."

Jake got up from his chair and paced. Madison watched him, keeping quiet.

Jake stopped and said, "And this is the first time you've been able to make out what he's saying?"

She nodded, her frightened eyes never leaving his.

Jake was struggling with whether or not to tell them about his dream last night. He barely knew Madison, but felt something between them. He had never spoken of his nightmares with Teri, feeling they were his own burden, his punishment, but he knew he could trust her. He decided they had to know. It was too much of a coincidence.

"This is going to seem a little far-fetched," Jake said, "but I need you two to hear this."

He proceeded to tell them about his dreams, and how they had been recurring repeatedly since Beth died. He at first thought they were the guilt he carried surfacing in his subconscious mind, but now he wasn't sure. He told them about last night's dream and how it ended with him being able to understand Beth's request, or whatever it was, and how her face frightened him.

"I don't like that vision of her in my head," he said. "I only want to remember her in a good light. Not this creepy, horror flick, kind of image."

"Wow!" Teri said, sarcastically. "You've got the whole scary visual thing. She's just got audio. My aunt died, maybe she'll send me a warning in an e-mail tonight. Come on guys, it's just a coincidence. You should hear yourselves."

Jake could see Madison getting a little angry and even though he was used to Teri speaking her mind, he couldn't figure out what was going on with her today.

"So you think I'm just making it up?" A decided edge in her voice.

"No, I didn't say that. I'm sure you had a dream of some sort, but you're making something more of it than it really is."

"You don't think it's relevant that Jake and I had the same dream in the same night?"

"You didn't have the same dream," Teri snapped. "You had yours, he had his. Yours was about your fiancé, his was about his wife. You didn't dream about his wife did you? No. He didn't dream about your fiancé, so how can they be the same? You came all the way down here to tell us that you heard Jake's name in a nightmare? I find it hard to believe that's the only reason you're here. What did you really come down here for?"

Madison stood up, clearly angry now.

"Apparently, nothing." She turned and stormed off, heading for the door.

"Madison!" Jake said. "Wait!" and then to Teri, "What the hell was that?"

And he took off after Madison. He caught up with her outside the lab's entrance.

"Madison…please…wait!"

She stopped and turned, her eyes shining, tears about to flow and said sharply, "Why, so you can make fun of me too? I thought you, of all people, would understand."

"I do," Jake said. "Please, wait. I don't know what's gotten into her. She had no right to attack you like that. I don't want you to leave like this. We need to think this thing through."

"I'm not going back in there."

"Ok, I don't blame you," Jake said. "But we still need to talk. Can I meet you later for coffee or something?"

She hesitated, considering. "All right," she said. "Where?"

"How about the coffee shop just up the street, it's called Java Joes. Say, seven o'clock?"

She nodded, looking a little better now, the tears drying up. "Ok."

"Good—I'll see you then and we'll sort this out, Ok?"

"Yes," she said, and she reached out and touched his arm. "Thank you."

Her touch surprised him causing a tingle to race up his arm. Uncomfortable now he said, "See you then," and turned to go.

"Just you and me, right?" she said to him before he could leave.

"Yes, you and me."
And smiling, she turned and walked up the street to her car.

10

January 10, 2010 10:00 a.m.

Orange Park, Florida

Back in the lab, Jake burst in, clearly upset at Teri.

"What was that all about? I can't believe you were so rude to her. What's the matter with you?"

"I just thought she was wasting our time. I guess you didn't think so."

"Whether she was wasting our time or not, I still didn't think it was appropriate for you to attack her like that. You're entitled to your opinions, but you were pretty rough on her. She was crying."

"I guess I was a little tough on her. She just rubs me the wrong way. Sorry. I'll apologize to her when I see her again."

Jake shook his head. He knew Teri, and he didn't think she would apologize. Something was bothering her, and eventually she would tell him what it was. At least he hoped she would.

"All right—let's get back to work," he said, and sat down at the desk.

They worked in silence for a while and then Teri said, "Jake, may I ask you something?"

"Sure. Shoot."

"Do you think we're doing the right thing? I mean, what if these things that keep happening are omens, or fate, or—I don't know.

Maybe we aren't supposed to know these things. Do you ever second guess yourself?"

He paused for a minute. "No, I believe I was given these gifts for a reason, and if I don't follow through, I will have wasted this talent."

She only nodded, but he could tell she didn't agree.

"Is that what's bothering you?" Jake said. "You're having second thoughts about our research? Is that why you jumped down Madison's throat?"

"Well—yes, sort of. She rubs me the wrong way, like I said."

"All right, you told me that already, but what's really bothering you?"

She paused, and then said, "What if both your dreams are like a warning or something? A message for us."

"I thought you said it was just a coincidence," Jake said, confused at her sudden flip flop. "Isn't that what set you off? You thought we were being stupid and childish?"

"Yeah, I made it sound like your dreams were no big deal, but it could be something different. Maybe you should stay away from her."

And there it was, Jake thought.

"Teri, I don't think meeting and talking with Madison McClaughlin is going to be dangerous. It might actually be worse if I don't talk with her. We might miss something." Jake shook his head. "Look at us. Jumping at every shadow like the bogeyman is going to get us. I think it will be fine."

11

January 10, 2010

Orange Park, Florida

They worked the rest of the day purging Peter's data from the system.

It took most of the afternoon for Andee to unlearn what Peter had taught her. They would get to Rachael's stuff tomorrow.

Jake locked up and walked Teri to her car, saying goodnight. He then walked the two blocks to Java Joes and ordered a large coffee while he waited for Madison. He was early. His sleepless night was beginning to take its toll and the coffee was just what he needed.

Madison arrived fifteen minutes late, but he didn't mind. He was glad she decided to show.

"Hi," he said, smiling, as she took a seat across from him, looking beautiful in jeans and a sweater.

Her hair was pulled back and held with a ribbon, her green eyes smiling as she said "Hello."

He signaled the waitress and she ordered a coffee with sugar.

She said, "Have you been waiting long?"

"No," he lied, "I just got here. I ordered without you, I hope you don't mind. I can't seem to wake up today."

"You look exhausted. Did you and Teri work all afternoon? We can do this another time if you'd like."

"No—no, I'm good. You'll keep me awake with your creepy dream stories."

She laughed. "What about yours? It seemed scarier than mine."

He nodded, serious now.

"I didn't like it at all." He paused. "I want to apologize for Teri today. She can be a little opinionated at times."

"A little? I don't know what I did to make her act that way."

"I'm not sure either. Later on she started talking about having second thoughts about our research, and she totally contradicted what she got angry about in the first place."

"What do you mean?"

"Well, remember, she kept saying she thought we were blowing our dream thing all out of proportion, right?"

Madison nodded.

"Later, she told me she was worried about what our dreams could mean, that maybe they weren't coincidences. She wasn't making sense. When I told her that, she said she was a little frightened and thought I should stay away from you."

"Do you think you should stay away from me?"

"No, I think we need to understand what these dreams mean and we can't do that apart."

The waitress brought Madison her coffee and she sipped it, savoring the taste. "Good," she said.

"Best coffee in town. Better than Starbucks and cheaper too. So, let me ask you something?"

"Anything."

"When you heard your fiancé say the name Jake, did you think of me right away, or do you know any other Jakes?"

"I thought of you. I woke up with a picture of you in my head, and knew you were the Jake he was talking about. My mom thought of you also. She's the one who said I should come down and talk to you about it. She thinks it's some kind of warning."

"Do you think it's a warning?"

"I'm not sure. When I woke up, I was scared. I had this ominous feeling, but it could have been from the way I heard your name in the dream. Ryan's voice didn't just come out of the cell phone's speaker. It was like his voice was all around me."

Jake nodded. "I usually wake up from my nightmare scared and lonely, but it's because I've lost her again. It's so real. This time, though, I was frightened because she looked so creepy. I can't get it out of my mind. It wasn't her at the end. My conscious mind could never imagine her like that, yet my nightmare did."

Reaching out and touching his hand she said, "She was everything to you, wasn't she?"

"Yes." He was barely able to get the word out. "She was the best thing to ever happen to me."

He had to stop. He didn't want to get choked up here, now. He squeezed her hand and then pulled his away, feeling a little guilty at how good her touch felt.

An uncomfortable silence hung in the air, and then they reached for their coffees at the same time, drinking in silence for a moment.

Jake broke the silence. "The thing that's bothering me the most, I guess, is the fact both our recurring dreams have similarities that seem too close for coincidences."

"Like what?"

"Like the fact we both have dreams about the accident which killed our loved one. We both feel somewhat responsible for their death and I know I carry a lot of guilt."

She nodded, solemnly.

"The recurring dreams both have Ryan and Beth saying things we cannot understand," Jake continued, "but on the same night, we both have our nightmare again, only this time we can understand a single word spoken to us."

"But is it a warning, a message, or just random words our unconscious minds are creating?"

"I don't know."

She paused for a moment, and then said, "What time was your dream?"

"I remember looking at the clock when I woke up. It was three thirty a.m."

"My clock read three thirty two. Another coincidence?"

Jake slowly shook his head. "I don't think so."

"This is getting weird. Do you really think we could be getting messages from the afterlife? I mean, until that day in your lab, my mom's Near Death Experience was this wacky story I heard as a kid. But can we be getting signals from people who have passed on?"

"If you had asked me that question two years ago I would have laughed in your face. But, now—with Andee and the research I'm doing, I'd be a hypocrite if I said no. I have to believe it's possible. It would take a hell of a lot of energy, but it could be possible—maybe."

"Energy?"

"Are you sure you want to hear this stuff?" When she nodded, he explained, "It's just a theory I have, but I believe it makes sense. All life is made up of some kind of energy. We take in some kind of fuel and it is converted into a form of energy so this biological machine can function. I've seen with Andee that a form of energy exists we've just become aware of, and when the biological machine that is our body expires, that energy is released. Since I was raised a good Catholic boy, I like to call it the soul, but you can call it whatever you like. When the soul is 'released' from the biological machine, it leaves this plane of existence and travels to another."

"Another plane?" she interrupted. "Like another world?"

"I don't know. I like to imagine it as bigger than another world. It's probably something beyond our comprehension, something so different than our current existence we can't even imagine what it would be. It could be vast and all encompassing, not somewhere, but everywhere. If we become pure energy, we could be anywhere and everywhere at the same time. Travel without traveling, no sense of time, only space. One little bit of energy that is part of all energy."

"Whoa! You're getting too deep for me."

"Sorry, I have a tendency to do that. My imagination is hopelessly skewed. But what I'm getting at is when the 'soul' leaves this plane, its energy signal is so small, so minute, it wouldn't be strong enough to impact this earthly plane. That's why I don't believe in traditional ghosts we like to scare ourselves with. The 'soul' wouldn't have enough energy here for us to even be able to notice it. Now, if in this other plane of existence we are able to call upon this all encompassing energy source that I think exists, then enough force could be produced to break through our earthly plane. We would have access to more power than we as humans have ever seen. Beyond nuclear!"

"That's amazing!"

"It's just a theory. I could be completely wrong, but I like to believe I'm close."

"Do you think Andee will be able to find a doorway into this other plane? Is that what you're trying to do?"

"Something like that. Right now I'm just trying to prove, scientifically, that this other plane actually exists."

"I thought you had already. I believed it when my mother was hooked up to Andee. It seemed so real."

"Yes, it did, didn't it? I just want to make sure it's not their imagination, or some chemical reaction causing hallucinations at death. That's the popular scientific theory, some kind of chemical bombardment causing nerve endings to fire uncontrollably creating vivid dreams or hallucinations."

"How can you prove it?"

"That's the million dollar question isn't it? I'm working on another theory I have and I'm hoping people like your mother are going to help me with it."

"How?" Madison asked, "I was wondering how Mom fit into all of this."

"Compared to a normal person, your mom is different. Something has changed inside her. Whenever someone has an NDE, that's what we call a Near Death Experience, something is altered inside them. Some switch or trigger has been set off or switched on prematurely, and that's what I'm trying to find. The switch, or trigger, or key if you want to call it that."

"When you find this switch or key, how will it help you see this other plane? Will it unlock something?"

"I'm hoping that the key will enable me to keep the conduit open between our plane of existence and the afterlife's, and then we can communicate with the other side or even interact with it."

She sat silent for a moment and Jake could tell she was thinking hard about something.

"I want to be part of this," she blurted.

Jake laughed. "I thought you were. These dreams have brought us together already."

"Well, yes, but I want to do more. I want to be involved in the research."

He looked at her hard, thinking he didn't need another assistant. She would probably get in the way. And Teri would probably have a fit! Still, something felt right about bringing her in.

"I really don't need another assistant. I'm not really sure what you would do besides get in the way."

She looked hurt at this and Jake immediately regretted saying it.

"All right," he said. "What can you do?"

She brightened a bit.

"Just about anything. I can do secretarial stuff, like typing reports or answering phones. I'm good with people and I can find you more subjects. Mom has contacts all over who have had similar experiences. She says they seem to find each other somehow. Could you use more NDE's?"

"Yes, actually we could. We've been having a hard time finding new subjects with these experiences. That would be excellent. You could locate new test subjects and do the preliminary interviews on them, then report to me so I can choose which would be good candidates. How does that sound?"

"When can I start?" she asked, excited.

"I don't know what I can pay you. The budget is a little tight and we just lost our two corporate sponsors."

"It doesn't matter. Gas money would be fine. I'd do it for free anyway."

"How about the day after tomorrow? Will that be all right?"

"That would be great," she said, smiling. "I haven't really done anything since—well, since Ryan died. I've felt so lost, but this seems right. I'm excited! Thank you!"

She jumped up and hugged him from across the table.

Surprised, Jake stiffened, but relaxed after a second. She felt warm and soft and her hair was clean and fresh.

She said into his ear, "Besides, now we can keep track of each other's dreams."

She pulled away, smiling.

12

January 11, 2010 8:30 a.m.

Orange Park, Florida

Jake slept like a log that night and thankfully, had no nightmares.

When he arrived at the lab, Teri was not there, which was unusual for her. Since their only other test subject, besides the now defunct Peter Vargas, was Rachael Swanson, and she was out of town, the only thing they could do was review previous sessions or perform maintenance on the system. Since he needed Teri here for the reviews, he started on some maintenance of the complex computer system which was essentially the heart of Andee. Teri showed up an hour later.

"Are you ok?" Jake asked as she walked in.

"Yeah. Sorry. I woke up late and there was an accident on I-295. Sometimes I hate living in Mandarin."

He nodded. "I was worried. Glad you're ok. I was just doing some much needed maintenance on the computer. I figured we would review Rachael Swanson's sessions after lunch. Sound good?"

"Uh huh, sounds good to me. Speaking of her, I e-mailed Rachael last night and she's back in town. She'll be ready to continue tomorrow if we want."

"Great! Perfect timing. We can only review so much. We need new data."

"I agree. Since we had to dump all of Peter's stuff, Andee is dying to be fed."

Jake couldn't figure out how to tip toe around the fact he'd hired Madison, so he just came right out with it.

"We may be getting some new subjects in the near future. Madison's mom, Sara, knows more people who share Near Death Experiences and I hired Madison to do the preliminary interviews on any new contacts she can find. She'll also do secretarial work and reception duties to free us up for research time."

She stared at him. He could see the wheels turning in there and braced for the impact, but it never came.

She said, "Fine."

Jake could tell it wasn't 'Fine' but he didn't push it.

They worked the rest of the day without any mention of Madison and even though Teri was somewhat distant, she was amicable enough. She only brought it up at the end of the day.

"So, when will Madison start?"

"Tomorrow."

"Oh—well I guess I'll have to come up with an apology then."

"That would probably be good. I want you guys to get along. Will that be a problem?"

"No, I'll be good."

Jake laughed. "I know you will. She really needs something to do. Apparently she's been cooped up all by herself since her fiancé died. And she's going to find us some new test subjects."

He walked her to her car and said goodnight. He wasn't certain, but he thought she was crying as she drove away.

13

Tallahassee, Florida

Rachael Swanson was a student at Florida State University in Tallahassee, Florida when she died. She tells people she's the reason the saying 'Party 'till you die!' exists.

Rachael and her boyfriend, John, were at John's Frat house for the annual hazing party during Rush week, and having a great time, when she finished her fifth Long Island Iced Tea and began seizing on the floor.

The first thing Rachael remembered was waking and finding she was looking down on her own body sprawled on a hospital gurney while doctors and nurses scrambled around her. She had tubes coming out of everywhere and people looked frantic.

Sounds from the scene below began to fade and she heard music, beautiful music that seemed to come from everywhere and nowhere at the same time. It felt like it was lifting her higher and for the first time she noticed glowing shapes around her. They slowly materialized into beings of warmth and light so bright they shimmered, yet it did not hurt her eyes to look.

Within the light, scenes flashed by, offering her views of her short life. Things she had forgotten and things she would never forget. They flew by at incredible speed but she saw and recognized every one. Her mother cooking dinner, her father helping her with homework, her sister breaking her arm after falling out of a tree, her grandma dying when she was eleven, she and her friends teasing Chloe Davis until she cried just because they could, her first car, her first kiss. It was all there and it was all so real, like it happened yesterday. It was then she realized this was her whole life flashing before her and she must be dead.

The beings of light began to merge into one glowing orb of golden light that beckoned and pulled at her. She heard voices calling to her from within the light but she couldn't tell what they were saying. She only knew she must follow.

Suddenly, the light faded a bit, as if it had a hiccup in power, and the hospital scene below her began to take focus again.

She could hear what the doctors and nurses were saying and the wonderful music began to fade. She could also hear what the doctor was thinking, which was really strange, and wondered if he was really pondering that left over pasta he had brought for dinner. One of the nurses was having an affair with the doctor and one of her co-workers knew this. Rachael's boyfriend, John, was still drunk, staring at a nurse's rear end and grinning, thinking things Rachael couldn't believe.

Rachael knew her relationship with John was over. Not because she was dead, but because he was an ass.

A roaring, tearing sound began to overwhelm her senses and then a voice in her head said "Go back!" and she sank from her lofty view back into her body with a whoosh. She awoke to pain and noise and a nurse saying, "The epi did it. We've got a good rhythm now." A male voice said, "Stop compressions! See if we have a pulse."

Rachael did.

Rachael was back from the dead.

And Rachael had the ability to see the future and read people's thoughts. It was strong in the first days after her death, but slowly faded with time. It never went away completely, but it was never as clear as those first few days.

Something had changed inside her and she would never be the same.

14

January 12, 2010 - 8:30 a.m.

Orange Park, Florida

Madison walked into the lab at 8:30.

Jake had arrived a little early because he wanted to be sure he was there when Madison showed up. He was still a little worried about Teri's reaction, but those fears were unfounded when Teri greeted her pleasantly enough and then proceeded to apologize.

"I wanted to say I'm sorry for the other day, Madison. I was way out of line. I guess I was a little stressed after all that's been happening. Forgive me."

"That's Ok," Madison said. "I was probably acting a little psycho myself. Who could blame you?"

"I was still not myself, and you didn't deserve it." Teri paused, "I want us to be able to work together. I was hoping we could start over again."

Madison stuck out her hand. "Hi, I'm Madison."

Teri laughed and took her hand in her own, "I'm Teri."

"Thanks," Madison said sincerely, "this means a lot to me."

Teri blushed. "Well, let me show you around."

"That would be great. By the way, I love your hair."

Teri smiled and said, "Thanks! I just had it colored at this little shop on the Westside…" And off they went, chatting.

Jake was relieved. He hoped it would last.

* * *

Madison felt a little apprehensive before arriving at the lab, but as the morning progressed, she relaxed. Jake was cute, Teri seemed amicable enough, and their test subject this morning ended up being someone she knew.

Rachael Swanson buzzed the door at a little after nine and she immediately recognized Madison. They were both the same age and had attended FSU at the same time, even took a couple of classes together. They spent some time catching up while Jake and Teri prepped Andee for the session.

When Madison realized Rachael was here because of a Near Death Experience she asked, "I remember when they took you to the E.R. after that frat party, is that why you're here? Did something happen in the E.R.?"

"Yeah—I died," Rachael said. "I had alcohol poisoning and croaked right there in the E.R. That's when I had my NDE. Not too many people know about it. They think I was just sick and then went home."

"Oh my god! That's what I thought. You know my mom had one too. I didn't believe her for the longest time until I came here with her last year. I'm a believer now!"

"What do you do here?" Rachael asked. "Did you just start, because you weren't here before?"

"Today is my first day."

"Don't you just love Dr. Jake," Rachael whispered. "He's so cute!"

Madison smiled but said nothing.

"So your mom had an NDE too?" Rachael asked.

"Yep," Madison said, nodding. "She fell in a pond in her backyard and drowned. Her grandma, who had died a year before, was there with her and told her what her children's names would be. Madison and Charlotte, my sister. Freaky huh?"

"I could read people's minds. I still can, periodically, but not whenever I want. It happens whenever it happens. I can't control it."

"Ok, girls," Jake said. "You can finish catching up later at lunch. We have to get going."

"Coming!" Rachael said to Jake, and then to Madison, "Watch my session. You'll see the mind reading part."

"I will."

Teri spent the next twenty minutes with Rachael, getting her hooked up to Andee, while Jake went over what he wanted Madison to do. Basically, she was to take notes on the whole session, paying special attention to comments made by Jake and Teri during the experiment. She said she could handle that.

Rachael's NDE started and very shortly into it, the distorted sound began and Jake said, "Two minutes and thirteen seconds into NDE, sound anomaly begins."

Madison remembered the same thing from her mom's session and started to comment on it, but decided she would wait until they were finished. She had heard this kind of distortion before, but wasn't sure if it was what she remembered from her mom's NDE or something else. She didn't want to interrupt, so she waited.

When Rachael's life review came up, Madison couldn't make out any of the images. They were somewhat distorted and went by so fast.

Jake said, "Life review anomaly begins at four minutes and thirty-seven seconds."

"They look more distorted today," Teri added. "I can hardly make out anything."

"I noticed that too," Jake said. "I wonder if we have a loose lead or something."

"I'll check it after the first run through."

Jake nodded.

When the NDE arrived at the section where Rachael could read the thoughts of the doctor and nurses, Madison laughed, then said, "Sorry. It's like watching a soap opera."

Jake and Teri nodded.

Just then a booming, thunderous, 'Go Back!' shook the room. They all jumped, and Madison screamed. It was very powerful.

Jake said, "Energy spike at eight minutes and twenty-two seconds."

The whine of the cooling system running at a high level could be heard in the background.

Teri said, "Coolant system at 85% and rising, should we stop?"

"No," Jake said. "She's almost done. Just a few seconds more."

Madison watched the coolant system gauge creep up toward 90%, then as the NDE ended, rapidly drop back to a range of 15%.

"That was intense," Madison said. "Do all of the sessions have events like that? I remember my mom's having something similar."

"Pretty much," Jake said. "They're all different in what the event is, and some are more intense than others, but they all have some kind of energy spike with an uncontrollable auditory feature. We've had water glasses shatter. Sorry, I forgot to warn you about it."

"That would've been nice. I think I peed my pants."

Teri grinned and said, "I knew it was coming, but I think I peed my pants too."

Madison laughed.

Teri continued, "They used to really scare me, but I've gotten a little used to them. It doesn't happen when we play it back. You can hear it, but it's at a normal volume and intensity. We haven't figured out why yet."

A muffled, "Everything Ok?" came from the other side of the lab.

"Yes, Rachael," Jake said. "I want to play back a part of the recording before we go through it again. Is that ok?"

"Yes," she said. "I just have to pee."

"What is it with everybody having to go to the bathroom whenever they get in there?" Teri said.

"It must have something to do with knowing you're stuck in there for a while," Jake said.

"Ok, play it back from the beginning. I want to hear something again."

Teri started the recording at the beginning and they all watched it play out again. Madison had moved up to the console and was leaning on it close to Jake watching the screen intently when Jake brushed against her and a tingle raced up her arm. Suddenly, Rachael laughed from across the lab.

"Thank you, Dr. Jake," Rachael giggled.

"Thank you what?" Jake looked confused as Teri stopped the playback.

"I could hear what you were thinking," Rachael said, giggling some more. They waited and she said, "You were thinking how lucky you were to have three beautiful girls in your lab, all to yourself."

Madison turned to him smiling and he blushed, looking away.

"I was—just—uh…" he stammered, and all three girls laughed. He smiled and said, "Sorry. It's true. I am lucky. You shouldn't be reading my mind anyway."

"It just happens," Rachael said. "I can't control it."

"All right. You're forgiven this time," Jake said. His expression changed as if something just occurred to him. "Rachael, what am I thinking now?"

"Uh—I don't know. It's gone. I've got nothing."

Jake rewound the recording back to where the distortion anomaly started and hit play. "What about now, Rachael?"

"Wow! I can see it! You're thinking about a big Philly cheese steak sandwich, covered in cheese and onions."

He stopped the playback. The distortion immediately stopped.

"And now?" Jake asked.

Sounding disappointed, Rachael said, "Nothing—I lost it."

Jake turned to Teri whose mouth was hanging open.

"She could see what I was thinking when we played this sound anomaly back. We can affect an ability by playing back a recorded session while she's hooked up to Andee."

He looked excited, pacing back and forth. "What did we just do? What is so special about this distortion? Why can't Andee decode it? We need to know what this is."

Madison knew he was just thinking out loud and not really expecting an answer, but she said, "Try it again. See if she can read my mind too."

Rachael could. And Teri's too.

They played around with it a little more and finally Rachael couldn't wait any longer for the bathroom. They got her out and she ran off to take care of business while Jake talked with Teri about the discovery.

When Rachael returned, she joined them at the console and Jake asked her, "The music you hear, when does it start? Is it right here?" He hit play at the point where the distortion began in the recording.

She watched and listened for a second. "Yep, right about there, but it's nothing like what you have recorded. You just have noise."

"That's it!" Madison blurted. "I knew I'd heard this type of distortion before."

"You've heard this before?" Jake asked.

"Not this exact sound, but something like it. It's a kind of digital distortion. You get it when the computer system you're recording to is not capturing or playing back the true waveform of the sound or music. I learned about it in a digital recording class I took at FSU. I majored in music and the class was an easy A." Madison felt embarrassed.

"So, what are you saying?" Jake asked. "The sound the computer is playing back is not the true sound that's in her NDE?"

"Sort of. It's the true sound, just not all of it. Parts of the true waveform are missing."

"How can they be missing? The computer is recording everything."

"I don't know anything about the software that's running your system, so I can't say one way or another if it's recording it all. What I do know is the sound we are hearing is distortion I associate with a compressed version of the original sound wave. The whole wave file may be in there, but it could be playing it back in a compressed form."

She paused, realized she was twisting her hair in her hands and stopped.

"It would depend on the software written to interpret the audio portion of the recording. Did you write the software that runs the system?"

Jake shook his head. "No, a friend at CRAY wrote the programs for me. His name is Bodey Jenson. One of the best software systems engineers in the country."

"He could tell you what the program is doing," Madison said. "He might even be willing to modify it so we can hear the true sound."

"I hope so," Jake said. "I'll try calling him after we eat. Ok kids, let's break for lunch. I'm buying. Good work."

* * *

At the restaurant, Rachael told them all stories of her life right after her NDE.

"I was having quite a few episodes of mind reading attacks. That's what I like to call them, attacks, because it felt like I was being bombarded. When you're taking a test in an undergraduate class of about three hundred, it can get pretty confusing. I bombed one English Lit exam when I kept hearing different answers in people's heads and then I would second guess my own."

She laughed to herself. "I kept hearing one kid louder than everyone else, and after the class, I went up to him and told him to stop thinking so loudly. He looked at me like I was a lunatic and said, 'Whatever.' He avoided me after that. I didn't care. He thought about porn a lot anyway."

"What about your boyfriend, John? What happened with him?" Madison asked.

"The next day when he came to visit me in the hospital, I told him he was an ass and I didn't want to see him ever again. He got all 'What's wrong babe?' and 'I love you' on me and wouldn't let it go, so I gave him explicit details of what he was thinking in the E.R. about a certain nurse. I'll never forget the look on his face. His jaw hit the floor and he got all freaked out. As he ran from the room, he kept looking over his shoulder like I was going to fly out of the bed on my broomstick and cast a spell on him. After that, he would run every time he saw me."

"You said the mind reading stuff slowly faded away. How long did that take?" Jake asked.

"About a year. It's never gone away completely, but now, it only happens every once in awhile. I can't control it. It happens when it happens—well, until today."

Back in the lab, Jake made the call to Bodey Jensen while Teri hooked Rachael back up to Andee. When Jake hung up he looked pleased.

"He's going to fly in first thing tomorrow and get to work on the software. He knew exactly what Madison was talking about and said it would be a breeze to update." He turned to her. "See, I knew there was a reason you were supposed to be here."

Madison felt a little embarrassed, but smiled.

15

January 12, 2010 3:00 p.m.

Orange Park, Florida

They ran through Rachael's NDE a couple more times that afternoon, but nothing new was discovered.

Andee's ability to learn seemed to be curbed. Jake hoped with the software update, things would accelerate and get them to the next level. As he watched Madison laugh and joke with Rachael, he smiled to himself. He felt the decision to bring her in had been the correct one.

That afternoon, Jake had Madison contact the one new subject they knew about here in the Jacksonville area, and Frank Lucas agreed to come see them first thing Monday morning. That gave Jake and Bodey three days to get things up to speed. He was pleased Madison was working out so well, and relieved Teri was behaving.

They closed up shop for the day and Jake told Rachael they would probably want her back late next week if she was available. She said that would be fine and to call her when he knew for sure what day. Rachael left and Jake locked up, setting the security system. He walked Madison and Teri to their cars and as he was about to get into his own, Madison came back over.

"Listen, Jake?" Madison said. "I was thinking about getting some coffee at the great place up the street. Did you want to join me?"

He paused for a second, thinking about it.

"If you're too busy, that's ok. I just thought it sounded good."

"It does sound good," Jake said. "Let's see if Teri wants to go, too."

He thought he saw a flicker of disappointment in her eyes, but he wasn't sure. Teri was pulling out of her parking space and Jake waved her over.

She pulled up, rolling her window down, and said, "What's up?"

"Madison and I were going to go get some coffee at Java Joes. Do you want to come with us?"

She hesitated. "No thanks. I've got to get home and get the dog fed. He gets mad at me if I'm too late. He's such a baby."

"Ok. Are you sure?"

"Uh huh. I'm fine. Thanks anyway. I'll see you two tomorrow."

She rolled up her window and drove off. Jake thought she had a funny look in her eyes too. What was up with these women? He'd never be able to figure them out.

"Looks like you and me," Jake said to Madison. "Do you want to walk or drive the two blocks?"

"Let's walk. I feel like I've been sitting all day."

"Me too, I'm exhausted from sitting. Does that make sense?"

She nodded. "I need a hike to wake up."

They strolled for a bit in silence, then Jake asked, "How'd you like your first day?"

"It was very exciting. I really liked it. I hope I wasn't too much of a pain for everybody."

"Are you kidding? We make one of the biggest breakthroughs in over a year and then you, all by yourself, after not even a day, figure out the distortion issue we've been wrangling with for months. I should be asking you if *I* was too much of a pain in the ass."

He stopped, turned her toward him and said, "I'm proud of you. I know I made the right decision bringing you on board. Not only are you smart, but I think you're a little lucky too."

She smiled, her green eyes shining in the crisp, early evening air. He was suddenly taken aback by her beauty. Standing there in front of him, radiant in the fading light, he had a strong urge to pull her toward him and hold her.

She looked into his eyes, smiling and said, "Lucky Maddy, is that me?"

Her eyes were mesmerizing. He couldn't look away. "Lucky Maddy. Is that what you like to be called? Maddy?" His voice seemed to be coming from far away.

Her eyes stayed locked on his. "Everybody calls me Maddy. Madison is just too formal, don't you think?"

"Maddy it is. I like it. It suits you." Finally looking away Jake said, "I don't think I've ever known any 'Maddys' before."

They turned and continued walking up the street toward Java Joes.

"Are you making fun of me, Dr. Jake?"

"No, I really don't know any 'Maddys.' And 'Dr. Jake' is not one of my favorite pet names. Rachael drives me nuts when she calls me that."

Maddy laughed. "She thinks you're cute, that's why she does it."

"Did she tell you that?"

"Yep. Well—she actually said 'Don't you think Dr. Jake is cute?'"

"And what did you say?"

"I didn't say anything."

"Nothing?" he asked. He feigned a hurt look. "My brand new employee, who I took under my wing under great strain and duress, risking bodily harm from my lab partner, wouldn't even stick up for me? I'm shocked."

She smiled. "It's because I was thinking you are very cute—in a scientificky kind of way."

"Scientificky—hmm—is that even a real word?" Jake asked. "Now I'm worried maybe I hired the wrong person."

They were at the coffee shop and Jake held the door open for her to enter.

"Ok—very, very cute," she said.

He felt a little embarrassed now, but she seemed to be enjoying herself. They grabbed a booth by the window and when the waitress arrived, both ordered coffee with sugar.

"I'm glad you took me under your wing, risking bodily harm from your lab partner," she said. "Although, I don't think she would do anything to you. Me, on the other hand…"

"I thought you two got along good today."

"Well, even though I can tell there is still something Teri doesn't like about me, she seemed pleasant enough. I just wish I knew what I've done to get on her bad side."

"She just gets into one of her moods," Jake said, not knowing why he was making excuses for Teri. "She's a great clinician, and an old, and close friend. I feel like I've known her so long, yet there are times I feel I don't know her at all. She has a tendency to keep to herself most of the time. It probably had nothing to do with you, personally. She was just having a bad day."

"Maybe," Maddy said, "but I can usually tell when someone is grumpy, or they don't like me. I get the impression Teri doesn't like me."

"Give her some time. She'll come around."

"How long have you known her?"

"Since my first year in college. We were paired up in biology as lab partners and we've been working together ever since."

"She's the brain and you're the brawn?"

"I think you have it backwards. I'm the brain and she's the brawn."

Maddy smiled. "She does seem like a tough cookie. She's definitely not afraid to say what's on her mind. You guys seem close, though."

"When Beth died, I was a wreck. She was my only friend at the time who wasn't all weird with me. No one knew how to respond so most of them avoided me."

"I know exactly what you mean. I had my mom. If she hadn't been there, I don't know what I would have done. My friends would try to get me to go out, or even try to set me up on a date, can you believe that?"

He shook his head. "I'm not making excuses for my friends, but I don't think they knew how to act around me. I mean, I was almost catatonic." He paused. "Teri at one point actually fed me with a spoon. She bathed me, dressed me, and even put me to bed. I was lost and floundering around aimlessly for weeks. She stayed with me until I could at least function. I owe her a lot."

Maddy was silent for a long moment then said softly, "Wow, I knew I was a mess, but you were so lost. I'm so sorry Jake. I wish I had known you then, I would have been there for you."

He nodded solemnly. Without even realizing it, he reached out and grabbed her hand and softly held it in his own. "I know you would have, but you had your own grief to deal with, too."

"She must have meant the world to you. Can you talk about it now? I'd like to hear."

Jake thought about Beth every day. Keeping the pain and memories to himself, he rarely spoke about her to others. It had been a long time since he had talked about the accident with someone else, and normally, he was reluctant to do so, but with Maddy, something felt different.

Yes, he barely knew her, but he felt connected to her somehow. Maybe it was because they shared a common tragedy in their lives. He wasn't sure, but he knew he hadn't felt this way in a long time.

He told her everything.

Maddy listened quietly, never interrupting him. He held on to her hand the whole time, sometimes squeezing so hard she winced, but she never stopped him and never let go. By the time he had told the whole story, she was crying.

"This was just supposed to be a cup of coffee," he said, getting himself under control. "How did we get here?"

"We're here because I wanted to know," she said. "And maybe you needed to tell me. I'm glad you did. She was someone very special and I feel I know her a little now. I wish I had been able to meet her."

Jake said, "You will."

"I hope so," Maddy said, "I hope so."

And Jake let her hand go.

16

January 13, 2010 - 3:32 a.m.

Orange Park, Florida

Jake sat bolt upright in his bed, gasping, a scream barely contained.

The sheets clung to his damp skin trying to trap him in the nightmare. His feet, tangled in the linen, struggled to break free and he slowly became aware of his surroundings as his frantic kicking subsided.

The nightmare had come again and this time seemed even more real than the last. Everything was the same, just more vivid. Beth's face right before he woke was terrifying. An image he couldn't stand to recall.

The room seemed to reverberate from the colossal 'Stop!' that had come out of Beth's mouth. Her lips had barely moved and so little effort had been made in speaking the word, yet the sound had been a deafening, booming, shout.

His phone rang and he jumped.

"Shit!" he said, running his hands through his hair. He took a deep breath and picked up the handset on the third ring.

"Hello," Jake said, softly, a little creeped out as to what might be on the other end.

"Jake! It's Maddy, Oh God—I can't take this!"

"Maddy, what happened? Are you all right?"

"I had the dream again. It was so real. Oh Jake, I'm so scared."

"It's ok, I'm right here. Just try and calm down. It's over—it's over."

He could hear her crying softly. She took a deep breath and said, "I'm sorry—I just…"

"It's ok," he interrupted. "Don't be sorry. I was awake."

"Mom and Dad went to see Nana and I'm here all by myself. I'm so scared."

"Do you have someone who can come over and stay with you? Do you want me to come over there?"

"Could you?" Maddy said, pleading. "No one else will understand. I don't think I can stay here by myself."

"Let me throw some clothes on and I'll be right there. What's the address?"

She gave him directions and they hung up.

Throwing on an old t-shirt and sweat pants, he grabbed his cell and wallet. It was only about a five minute drive and he was knocking on her door. He could see a shadow looking through the peephole and then the door was unbolted and thrown open.

She threw herself at him and hugged him tight.

"Oh Jake! I'm so glad you're here!"

He could feel her trembling, "Whoa!" he said. "Hey…" he pulled away slightly, and tilted her chin up. "It's ok now. I've got you. What scared you so badly? It's a dream remember?"

"It was so real," she said again, "and there's something else."

"What?"

"Come in, I'll show you."

She grabbed his hand and pulled him inside. It was as if she didn't want to be more than a few inches away from him. He let her cling to his arm as she led him through the small, single story, ranch style house.

Every light was burning bright and he could see clean, but dated furnishings in a comfortable and cozy country décor. Family pictures hung on the hall wall where he found Sara and Maddy, and what must also be her father and sister, Charlotte. She was another stunning beauty favoring her mother's blond locks where Maddy shared her father's red hair.

He'd never met the man and had no idea what he did for a living, but he looked somewhat industrial; medium height and stocky with large hands and bulging forearms. One picture showed him in greasy coveralls standing proudly in front of a blue '69 Chevelle.

They passed through a medium sized kitchen with older appliances, the exception being a brand new stainless fridge, which looked somewhat out of place. They continued down a long hallway and Jake had the impression the place was bigger than it first appeared. As she pulled him along, they passed three doors on the left and two on the right. They were closed except for the last one. Jake caught a brief glimpse of a bathroom.

The last door at the end of the hall stood open and Maddy led him inside what was surely her room.

"See," she said, but Jake did not.

The room was small and tidy, decorated in the country theme that carried throughout the house. The walls were a muted yellow with pictures of Maddy and her friends from days past. The bed was a queen with a large canopy, the sheets rumpled and slept in. A dresser with a mirror was to the left of the doorway and there were snapshots of people and places stuck in between the mirror's glass and the frame. Two nightstands with lamps burning brightly were placed on either side of the bed framing a large window draped in a sheer purple fabric. An older desk of dark wood stood against the wall opposite the bed and held a small TV and laptop computer. Knickknacks and collectibles adorned a few shelves scattered around the room and Jake thought, *Thank God there were no unicorns.*

Jake noticed that every other picture had Ryan, her dead fiancé, in it. There were shots of them together with friends in a club, everyone holding their drink up in a toast to the unknown photographer, tongues hanging out in that gesture the young seemed to think was cool. There was one with Maddy and Ryan in cold weather gear, holding each other tightly in front of a ski lift with the winter sunshine framing them from the side. She looked so happy.

He found another one with Ryan, tanned and shirtless, standing with a beer in his hand next to Maddy's father who also had a beer. They were in front of a sparkling pool with Maddy floating on a raft in the background waving at the camera. There were so many more. The two at the beach, at Disney World, driving with the top down, on a fishing boat, on a pier somewhere with the sun setting behind them, so happy.

These scenes only reminded Jake of his own loneliness and his longing for Beth. He had pictures just like these but couldn't bear looking at them.

Jake realized there was something missing.

Where was the picture of Ryan holding the big fish he had caught the day he died? The one he had seen the day Maddy visited the lab during her mother's sessions. He looked all around the room scanning the wall.

Maddy let his hand go and walked over to the wall opposite the door. She bent down looking at something on the floor. Jake walked over and knelt beside her. The fish picture lay on the floor between them, the glass shattered and scattered in sharp pieces around the frame. Jake thought it odd that it broke into so many small fragments, like it had been crushed. He went to reach for a piece of the glass, but Maddy grabbed his wrist.

"Don't," she said.

"Is this what you wanted to show me?"

She nodded.

"What happened?"

She stood looking around the room as if searching for something, but finding nothing, said, "At the end of my dream there was a loud thump that shook the whole room. The room that was in my dream. My room." She looked around warily again and wandered over to the dresser. "When Ryan said your name, even though it was coming through the cell phone speaker, it was so loud it shook the room, too." She looked up at him with haunted eyes. "In my dream, pictures rattled and fell off the wall and one shattered as if smashed, then fell off the wall. I woke up, about to scream, and the sounds seemed to follow me out of the dream." She paused, walked back over to Jake and whispered, "This picture was lying on the floor and I swear I could hear the glass tinkling like it had just finished breaking."

Jake knelt down again looking at the broken glass and the fragmented picture of Ryan distorted through the shards. He picked up a piece and she did not stop him this time. It seemed like ordinary glass.

"Could you have broken it in your sleep, like sleep walking or something?" he said, standing.

"No. I'm not imagining things, Jake." She paced. "I was in my bed when I woke, how could I have broken it from in my bed?"

"Could you have thrown something over here in your nightmare?" he asked, looking around for something that might have broken the picture.

"No! You don't believe me?"

"No—I mean yes—yes I believe you. I'm just playing devil's advocate, I guess. Sorry, don't be upset at me. I guess this scares me a little too—because I had my dream tonight. I had just woken up from it when you called."

"And you didn't tell me?"

"I never really got the chance. I rushed over here and you brought me right here. I'm telling you now aren't I?"

The edge in his voice visibly upset her and she turned away from him with fresh tears springing in the corners of her eyes.

"You're right, Jake. I'm sorry. I never gave you the chance to tell me. I guess I was just frightened."

He walked over and turned her toward him.

"Hey," he said. "Maddy, look at me. I didn't mean to snap at you. I guess we're both a little freaked out, huh?"

She nodded her head, still unable to look at him.

"We'll figure this out, I promise."

She looked up at him, eyes red and wet, her face flushed. "Promise?"

"Promise," and he crossed his heart, smiling.

She moved inside his arms, pressing against him, and he closed them around her. Even though she had been asleep, her hair smelled clean with a hint of some flowery shampoo. He could feel the heat from her body through the thin t-shirt he wore and he held her tighter to him marveling in how good she felt against his body.

She was wearing a thin one piece nightgown which felt slippery against her skin as he caressed her back trying to comfort her. She had been holding her arms curled up against herself as he held her, tense and upset, but as he stroked her back, she began to relax. She lowered her arms and then encircled his waist holding him, pressing harder against his body, melding hers into his, and he could feel her firm breasts pressing against his chest through the thin nightgown.

Their lower bodies came together naturally and the warmth of her against his groin assaulted his senses and he became aroused so quickly he barely had time to think about what was happening.

She picked her head up off of his chest and looked into his eyes. Her lips parted slightly, and her sweet breath played softly across his lips.

She was so close.

She stood slowly on tiptoes, sliding her body exquisitely against his as she rose up, and brushed her lips softly against his. All his anguish over Beth, his devotion and abstinence, melted away as he let go and pressed his mouth firmly against hers, feverishly and hungrily satisfying his urge. His desire rose so quickly, there was never a chance to quell it and she seemed to find as much urgency in her own response as his.

Her lips parted and his tongue found the softness of her mouth as their passion grew. He pulled her to him harder, thrusting against her as they both gasped in the pure electric shocks that coursed through their bodies.

His right hand slid up and cupped her breast through the thin material of her nightgown, his thumb playing against her hard nipple. She moaned against his lips and pulled away, breaking the kiss, and gasping for air. He pulled her back to him and as he thrust his tongue even deeper into her eager mouth, she slid her hand up under his t-shirt and caressed his chest with her warm hand.

She broke away again and stepped back.

Keeping her eyes locked on his, she slipped the nightgown off of her shoulders and it fell to the floor in a soft whisper of fabric. Her breasts were full and slightly upturned at the nipples, which stood hard and thrusting in the cool room. Her panties, pink with a small purple flower at the hip, could not conceal the reddish blond hair showing through the thin fabric. Her neck was flushed and her lips full and red from the eagerness of their kiss.

She took his hand in hers and pulled him to her, sliding his fingers under the elastic of her panties and against the heat between her legs. She shuddered and gasped. Her green eyes were blazing and he could see himself in them.

Sliding her hands up inside his t-shirt, she pulled it over his head. She kissed his mouth hard and then moved down to his neck and chest. Reaching down, she felt him through his pants and he thought he would explode.

He fumbled with his drawstring and she helped him, fumbling with it too and they giggled, breaking the tension a bit. He finally got it untied and she slowly, deliberately, pulled his pants down, keeping her eyes locked with his, a sexy little grin on her lips.

She let his pants fall the rest of the way to the floor, bringing her fingers slowly up his legs and then grabbing him firmly with both her hands. A moan escaped his lips.

He slipped her panties all the way off and they joined the pile of clothes at their feet. Pulling her toward him, he pressed his body hard against hers, feeling the glorious warmth of her nakedness from head to toe.

She pulled him backwards to the bed and they fell in a heap together, limbs entwined, mouths eagerly kissing and hands feverishly stroking. His mouth found her erect nipple and she moaned loudly as he suckled it hard, nibbling a bit. She rolled on top of him, straddling his hips, caressing his thighs with her fingers and kissing his chest and stomach as her long hair draped over his body.

He gently pulled her face back to his and kissed her sweetly at first and then ever more urgently. She reached down and guided him into her, slowly sliding the length of him with her warmth. He was so close to losing it, he felt like a schoolboy. They slowly moved together, him thrusting ever deeper, the pace quickening as their desire built.

She raised up on her arms, head back and breasts thrust forward as she rocked rhythmically with him, her urgency rising. He couldn't hold much longer and she seemed to sense his closeness and thrust that much harder.

She was gasping and making small noises of pleasure as he held her, driving harder and deeper into her, his climax building. As his first explosion rocked her body, she let out a small cry and her body shuddered, joining his in her own climax, pulsing up and down along him, her body collapsing to his as they released years of built up tension in a wonderful rush of desire.

He held her against him as she cried softly against his neck.

Shortly, he fell fast asleep, still locked together, their bodies cooling in the night air.

One thought kept repeating in Jake's mind over and over, and it followed him into sleep. *What have I done?*

17

January 12, 2010 - 9:12 a.m.

Orange Park, Florida

When Maddy woke, Jake was not there.

At first she thought he had slipped out in the night and her disappointment was palpable. How could he leave, without even a word, after what happened last night? Their bond had been so intense. She had never felt anything like that with Ryan. She felt like crying again as the brief guilt she felt after they made love came back with an intensity she didn't expect.

It was then she heard small noises coming from another part of the house. Kitchen noises. Her spirits immediately lifted and she got up, found her panties and nightgown, slipped them on, and padded softly down the hall in her bare feet. She found Jake searching through the cupboards for something and as he closed the door, she startled him. He laughed at his own jitters and she smiled coyly, coming around the counter, stepping to him and letting him enfold his arms around her, holding her against his warm body again.

She sighed.

* * *

"I thought you left," she said.

"Leave?" he said, unwrapping himself from her and continuing his search for coffee and mugs. He could tell she was disappointed he was no longer holding her. "I was trying to find coffee. I was going to surprise you with breakfast."

"I thought you might have been upset about last night and left before you had to face me."

She watched him closely and he knew this was a test, yet he couldn't look at her. His hesitation said it all and she looked crestfallen. He had already gotten a 'D' on the test.

"Maddy…" he began, searching for the right thing to say. "How are you feeling about—you know…?" He was making some foolish gesture with his hands and stopped. "I mean—are you ok with what happened last night?"

She simply said, "Yes."

She was so direct, he had to smile.

Her face brightened a bit and he said, "I need to be honest with you Maddy. I'm a little confused right now. I haven't been with anyone since Beth and…"

"Neither have I," she interrupted.

"…and I'm not sure how to feel. There is definitely something between us, because last night was, uh…"

She smiled and nodded.

He smiled too. "I guess what I'm saying is…"

She walked over and pressed her finger to his lips.

"Sshh. Did you feel anything last night?" she whispered.

He nodded.

"So did I. Do you care about me?"

He nodded again.

"I care about you," she said. "Do you regret anything about last night?"

He hesitated, and then nodded slowly.

"So do I," she said. Her finger was still pressed to his lips and he furrowed his brow, confused.

"Jake, I think we both needed this," she said, dropping her finger from his lips. "I have felt so empty and lost for so long, it was becoming unbearable. When I had my nightmare last week and heard your name, I knew we were meant for something. I didn't want to admit it to myself at first, but now I know."

He wasn't as convinced as she and he remained silent.

"When we—after we were together last night," she said. "I cried because I felt so guilty. I felt like I had betrayed Ryan somehow. That I had cheated on him. Even though he has been gone for almost two years, I still feel connected to him and wanted to remain faithful to his memory. I regret feeling that way, but I don't regret what we did last night."

She stepped closer to him and looked up into his eyes. "Jake, what we had last night was beautiful. We were connected. I felt it with you and I know you felt it with me. I love Ryan and always will, but I never had with him what we had last night. It was magical."

Jake wanted to pull her to him and hold her until it stopped hurting, but that hurt, that guilt was what was stopping him. He knew she was right. What had happened last night was special, but he wasn't sure if it was the result of two years worth of pent up energy or the magic she described.

She was waiting, looking up into his eyes. She was so vulnerable and so beautiful.

"Maddy, I have to be honest with you. I felt so guilty this morning, that I almost did bolt and run. You're so beautiful and special that I felt I not only betrayed Beth, I betrayed you." He reached up and held her face in his hands. "Maybe we should stop this before it goes any further and we both get hurt." He felt like an ass as the words left his lips.

She pulled away from him, clearly hurt. "Fine," she said, turning away.

She stopped and turned back and he saw a little fire in her eyes.

"You know Jake, I expected a little more from someone like you. If I had wanted a cheap line like that, I could have picked up any Joe Blow in a bar and brought him home. Is that all you can say, 'We should stop before we get hurt?' Well, I'm already hurt."

"Maddy, you're right, that was a dumb thing to say and it came out all wrong. What I know in my heart is that I don't know if I can give you what you want. I don't know if I'm capable of loving someone right now."

"Who said anything about love? We've only known each other for a few days. But I feel something for you and it's something stronger than just two lonely people needing sex. I just want to know you. Don't you want to know me?"

"Yes. Of course," he said, taking a step toward her. "I'm just confused right now. I've spent the last two years of my life trying to find a way back to Beth. I've done nothing but work on a way to talk to her. To see her again. The last thing she said to me as she died in my arms is a mystery and I need to know what she meant. And now, I'm getting messages from her in my dreams that raise more questions than answers. I loved her..." he stopped. "I love her so much. I can't deny that and just throw it away and start over again. It's not fair to you for me to lead you on. You asked me if I felt something for you. I do. You also asked if I care for you. I do. I just don't know if I can go any farther than that right now."

She no longer looked angry. She went to him and he took her in his arms and held her.

"Jake, I don't know if I can go any farther than this right now either. I want this to be what it is. Nothing more. Can we do that?"

"Of course." The tension was leaving him. "Besides, who else do I have to rescue at 3:30 in the morning?"

She hit him playfully in the butt. "Nobody, you lecherous old man."

"Me? Lecherous? And old?"

"Yes—you. I needed your help," she teased, "and you came over and took advantage of a helpless, lonely girl in need."

"Hey, who kissed who first?"

She lifted her head off of his chest and looked into his eyes. "I did." And she lifted up on her toes and kissed him again.

"Is that against the rules?" she asked huskily.

"No," he said and kissed her back. He broke the kiss and joked, "You're killing me!"

"Horrible way to die isn't it?"

"Look at me!" he said, wriggling his erection against her. "This is what happened last night."

"I know," she said. "I like it."

"Me too," he said kissing her again. He picked her up playfully and spun her around while she squealed and beat on his back. He set her back down and said, "You're something."

"Something what Dr. Jake?"

"Something special."

"Are you getting all mushy on me? That might be against the rules."

"What are the rules?"

She thought for a second and said, "We're only allowed to have sex and be friends."

"Do you know you've just described every college guy's dream girl?"

She laughed. "Are you complaining?"

"I'm not in college," he said dryly, "but I'll take it."

"Now?" she asked, mischievously.

"Now."

He picked her up and carried her into her bedroom. He was surprised how eager he was even after the argument they just had about keeping it low profile. Afterwards, she lay atop him and he caressed her backside, enjoying the afterglow.

After a bit she said, "What did Beth say?"

He didn't answer right away so she said, "You said she told you something you had to find the answer to. Something you didn't understand as she slipped away in your arms. What did she say?"

"She said, 'Be good to Madison and Lucas,' and then something I couldn't understand."

She picked her head up and looked at him surprised. "Me?"

He shook his head. "I don't know. I always assumed she was talking about our unborn twins. She was pregnant with them when she died, but I didn't find out until after the ER doctor told my family and they later told me. A boy and a girl. She was talking so faintly when she went, I had a hard time understanding what she said. The only thing I heard was 'Be good to Madison and Lucas.'"

"Maybe she saw your future and you're supposed to be with me. It would make sense. That's why my Ryan keeps saying your name in my dream."

"I don't know. Who is Lucas? And why does she tell me to 'Stop!' in my dream? What am I supposed to stop? At first I thought she was telling me to stop trying to hear what she's murmuring in the dream, but now I don't know. Maybe she wants me to stop being with you."

It was out before he could catch it.

She shook her head. "I don't believe that. I'm being told to find you in my dream and you're being told to stay away? It doesn't make sense." She paused. "Your dream tonight, what happened?"

"The same as the other night, but a lot more vivid and real. Her face was so horrible, like I didn't know her. The thumps were louder and when she said 'Stop!' it was thunderous, even though her mouth barely moved. As I woke, the sound seemed to be reverberating in the room. Like it had followed me out of the dream. Nothing was broken in my house though."

"We're missing something. It doesn't make sense."

"I know. I wish I knew what it was."

"Do you want to stop being with me?"

"No. I think we're supposed to figure this out together."

"Good," she said, laying her head back down on his chest. "I was hoping you would say that, because that's what I think too."

They showered together and then, after she showed him where everything was in the kitchen, he finally fixed her the breakfast he promised. Afterwards Jake asked her if she wanted to go to the airport with him. He was picking up Bodey at noon out of Chicago.

"Ok. Will he mind? He doesn't know me."

"Are you kidding?" Jake laughed. "He'll be hitting on you from the second he sees you."

"Maybe I don't want to go then."

"Come," he said. "You'll like Bodey and I'll like the company on the drive."

She smiled and said, "Ok."

18

January 13, 2010 12:15 p.m.

Jacksonville, Florida

Bodey's flight was a half hour late and as Jake spotted him coming down the ramp, he waved and yelled, "Bodey! Over here!"

Bodey was short and stocky, five foot four with curly brown hair and a full beard which was in serious need of trimming. He wore a Sherman Oaks Physical Education t-shirt with a thin blue windbreaker, purple with white striped jogging pants, and dirty gray sneakers. His luggage consisted of a beat up old duffel bag which he dragged along the ground behind him.

"Jake! What's up my man!" Bodey said extending a hand and going through a complicated handshake ritual that never seemed to grow old.

"Bodey," Jake said. "Glad ya' made it. You're looking good."

"Bullshit!" Bodey said. "I look like crap, but hey, I had to get up at three this morning to get here. You owe me." He grinned, showing crooked, but surprisingly white teeth.

"I do," Jake said. "But wait 'till you see what you've got to work on. I'll owe you big time for that."

"Hey, who's this?" Bodey asked, looking Maddy's way. "Is she a new assistant or is this your sister?"

"Bodey this is my new lab assistant, Maddy, so be good. Maddy, Bodey Jensen."

"Hi." Maddy smiled and extended her hand. He waved it away, grabbed her and gave her a big hug.

"Maddy," he said, trying it on for size. "I like that name, it's cool. Fits you too. Has anybody ever told you you're stunning?"

"Come on Bodey," Jake said. "I told you to behave."

He gave a look like 'What!?' but Maddy said, "He is behaving. I can live with stunning."

"See," Bodey said, "she likes me." He looked around and said, "So where's Teri? She didn't miss me?"

"She'll be at the lab when we get there," Jake said, "and she can't wait to see you."

He looked disappointed, but said, "I can't wait to see her either." He winked at Maddy. "I think Teri likes me."

"In your dreams, man," Jake said. "Come on. Let's get you out of here."

"New lab assistant, huh?" Bodey said. Then he stopped and Jake and Maddy did the same, turning to look at him. "Wait a minute," he said. "You two got something going on, don't you?"

Jake felt his face flush and Maddy looked down and away, blushing.

"I knew it. Good for you Jake," Bodey said. "It's about time you stopped hanging around dead people."

Maddy looked shocked, but Jake laughed and took it in stride. Bodey had a way of saying it without offending him.

"We're just friends," Jake said, but smiled at Maddy and she smiled back. "So don't get all worked up."

"Nope," Bodey said. "You guys are more than friends," and left it at that.

"How was the flight?" asked Jake, changing the subject.

"Bumpy and long. The pilot kept getting on the P.A. and saying air traffic needed us to do this and there was weather over the Appalachians and air traffic needed us to do that. I just wanted to sleep and the guy would not shut up. I finally asked the stewardess if he was always this talkative. She said, 'You have no idea.' So I told her to feed him or something so he would let us passengers get some shut eye. She laughed and said, 'Let me see what I can do.' I never heard a peep out of him the rest of the flight."

"Did you get to sleep?" Maddy asked.

"Nah—it was like trying to sleep on a rollercoaster. Then everybody was hurling all over."

"Oh, man! That sucks!" Jake said. "What a crappy flight."

"Depends on how you look at it," Bodey said with a grin. "I got to hold this beautiful blond girl's hair out of the way while she puked in an airsick bag. She loves me now."

"Bodey—only you man," Jake chuckled.

"Hey, I got her number! She's here in town for a few days visiting her parents. Her name is Robin." He was waving a scrap piece of paper in the air proudly. "I figure if you hold a girl's hair out of the way while she hurls, you're practically her boyfriend already. Pretty intimate stuff."

Maddy was laughing hard at this and said, "Jake was right. I like you already."

Bodey grinned.

As they walked down the concourse toward the baggage area, a guy with a luggage cart ran smack into Bodey's duffel bag as he dragged it behind him.

Bodey didn't even seem to notice, but Jake said, "Whoa! Did that guy just kill your laptop?"

"Nope, it's not in the bag."

"Did you check it?"

"Nope," Bodey said, with a smirk on his face.

They all stood around staring at each other for a second and finally Jake said, "Did you bring it?"

Bodey shook his head but still had a smirk on his face.

"Well, then how are you going to...?" Jake started to ask but Bodey held up his hand, palm down.

With a flourish, he turned his hand over and opened it revealing a small device the size of a cigarette lighter. It was black and smooth and seamless. It looked like a polished domino without the dots and designs. Jake and Maddy both crowded in closer to look and Jake smiled.

"You did it?" Jake asked.

Bodey grinned and nodded.

"It's beautiful," Jake said. "I can't believe it."

"You're looking at the next generation of laptop," Bodey said, glancing around conspiratorially, and talking in a subdued tone. "It's actually more of an interface, but it has Wi-Fi capability, enabling it to access its home processor from anywhere. It's top secret," he whispered.

"This is a computer?" Maddy asked.

"SSHHH!" Bodey shushed, then grinned. "I'm not supposed to have it here with me, but I couldn't resist."

"How does it open?" asked Jake.

"Not here. I'll show you back at the lab."

He put it in his front pocket and started walking toward the exit dragging his beat up duffel bag behind him.

19

January 13, 2010 12:30 p.m.

Jacksonville, Florida

As Peter watched, the small group passed him by.

He was standing just inside the art gallery of Jacksonville International Airport, and they never turned his way. Set in a small section of the center food and shopping court, it was a feature of the airport rarely used. Most travelers were in too much of a hurry or couldn't care less about art. There were too many other distractions in the court such as alcohol and food. He pulled a cell phone out and dialed a number from memory. It was answered by the General on the third ring.

"Yes."

"I'm at the airport," Peter said. "The computer geek just arrived."

"Bodey Jensen?"

"Yes. They're heading to the lab now. The girl I told you about is with them also."

"All right, stay on them. I want to know everything that is said in the lab and on his cell. And I guess we'll need some equipment on the girl."

"Yes sir."

"Keep me informed," the General said and the line went dead.

Peter then dialed another number from memory and a gruff voice answered, "Yeah."

"It's me. I need some equipment."

Peter gave his instructions to the individual and concluded the conversation with a place and time to pick up the supplies. He could only safely use each outside asset three or four times and then it became too much of a risk. Peter had used this asset three times already and he would have to terminate the relationship after this drop.

Peter pressed end. The phone was now compromised.

He removed the back cover from the phone and took out the battery. He pulled a small, thin metallic object from his pocket and ran it along the electronics exposed inside the battery compartment of the phone. A small spark erupted, but nothing anyone standing within three feet would notice. The phone was now useless. He deposited it in the nearest trash can. The battery he disposed of in the men's room and the small metal tool he threw away as he exited the airport.

20

January 13, 2010 2:00 p.m.

Orange Park, Florida

Bodey, Jake, and Maddy entered the lab at two o'clock in the afternoon. The three were laughing and joking around as Teri yelled, "Bodey!" and came running over.

"Hey girlfriend!" Bodey said, and gave her a big hug. "How 'bout a big kiss for the geek?"

Teri laughed and said, "There's nowhere to kiss. It's all too furry."

Bodey laughed too. "How 'bout here?" indicating his forehead. She gave him a big smooch. "How are you?"

"I'm better now that you're here. I've missed you."

"Me too. Where are you staying?"

"I don't know." He turned to Jake. "Where am I staying?"

"With me, or we can get you a hotel room if you'd like."

"I was kind of hoping to stay with Teri now that she's asked."

"You know you can't stay with me," Teri said. "I don't trust you alone with me." But she smiled and so did he.

"I'll call Robin," Bodey said. "She'll probably let me stay with her."

Jake and Maddy laughed and Teri said, "Who's Robin?"

"She's the girl I met on the plane. I held her hair while she barfed."

"Never mind," Teri said. "I don't want to know."

"Bodey, you're with me, is that ok?" Jake asked.

"That's great Bro'."

"All right," Jake said. "Are you ready to do a little work?"

"Let's get to it," Bodey said.

He pulled out the palm sized computer he showed them at the airport. "Let me get this thing synced up to the CRAY and we'll be in business."

Bodey pressed some hidden button or sensor on the computer and it sprang open like a folded up piece of paper. It kept unfolding on itself until it was the size of a hardcover book laid open. He pressed another area in the upper right corner and the computer came to life. A screen appeared in the upper half and a keyboard in the lower. He tapped a few keys on the now visible keyboard and the CRAY emblem appeared with a query asking if the user wanted to log on to unit JT00004CR2, which was the identification number of Jake's CRAY.

"Bodey," Jake said, "that is truly amazing. How did you guys get past the circuitry issue in the keyboard?"

"We just skipped it."

"Skipped it?" Jake asked. "What did you do?"

"We modified a design of yours, actually," Bodey said, grinning. "We took the sensing material you used in the body mold of Andee, layered it with pliable LCD material, and now there is one subatomic connection between the lower part of the unit and the screen. The keyboard doesn't react to my touches. It reads what I am thinking and reacts by sending the correct key input. I don't even have to type if I don't want to."

"What?! You're kidding right?" Jake was floored.

Bodey shook his head and said seriously, "Buddy, your shit is the most amazing stuff we have to work with. We've made leaps and bounds with your discoveries. Why do you think I was able to drop everything and come down here? You're invaluable to the company and we want to make sure we have access to your noggin. Watch this."

Bodey looked at the screen and the cursor moved over the query and then clicked 'OK.' A password screen appeared and a series of letters and numbers filled the line quicker than any of them could see. The cursor moved and clicked 'OK' again and the computer was now logged on to Jake's CRAY. All this without Bodey lifting a finger or moving an inch.

Jake, stunned, giggled like a kid. Maddy was grinning from ear to ear and Teri had her hand over her mouth but you could see her eyes smiling.

"And it's protected by the most powerful encryption known to man," Bodey said. "It's linked to my individual brain waves and will only respond to me. We don't think it can be hacked, but we've been trying. No luck so far, so it's virtually secure. Cool, huh?"

"I don't think 'cool' is the right word, dude," Jake said. "I'm speechless."

"I told you it was sweet," Bodey said. "Now, let's take a look at your problem…"

21

January 12, 2010 3:30 p.m.

Orange Park, Florida

Jake and Bodey had been working with Andee for over an hour and Jake was feeling a little anxious.

Bodey was awfully quiet, but Jake was trying not to let it bother him. He knew it was the way Bodey worked.

Bodey was in the process of writing code to address the sound anomaly issue. He said he knew exactly what the issue was, but first needed to see if the software he had originally written for Andee was recording the whole sound wave. As he viewed the existing data, he looked concerned.

Jake was watching him and said, "What?"

Bodey shook his head. "This file is huge. No wonder you can't hear the whole wave. I've never seen a sound file this big."

"Why is it so big?"

"That's the question of the day, isn't it?"

"What's considered big?"

"I'll explain it like this—you take a normal music CD, it's formatted at 16 bits, and 44Khz, which is good, but not the best sound quality..." He stopped and stared at Jake. Jake must have had a funny look on his face because Bodey said, "Do you understand what is going on digitally with a CD?"

Jake nodded his head. "I remember basics, but refresh my memory."

"Ok—basic sound 101. An analog sound, the sound waves you and I hear through our eardrums is basically just that, a wave. A sine wave to be more specific. Look…" Bodey took a pen and a piece of paper and drew and wavy line which looked like a snake. "The wave has rounded peaks and valleys as the sound is produced. When the digital revolution came along, the computer was programmed to try and represent this linear wave in a computer's world, which is not linear. Because computer language is a series of ones and zeroes, you'll never have a completely linear wave. Get it?"

"Partly," Jake said.

"All right, let's try it this way. When I say CD quality sound is 16 bit and 44Khz., what that means is the wave is represented by a number with 16 zeroes in it and each number has 44100 samples of sound per cycle. The computer assigns each sound sample a number which is 16 places long. That sixteen place number is a series of ones and zeroes. When you add that all up, 44100 sixteen place numbers per wave cycle, is a lot of numbers, right?"

Jake nodded.

"But it still has flaws because it is not linear," Bodey continued. "The computer's wave looks jagged, like a set of stairs going up and down along the wave's peaks and valleys. There are gaps of true sound missing where each step in the wave is. In CD quality, the human ear can barely detect these gaps, that is why the CD is so popular, but some people can still hear it and don't like it. They say it's tinny sounding or some of the nuances of the music are missing and they would be correct because some of the true analog wave form is missing. DVD quality is better sounding because it's represented by bigger numbers thus a bigger file. A DVD is recorded at 32 bits and 96Khz, which, if you follow what we talked about, is a file with each cycle having 96000 samples of a number with 32 places in it. You see, in DVD quality, the little steps, or blanks in the wave are smaller, thus a better representation of the true sound wave? Get it?"

Jake smiled and said, "Yeah, I get it now. So how big is our wave file?"

"That's the problem," Bodey said. "I'm not sure, but it's bigger than 256 bits and 96Khz which is a truly complex computer representation. I have to work on this a bit to extract it all. Take a break Bro' while I crunch some numbers."

Jake walked over to where Maddy was working on a few contacts her mother had given her and said, "Any luck?"

"Not really," she said. "Two answering machines and one wife who said she would give her husband a message. Mom says 'Hi' by the way. They got back this afternoon and she asked what happened to the picture in my room, so I told her everything including the fact that you stayed with me last night."

"You told her everything?" Jake asked.

"Not everything," Maddy said, playfully. "She wanted to make sure I said, 'Thank you' from both of them for watching over me. She wants to make you dinner tonight."

"That's awfully nice of her, but I have Bodey with me."

"I told her that, and she said bring him. And Teri too."

"Ok. Sounds good."

"I'll call her back and tell her," Maddy said. "How about six thirty?"

"That will work. Its four thirty now and I don't want to overwork Bodey. He's had a long day, what with the barfing blond and all."

Maddy laughed. "He's a trip."

"Yes he is. Where's Teri?

"I don't know. I haven't seen her in a while. She's hardly said two words to me today."

Just then, Teri poked her head from around the partition separating the sensing chair and the control desk and yelled, "Jake, come here for a sec. I want you to see this."

Jake and Maddy both walked over and Teri bent down next to the chair and pointed at something attached to the underside of the pedestal. It was a small, silver, metallic object with a very fine hair-like filament protruding from the side. It was the size of a hearing aid battery.

"What's this?" Teri said.

"I don't know," Jake said.

"Well, I think I do, now that you seem surprised it's here," Teri said.

She pried the small object from the pedestal, stood, and carried it over to the sink where she proceeded to fill a glass with water and drop it in.

"There," she said. "That'll take care of that."

"Take care of what?" Bodey said, joining the group.

Teri held the glass up for Bodey and he peered inside.

"That's a bug," Bodey said. "And a nice one. Somebody spent some money on this."

"Breckenridge," Teri and Jake said at the same time.

"Who's Breckenridge?" asked Maddy.

"General Breckenridge is the head of the government organization funding our research. They're our sole source of income right now," Jake said. "Apparently he doesn't trust the reports I've been filing with him, so he's taken it upon himself to get accurate intel his own way."

"Peter probably planted this," Teri said. "I'll bet there are more. Should we look?"

Jake thought for a moment, then shook his head. "No, we don't have time right now. It would be like looking for a needle in a hay stack. We'll start tomorrow. Bodey's probably exhausted and I should get him to the house and cleaned up. We're all invited over to Maddy's place for dinner. Maddy's mom, Sara, is going to cook for us."

"I am beat. Hungry too," Bodey said. "Sounds good. Does she know how to cook?"

"Yes sir," Maddy said with a twang. "Good 'ol southern cookin'. Fried chicken and sweet tea, corn bread and collards."

"What's a collard?" Bodey asked.

"You'll love it," Jake said, clapping Bodey on the back. "It's like wilted salad."

"Great," Bodey said, sarcastically. "Can't wait."

22

January 13, 2010 6:12 p.m.

Orange Park, Florida

Jake and Bodey arrived at Maddy's a little after six. Teri was there already, drinking a Corona with a lime in it and talking with Sara.

Sara came over, gave Jake a big hug and kiss and said, "Thanks so much for keeping my Madison safe. It means a lot to me."

Jake was a little embarrassed. "No problem. My pleasure."

Maddy's father came into the kitchen and he looked the same as he did in the pictures, except, maybe a little older. "Is this him?" he said, gesturing toward Jake and speaking to Maddy.

"Yes, Daddy, this is Jake. Jake, this is my father."

"Very nice to meet you, Mr. McClaughlin," Jake said. "You have a fine family."

"Well, thank you. Call me Mike," he said shaking Jake's hand. "And thanks for keeping an eye on my daughter while we were out of town. She said she had quite a scare." He leaned in close and said, "She's still having nightmares from the accident where her fiancé was killed. She wakes us up in the middle of the night like a scared little girl. It's been tough on her. I was hoping they had stopped, but I guess not."

"Yes, sir." He turned to Bodey and said, "This is Bodey Jensen. He is helping me in the lab with a computer issue."

Sara said, "Hello Bodey, welcome."

Mike shook Bodey's hand and said, "You boys want a beer?"

"Yes, sir!" they both said a little too quickly and Mike laughed.

"All right—let's get you one." He went to the fridge and pulled out three Bud Lights and handed one each to Jake and Bodey, keeping the third for himself.

Sara asked, "Where are you from, Bodey?"

"Chicago, ma'am. Suburb called Wheeling."

"It's gotta be damned cold up there right now," Mike said.

"Yes, sir. When I left it was eight degrees. I like it better here."

While Bodey made small talk with Sara and Mike, Jake sat down at the table with Teri. Maddy was helping her mom prepare the meal and she looked up, catching Jake's eye and rolled her own eyes, smiling. Jake smiled back, laughing to himself a little.

Teri noticed the exchange and said, "So, you stayed here last night?"

Jake didn't like the look on her face, but nodded and said, "We both had the dreams again and hers was particularly bad. She called me pretty scared. I came over so she wouldn't have to be alone in the house."

"What about Beth?" Teri asked.

Jake visibly winced. "What do you mean?"

"Come on, Jake. You're already playing around with the hired help? I can see it."

"It's nothing," Jake said, lying. "You're imagining things and I don't appreciate the comment."

"Then why does she keep making googly eyes at you and smiling all the time? Jake, why would you be doing this now?"

"You, of all people should know what I've been through the last few years. Now, let it go."

She said, angrily, "I need another beer."

She got up from the table and stomped to the fridge.

Maddy saw the discussion and came over, sitting down next to him. "Everything Ok?" she asked.

"Teri's being an ass. I don't know what's gotten into her lately."

"What did she say?"

"She senses something between us and was pressing me on it."

She nodded. "Have you ever thought that maybe she might be jealous?"

"No. Why would she be jealous?"

"Because she likes you, silly. She may even love you. I think I just figured out why she's been acting the way she has toward me. She feels threatened. Trust me. It's a woman intuition thing."

"But I've known her for forever and she's never remotely shown any interest in me before."

"Or maybe you've never noticed. Don't be hard on her, Jake. She's done a lot for you, remember?"

He nodded, but was clearly bothered by this new revelation. *Teri in love with him? What the heck?*

Maddy squeezed his hand, got up and went back to the counter to finish helping her mother. Teri had recovered from their spat and was joining in on the conversation in the kitchen. They were all laughing at the story of Bodey and Robin, the vomiting girl on the airplane, as Jake stood and rejoined the group.

Bodey suddenly switched tracks. "So, what's collards?"

"Boy, you mean to tell me you've never had collard greens?" Mike said.

"I don't even know how to spell it, sir."

"Well, you're in for a treat. We'll give ya' an extra helping," Mike said, slapping Bodey on the back, hard. "Come on boys. I got something to show you."

Maddy said, "Oh no, Daddy. You'll bore them to death."

"I can't imagine any man worth his salt being bored by a car," Mike said.

"The Chevelle?" Jake asked, brightening.

Mike, surprised said, "You've seen it?"

"Just the picture in the hall, sir. I'd love to see the real thing."

"See?" Mike said to Maddy, "You ladies worry about the kitchen stuff and I'll keep the men entertained."

Maddy threw a carrot at him and stuck her tongue out, then grinned at Jake.

Sara said, "We're going to eat in twenty minutes. Don't make me come find you."

"Yes, Mamma," Mike said obediently, and led them away.

In the garage, next to a Chevy Equinox, a large green tarp covered what was obviously a car. Mike raised the door so they could get around to it and slid the cover off the Blue '69 Chevelle SS. It was immaculate with two fat, white, racing stripes running from front to back down the center of the vehicle. All the other badging looked original.

Jake whistled and said, leaning over looking into the car, "1969 Chevrolet Chevelle SS coupe. Is this the 402?"

Mike shook his head no, and Jake stood up quickly and said, "The COPO with the 427 V8?"

Mike nodded, grinning. "You know your cars. Everything is stock. I restored her last year. Her interior was a mess."

"Oh my God," Jake said. "They only made like three hundred of these, right?"

"Three hundred twenty three," Mike said.

"What will she do?" Bodey asked, looking into the interior.

"0-60 in 5.1 seconds," Mike said. "1/4 mile in 13.3 seconds at 108 mph. She'll put you in the seat back. Wanna take her for a spin?"

"Do we?" Jake said. "Hell, yeah!"

* * *

The men returned from the joy ride ten minutes late and Sara playfully scolded her man for making them wait. He apologized profusely and said it would never happen again, but Sara just smiled. Jake must have had a huge grin on his face because Maddy laughed and shook her head when she saw him. He loved classic cars.

The collard greens were a hit with Bodey. He had three helpings.

"Be careful," Mike said, "they may go right through ya' if you're not used to 'em."

"Yes, sir," Bodey said and put a spoonful back. Mike chuckled.

After dinner, they went outside on the deck where Mike built a fire in the pit. Bodey and Teri sat together and caught up on old times while Mike and Sara joined Jake and Maddy, close to the fire. It was a little cool for Florida and the blaze kept the chill away.

Maddy sat close to Jake and they shared a smile. Jake saw Sara watching them and felt his face turn red as Maddy snuggled closer to him getting warm. Sara glanced at her husband and they shared a look. Jake also thought he saw something in Mike's eyes that made him feel a little uncomfortable. Like a warning.

"So Jake," Mike said, "what've ya' got my daughter doin' down there at this lab of yours? It's not anything dangerous is it?"

"Daddy," Maddy protested.

"No, sir," Jake said. "She's helping with research and assisting with some secretarial duties. The lab is completely safe and Andee wouldn't hurt a fly."

"Honey," Sara said to Mike, "I've been there, remember? It's fascinating. I tried to get you to go, but you wouldn't."

Mike nodded and said, "Who's Andy?"

"N-D-E-E-E," Jake spelled, "pronounced Andee. She is the computer system and hardware I developed to advance our understanding of the human brain."

"Hmm," Mike said. "But what's all this hoopla about dead people and seeing ghosts and stuff. What has that got to do with brain research?"

"Honey," Sara said, "I told you, it's not about ghosts. He's helping people who have had experiences like mine. Near Death Experiences. He's a scientist."

"Let me explain," Jake said. "Some of my research is classified, but I can give you a general idea of what I'm doing. I began developing a system which would analyze brainwaves of people who were having some sort of sleeping disorder in order to evaluate if a safe alternative to their drug therapy could be utilized to help them sleep better. I stumbled upon an energy source in the body previously undiscovered. The particulars of this I can't discuss, but basically it allowed the equipment I was using at the time to interpret what the brain was doing."

"You were reading people's minds," Mike said.

"Very good, sir," Jake said. "The equipment I used back then would not allow the full potential of this energy source to be discovered, so I developed a much more complicated system, with the help of Bodey here and his company, and now I can view, in a visual and auditory format, whatever someone is thinking. I can read people's minds, but with some limitations. I'm now a sophisticated carnival sideshow," Jake joked.

Mike smiled and said, "But what does that have to do with my wife?"

"Good question, sir," Jake said. "The system, though highly advanced, has some limitations like I mentioned. For instance, it can only read what the person is actually thinking or dreaming at that time. It cannot read what the subject does not want us to know."

"Daddy, I've seen this with Mom. It's pretty cool."

"I have parties who are interested in assisting me with getting past this limitation, and that is what I am working on now," Jake said.

"Parties?" Mike asked.

"I can't discuss that part, sir. I'm sorry."

"I was in the special forces in 'Nam, Jake," Mike said, "I can see the military and covert implications of what you are doing. I'm still confused about how my wife fits in?"

Jake nodded. "Sara and others like her have had something altered in their bodies. Having the body cease its biological function and prepare itself for death causes a change we don't understand fully yet. And then if that body is brought back from a biological death, something permanent has changed within them. They are special and unique and I believe they may be the key to unlocking the limitations we have."

"Is that all you believe they can help you with?" Mike asked.

Jake hesitated.

Maddy's father seemed to have the uncanny ability to see right through him. It made him a little uncomfortable. He contemplated how to say what he wanted them to know, and then decided to just be honest.

"Sir, this part of my research may not seem very scientific to the common layman, but to put it bluntly, I believe there is life after death, and I want to prove it."

Mike didn't seem surprised by this revelation at all. He said, "What's wrong with good old fashion faith?"

"Nothing, sir," Jake said, "but faith can't let me speak to my wife. And there is something important I need to ask her."

As the words fell from Jake's lips, this revelation, put into such simple terms, sounded weak and thin, even to him. His resolve faltered the smallest fraction, and somewhere deep inside something cracked. Jake felt himself wince. A loose watery feeling settled into his stomach and he probably looked a little pale at that moment.

Silence fell on the small group for an uncomfortable minute, and then Mike said, "Jake, I really like you. This little bit of time we've spent here tonight has made a very favorable impression on me, but I have to say I'm worried you're into something that may not be healthy for you, my daughter, or the rest of us for that matter. You don't want to go messin' with God."

"No sir, I don't," Jake said, "but I believe someone wants me to do this. Why would I be given the knowledge and the foresight to get to this point if I'm not meant to follow through? What If I'm supposed to do this and I give up or quit? What would I have missed or failed to do?"

"Even if you think you've been given divine guidance," Mike said, "you must still make decisions for yourself. You must ultimately choose whether this path you're going down is right and good and you must someday answer for the decisions you make."

"I know, sir," Jake said, solemnly. "I think about that every day."

"I hope so," Mike said. "I hope so."

Breaking the tension, Maddy said, "Mom? Don't we have dessert?"

"Yes, sweetheart, we do," Sara said, standing. "Does anyone want peach cobbler?"

A hardy 'Yes!' from everyone brought them all back to the kitchen and warm peach cobbler. Later, after an hour of Bodey and his stories, they were all saying goodnight. Teri left first, and while Mike was explaining to Bodey the intricacies of fly fishing, Maddy pulled Jake off to the front room for a moment.

When they were alone, she moved close and he held her tight.

"God, I've wanted to be right here all night," she said, snuggling closer. "Maybe Bodey needs to stay at a hotel."

"Don't tempt me," Jake said. "I might kick him out."

She looked up into his eyes and said, "I'm sorry about my dad. He can be pretty overbearing at times."

"I like your dad, and I respect his opinion. He was right on a lot of things, but I'm pretty committed to this project."

"I know you are, Jake. But what if he's right? How will you know if you've gone too far?"

"I don't know. I'm kind of playing it by ear right now."

She nodded and put her head back on his chest.

"How are you with all this?" Jake asked. "Do you believe I'm doing the right thing?"

She was quiet for a moment and then said, "I trust you Jake."

She reached up and kissed him softly, and then more passionately until Bodey yelled from the kitchen, "Yo! Bro! I'm exhausted. Take me home and put me to bed."

Jake and Maddy both laughed into their kiss and he yelled back, "Coming!"

She kissed him once more and said, "Sleep tight. Sweet Dreams."

The irony of that request would haunt them both until morning.

23

January 14, 2010 – 3:31 a.m.

Orange Park, Florida

Maddy woke screaming.

Sara was right there, quickly, as a booming sound rattled the windows in the house. Mike followed shortly behind her, his hair sticking up in spikes and clumps, sleep still lingering in his face and eyes.

"What the hell is going on?" he said.

Sara held Maddy, trying to calm her down. "Another nightmare," she said.

"But what was that loud bang?" Mike asked.

Sara shrugged, looking afraid.

Mike said, "Is she all right?

"She's frightened, Mike, but I think she's ok."

"All right, I'm going to look around. Yell if you need me."

Sara held Maddy and stroked her hair. "Are you all right, sweetie? Do you want to talk about it?"

"I'm ok now, Mom, thanks. I need to call Jake."

Sara looked concerned and stopped Maddy as she reached for the phone. "Honey, what's going on? Why do you need to call Jake at this hour? He's probably fast asleep."

"Because he's having his dream too."

"You're not making sense, Maddy. How do you know Jake is having a dream?"

"Because we've been having dreams about Ryan and Beth, and we've been having them at the same time. Remember, I told you about it? Ryan said something else to me, in my dream, and I need to tell Jake."

"You're having the same dream as Jake and at the same time as he is?" Sara asked, incredibly.

"Sort of, Mom. I'm having a recurring dream about Ryan and he's having a recurring dream about his wife, Beth. But yes, we have them at the same time, about 3:30 in the morning."

Sara looked perplexed, but let her hand go and Maddy picked up the phone and dialed Jake's number. He answered on the first ring.

"Hey," Jake said, as if he knew who it was without waiting for her to tell him. "Are you ok?"

"Yeah, Mom is here with me. I woke up screaming and she and Dad were awakened by a loud bang. Dad's checking the house out now. Jake—Ryan said something new to me tonight."

"Beth did too. She said, 'The balance.'"

"The balance?" Maddy said. "Balance what?"

"I don't know, but I do know the dreams are getting worse and stronger. Bodey woke up. He said he heard a loud voice. He wasn't sure, but he thought it said, 'balance.' He was just waking as it ended."

"Ryan said 'must not.' And Jake?"

"Yes, Maddy."

"I could see him this time."

"Who? Ryan?"

"Yes," she whispered, a tear trickling down her cheek. "After the sounds of the crash ended, instead of the mumbling voice I normally hear, I could hear scraping noises, as if someone were crawling through gravel and broken glass. Then I could hear someone trying to pick the phone up. When I looked down at the phone in my hand, the screen was showing a video. It was Ryan, bloody and broken, crawling across the pavement toward his phone. He had a horrible grinning, blood streaked face and as a tattered hand reached for his phone, he said 'Jake... must not.'"

"Honey," Sara said, "how horrible."

Ignoring her mom, Maddy said into the phone, "What did he mean by 'Jake must not?'"

"I have no idea," Jake said. "This is becoming more confusing than ever. I wish I knew what this was all about."

"Me too."

"Will you be ok there with your parents?"

"Yes, I'll be fine."

"All right, we'll figure this out in the morning. Try and get some sleep."

"Jake?" she said before he could hang up.

"Yes."

"I wish you were here."

"I do too," and they said goodbye.

24

January 14, 2010 8:33 a.m.

Orange Park, Florida

Jake walked into the lab feeling exhausted.

Bodey and Maddy followed shortly behind, her eyes red rimmed and droopy, the last two nights seeming to catch up with her. Bodey's sneakers shuffled across the vinyl floor making harsh squeaking noises.

Teri was on a ladder running her hands along the top of some cupboards and storage shelves. She jumped down when they came in. Looking refreshed and full of energy, she said, "What? Did you guys stay and party all night after I left?"

Jake said, "Nightmares again," and walked to the coffee pot.

Bodey said, "Jet lag and someone else's nightmare," and followed Jake to the coffee.

Maddy said, "Me too," and stood in line for coffee.

"Well, I slept great," Teri said. "I got here a little early to start looking for—you know." She looked around the room suspiciously. "I found one too," she whispered.

She held up another one of the small battery shaped devices, only this one had been crushed by something.

"I stepped on it to disable it," she said.

"Good work," Jake said. "Do you think there are more?"

"Probably. If I was hiding these, I'd put more around. I've been looking over here," she said, pointing to where the ladder stood. "When you guys wake up, we should split up and cover the whole lab. I'll continue searching the cupboards. Someone needs to check the kitchen and bathrooms. Jake, do you want to look over the console area?"

"Yeah, I'll get it. Bodey, can you keep working on the software? I hate to waste your valuable time with this crap."

"Sure."

"I guess I get the bathrooms," Maddy said, sounding a little irritated.

"I'll help you when I'm through with the consoles," Jake said.

Maddy smiled and said, "Ok."

They all went to work.

25

January 14, 2010 9:30 a.m.

Mandarin, Florida

Peter was livid.

How could he have been such an amateur? He had never botched an assignment as miserably as this one. First, his training had failed him during the ruse as Peter Vargas. That piece of shit Jake Townsend had seen right through him and the General had been highly disappointed in him. He had reamed him a new asshole.

Now, the listening devices he had placed in the laboratory while impersonating some stupid Near Death clown were slowly being discovered by that lab tech bitch, Teri.

They hadn't found the video camera yet and he was watching and listening closely to them as they searched the lab trying to find it. If they discovered this last piece of equipment, he would be blind in there for a day or two while he made other arrangements.

After watching the activity for a few more minutes, he decided he'd better start putting alternative plans in to motion. He did not like to rely on luck for a mission's success, and at the rate they were thoroughly exploring every nook and cranny, it was only a matter of time before the fiber optic camera and microphone were found.

He picked up one of the new secure cell phones he bought at the kiosk in the mall and made a call to a number provided to him by The Organization. It was answered on the fourth ring.

A woman's voice said, "Hello," and this surprised Peter. Either, he had dialed the wrong number, or the operative was the rare female The Organization used. He hoped it was the latter. She had a great voice, and this particular job would require the operative and himself to perform the work together.

Peter said, "Hyperlink."

If the operative was genuine, he or she would respond with seven tones played by the pressing of the number pad on the phone. The numbers would correspond to the music of 'Mary had a little lamb.' If the person on the other line did anything else, Peter would terminate the call and dispose of the now compromised phone in the same manner as the one at the airport.

He had purchased five phones at the kiosk in the mall, but he did not like wasting the time or exposing himself to possible discovery if he had to return and purchase more prematurely. He was hoping the number had been dialed correctly.

Nothing happened for a moment and then he heard the familiar song being played by the keypad tones. He hadn't realized he was holding his breath, but he let it out slowly and grinned at the prospect of working with a woman. Historically, the type of female who would be involved in this line of work could be very stimulating. He hoped so.

He said, "Ten Pin Lanes, Mandarin, 7:30."

The woman responded with, "Yes."

"Are you familiar with biometric cipher combinations?" Peter asked.

"Very," the woman said.

"A local alarm monitoring system will be involved too," Peter said, "but it should prove simple. The main problem will be the cipher lock."

"That will not be a problem."

Peter was distracted by the face of Teri looming large in the video monitor. A hand reached up and the view moved in a dizzying spinning motion as the camera was removed from the A/C vent overlooking the main chamber of the lab. Teri's angry face came into view again and a hand came up with an obscene gesture directed toward the lens of the camera. Then the screen went blank.

Bitch! He thought.

The woman on the other end of the line said impatiently, "Hello?"

Peter looked away from the monitor and said into the phone, "Uh—good. See you tonight," and ended the call.

He swore loudly and almost threw the phone through the window, but caught himself in time.

"All right, bitch," Peter referred to Teri, "let's see how you are the next time we meet."

He relaxed and waited for 7:30 to arrive.

26

January 14, 2010 11:00 a.m.

Orange Park, Florida

After Teri found the fiber optic video camera and disabled it, they searched for another hour, but found nothing.

Jake decided enough time had been devoted to the hunt and went back to pursuing the problems with the sound anomalies.

Bodey had just finished writing the software which would allow them to hear the true sound of the recorded sessions and Jake anxiously waited for the program to boot up.

"This mother was huge," Bodey said, referring to the sound file. "I've never seen anything this big."

"Is it going to work?" Jake asked.

"Yeah. I had to program the main frame to handle these large files. Part of the problem was I had this workstation here networked with the CRAY and it was processing the audio and video display. It's way underpowered and can't handle this kind of conversion, so I routed the audio and video crunching into the CRAY system. You'll have plenty of compute cycles now. Let's give it a whirl."

Bodey hit play.

The video of Sara's NDE began like it always had and then they heard music. A complex chord was playing in the background as the video continued. The chord did not change or move up and down in the register of notes, but it was full and beautiful all by itself.

Maddy came over and said, "Now that's a chord."

"It's music," Jake said a little surprised even though he had heard Sara and others describe music in their NDEs.

"You sound disappointed," Maddy said.

"I guess I expected more."

Teri had joined them and said, "It's beautiful."

Maddy smiled and nodded her head. "Yes, it is, isn't it. I've never heard such a beautiful chord of music and I'm a studied musician. I'm not sure, but this may be unique in all the world."

"What are you saying?" Jake asked.

"When I took music composition, the instructor told us that all the music in the world had already been written. Mathematically, every combination of notes and chords had more than likely been played together by someone before us. Our job in the class was to arrange those combinations into something original. But this chord is something I've never heard before. It almost overwhelms me with its complexity. Don't you feel it? It's as if the music is right there in front of you and then it slips away. I can almost hear all the notes in the chord and then some of them escape me."

Bodey said, "I was wondering about this…" and typed something into his fancy laptop.

"Wondering what?" Jake asked.

"What she said about the notes escaping her gave me an idea," Bodey said. "I had a feeling this sound file was going to be beyond our human ability to hear, but she may have just confirmed it. Let me run it through this tonal analyzer and see what we get."

He pressed a few more keys and then a waveform appeared in the analyzer.

"Whoa!" said Jake. "Look at that."

Bodey whistled. "Off the scale. The gauge on this analyzer doesn't measure above a certain note, and this thing has notes way above and below the capacity for human hearing. Or even dog hearing for that matter. And look here," he pointed to a section in the middle of the cycle. "There are harmonics in here that aren't even true notes as we know them. They're notes in between notes if that makes sense."

"Well," Jake said. "This is fascinating stuff, but it doesn't give me the breakthrough I was hoping for. At least we don't have to listen to the distortion anymore."

The recording was still playing and Jake saw something on the monitor which caught his eye. "Hold it, Bodey," Jake said. "Back that up."

Bodey rewound the segment until Jake said, "Hold it!—right there. Now hit play."

They watched the video and Jake said, "There!" and pointed to the screen.

Bodey said, "What am I looking for?"

Maddy looked puzzled. Teri had a smile on her face as she bent forward and used the controls.

"Let's slow it down," Teri said, and she backed it up a bit and played it back at about a quarter of the normal speed.

The life review had cleaned up a lot. It was still not perfectly clear in places, and it seemed to be jumping and skipping a lot, but you could make out images and scenes, instead of just blurred colors.

Maddy gasped as she saw a scene with her nana in it. She was so young.

"That's my nana," Maddy said. "She's so beautiful and young. Look! My grandpa." Maddy was giggling. "Mom needs to see this. But where are the scenes of me and Charlotte? Or my dad?"

"They wouldn't be here," Jake said. "Remember, your mom had her NDE very young and her life review would only contain images of her life up to that point. You guys didn't come along until much later."

Maddy nodded, understanding now. "It's like a home movie."

"Bodey, it's skipping around a lot, isn't it?" Jake asked. "How much information is in this video?"

"Yeah, it's skipping pretty good even slowed down to one quarter speed. I didn't look at the video file, but the software right now won't slow it down any more. You want me to work on that? It would be fairly easy to make adjustments."

"Do it," Jake said. "This might be what I'm looking for."

"On it," Bodey said, and started typing commands.

"Who wants lunch?" Jake asked. "Maddy and I will go pick it up."

Everybody was hungry, so they put in an order for barbecue and Jake and Maddy headed off to get it. Maddy seemed happy to be alone with him for a minute and they rode to the restaurant holding hands and sitting close.

"Jake, you never told me about your dream last night," Maddy said. "I mean you told me what Beth said, but was there anything else?"

"Yeah—are you sure you want to hear?"

She nodded.

"You remember me telling you I'm holding her in my arms and she's saying nonsense words, right?"

"Yes."

"And then I hear loud thumps and look around. When I look back at her, she's staring up at me and says 'Stop!' That part didn't change. But last night, after she spoke the word, she slowly stood up. Her neck was pouring black blood from the gash. She looked down on me and pointed. That's when she said, 'The balance.'"

Jake's hand had become cold and clammy and she squeezed it tighter.

"Her face became this mask of pain and anger," Jake said. "Something I could barely recognize as Beth. Bodey said I screamed. I don't remember."

Jake felt Maddy shudder.

"Oh—and something else," Jake said. "I could hear a cell phone ringing, faintly. I'd never heard that before in any of my dreams."

"Was your cell going off, or even Bodey's, and it invaded your dream?"

"I thought that too, but it wasn't my ringtone. Bodey's either. He thought I was crazy asking him to play his ringtone in the middle of the night."

Maddy had a strange look on her face. "What was the ringtone? Do you know?"

"Yeah—it was that T-mobile ring tone. I think they call it 'T-Jingle' or something. Do you know the one I'm talking about?"

She turned white as a ghost and let go of his hand as if it had turned to ice. She hugged herself.

"What?" Jake said. "What's wrong?"

"That was Ryan's ringtone. I can hear it ringing in my dream."

Just then, Jake's cell phone went off and they both jumped. Jake almost drove off the road. They both laughed nervously and Jake asked Maddy if she would get it. He never talked on cell phones when he drove anymore. Not since Beth.

Maddy pressed the speaker button so Jake could hear. "Hello?"

"Maddy? It's Bodey. Could you guys get me some collards if they have them? I forgot to ask."

"Yes, Bodey," she said. "We'll get you some collards. Anything else?"

"Sweet tea."

Jake was laughing now and Maddy giggled.

"Sweet tea," she repeated, hardly able to get it out.

"What's wrong with you guys?" Bodey asked.

"Nothing," she laughed. "We'll be back in a few with the collards."

"Ok, great," Bodey said, and hung up.

Jake and Maddy were still giggling as they arrived at the restaurant. In a better mood, he stopped her from getting out and turned her toward him.

"You're something," he said, leaning close to her.

"Something what, Dr. Jake?"

"Something special," he said and kissed her.

"Are you getting all mushy on me, again? You're breaking our rule."

"I don't care."

"I'm glad."

A car drove by and someone yelled, "Get a room!" and they laughed, embarrassed.

"Should we?" she asked.

"Get a room? Hell, yes! What about the food?"

"We'll call them back and tell them they ran out."

They touched foreheads and he said, "Later?"

She nodded, smiling. "Later."

They got the food and headed back, making small talk and joking about Bodey's collards. Everyone wolfed the food down and Bodey was disappointed there was only one serving of collards for him.

As they worked, Jake would look up to find Maddy staring at him and they would enjoy a moment between them. Once, Maddy walked by and whispered in his ear that she would be in the bathroom, alone.

He said, "Tease!" and she gave him a sexy, sly, look as she sauntered away. He saw Teri glaring at her and had a flash of anger, but he let it pass.

Later, Bodey was discussing some property of digital film compression with him when Maddy came over and whispered in his ear, "I'm not wearing any panties," and turned and left.

His jaw about hit the floor.

Bodey hadn't heard what she said, but he grinned anyway. He watched her walk away and whispered to Jake, "Damn!"

Maddy did look great in her short skirt and pumps. Jake hoped he could make it the rest of the day.

A half hour later, Bodey was ready with the program updates. They all gathered around to see.

"These files were even bigger than the audio files," Bodey said. "But you would expect that with video. A lot more stuff going on."

He hit play and when the scene arrived at the life review he stopped it and restarted it at one thirty-second of the normal speed. He had hit the mark. The view was seamless and the gaps and skipping had stopped.

"There's a lot of information here," Bodey said. "If I were to guess right now, we would be here eleven years watching all of it."

What Bodey said didn't immediately sink in until Maddy asked, "You mean my mom's whole life is there? I mean everything? At least up to age eleven when she died?"

"I don't know," Bodey said. "I was being facetious."

Teri said excitedly, "Fast forward it."

Bodey jumped ahead some and the scene changed to a little girl of about four playing on a swing set.

"Again," Teri said.

It jumped again and a man and woman were singing happy birthday to Sara on her seventh birthday.

"Nana," Maddy said.

"Again," Teri said.

It jumped to a funeral. Sara was crying into her mother's side as her mother cried into a handkerchief.

"That must be my great grandma's funeral. The one who predicted mine and Charlotte's names," Maddy said.

Teri was smiling and then she was exuberant. "Jake! We did it! We cracked it. I can't believe it!"

Bodey was high fiving Maddy while Maddy clung to Jake's neck and Teri was hugging Bodey, but Jake was a little more subdued.

Maddy noticed first and said, "What is it Jake?"

"This is a breakthrough," Jake said, "but there is a problem."

"What?" Teri asked.

"Think about," Jake said.

They all looked at each other, but none of them spoke.

"Everything is there up to the time of the NDE," Jake said, "but nothing after that. We've managed to access everything in her mind from her first day of life up until her body thought it was her last, but everything ceases after that."

"But that's amazing, Jake," Maddy said, still smiling. "You can now access that information like a computer. Isn't that what you've been working for?"

"You guys are missing one thing," Jake said.

Teri was nodding now, pulling on her hair.

"This only works on people who have had an NDE." Jake paused. "Don't you see? The person will have had to die for us to be able to access their memories. They will have had to die and have a Near Death Experience for us to do anything with them."

27

January 14, 2010 1:30 p.m.

Orange Park, Florida

"So—we kill people," Bodey joked, but no one made a comment.

Jake was pacing and thinking, but finally shrugged and said, "Well at least I can tell the General we've had a breakthrough and we're making progress. I'm sure he'll be glad about that. Good work, Bodey. You pulled out all the stops today to get me to this point. Feel like going home? We can get you on a flight back tonight if you'd like."

"Yeah, I should get back. I have lots of stuff on my plate back home. I don't want to get too far behind."

"Maddy," Jake said. "Can we get him booked on a flight out to O'Hare?"

"Yep, I'll get right on it." And she left to make the reservation.

Teri told Jake, "This is big time. Don't belittle what we've done today. We'll get the rest soon. I can feel it."

"I can too," Jake said. "Something is bothering me and I can't figure out what it is. It's like something that is on the tip of your tongue, but you can't quite get it out."

She nodded and said, "It'll come to you."

"Teri?" Jake said, "I'm proud of you. You did good work today and I couldn't have done any of this without you. You know that, right?"

She smiled and gave him a tender kiss on the cheek. "Yeah, I know it."

Jake and Maddy took Bodey to the airport and walked him to the plane.

Before Bodey left he told Maddy to take care of Jake. "I see how you two are. I wanted to let you know I haven't seen him in this good a mood in—well—never."

"I will. Don't worry." And she gave him a big hug and kiss on his non-furry forehead.

"Maybe it'll be a rough flight and a redhead will need her hair held for hurling," Bodey joked. "I like redheads."

She laughed.

Jake shook his hand and said he would call if he needed anything else. Bodey turned to go and then stopped and put his hand to his head.

"Jeez—I almost forgot," Bodey said. "You're going to need this."

He pulled a CD case out with a disc in it and handed it to Jake.

"The new software modifications will not work without this disc. I didn't have time to properly modify the system so this is just an add-on until I code the operating system back in Chicago. I'll send you the new one when it's ready. Don't lose that."

"Important," Jake said. "Got it."

Bodey waved and left.

As Jake and Maddy walked back through the concourse holding hands, they didn't talk. It was as if speaking would break the spell, and the glances and smiles they shared were more powerful than anything that could be spoken.

When they got to the car, she slipped in next to him and they left the parking garage for the interstate. She kept running her fingers through his hair and softly kissing his neck, teasing him as they drove. It was driving him crazy.

He had his hand on her bare thigh and she opened her legs a bit. He took the hint and slid his hand between her warm legs, surprised to find what she had whispered earlier in the lab to be true. She wriggled against him and then teased him through his pants as they arrived at his place.

They jumped out of his car and as he fumbled the front door open, she attacked him before he could get it all the way shut. She laughed as they fell to the couch and as she slowly pulled the blouse over her head, he unzipped her skirt, tugging at it. She playfully shook her head 'No' and he stopped, letting her slowly slide the skirt up so it bunched at her waist. She slid onto his lap, straddling his legs, unbuttoned his trousers and loosened his fly. She grabbed him and rose up, guiding him slowly inside her. He finally spoke two words.

"You're something."

Afterwards, as he held her from behind, caressing the nape of her neck and languishing in the curve of her hip, she said, "Do you realize what you did today?"

"What do you mean?" he said.

"You achieved two of your goals."

"Was one of my goals bending you over this coffee table?"

She slapped him playfully and said, "Will you behave?" but then she wriggled her rump against him as he spooned her.

"Me behave?" he said, enjoying her tight rear against him.

"Seriously."

"Ok—two goals?" He asked. "I didn't even get one right."

She turned over, facing him, and placed a hand on the back of his neck.

"You accessed the human brain and can now pull information from it like you were accessing files on a computer."

"But the brain has to have died for me to do that. I don't know if that's a victory or not."

"You'll get the rest of it, I know it."

"Maybe."

She waited and finally said, "You have no idea the other one do you?"

He shrugged. "No."

"You proved that there is life after death."

"How?"

"By showing the Life Review is a real thing, that when you cross over, your life is shown to you in its entirety. We now know it's real, because we have video proof it exists."

He thought about this for a minute and then held her eyes with his own, smiled and said, "You're something."

* * *

They ate dinner in, ordering Chinese and drinking beer, then they relaxed watching a little TV. He thought it cool she could drink like one of the guys.

She belched loudly, not seeming to care, and he said, playfully, "OMG, you're a pig!"

"OMG?" she laughed. "Did you just say OMG? The old man trying to be cool. And do I look like a pig to you?" She playfully threw a pillow at him.

"Old man?" he said, throwing the pillow back at her and then pinning her under him on the couch. "I'll show you an old man."

He tickled her and she squealed, thrashing around and spilling a little beer. She managed to get him off of her, but he lost his balance and fell off the couch, hitting his head on the coffee table. She fell on top of him giggling and said, "OMG, is your head ok?"

"You tried to kill me," he said, rubbing his head.

"You were tickling me. I have to warn you I lose all control of my bodily functions when I'm being tickled. The tickler beware." But she kissed his head.

"All control?" he asked, a little sneaky smile on his face.

"All control."

He kissed her and liked the taste of the beer on her tongue. It was kind of sexy and bad girl all at the same time.

Somehow, they ended up naked again on the floor and when it was over, he said out of breath, "Girl, you are killing me."

"Horrible way to die, isn't it?"

"Will you stay here tonight?"

"I really want to, but my mom would give me this look of disappointment all week."

He nodded.

"I don't have to leave for awhile though," she said.

"Do you think they would be upset if I called Mike and asked him to take your mom back to your nana's for like a month?"

"Yeah—that would probably go over well," she said, playfully punching him. "You really want me to stay that bad?"

He nodded.

"We might be breaking our own rules," she said.

"I look at it as an opportunity to know you."

"Are you making fun of our rules?"

"No—I respect the rules. Our first one seems to be going really well."

She punched him again.

"Ow! This arm is getting sore."

"How much can you 'know' me while I'm sleeping?" she asked, still joking with him.

"I already know a lot," running the back of his fingers casually down the curve of her face. "You have this little happy grin while you sleep, and you twirl your hair a little too. It's cute."

Her eyes moved to his.

"And this little dimple right here," he touched the corner of her mouth, "comes and goes as your smile grows."

She smiled.

He touched her earlobe softly and said, "This ear has three piercing holes where this one has only two," and he touched her other lobe just as softly. "But my favorite thing is this mole right here," and he placed a fingertip on a small mole next to her bellybutton, "it's shaped like a heart when you look at it upside-down."

She was staring at him intensely now, and said softly, "How do you know this?"

"I watched you sleep the other night," he said, a little embarrassed. "I couldn't keep my eyes off of you. You were like an angel lying in my arms."

"Jake…" she said, softly. "I…" but she didn't finish. A single tear traced a line down her cheek and hung on the corner of her mouth, trembling. He kissed her softly there and brushed it away.

"Well, I'm good at making girls cry."

She smiled and then said, "You're making it very hard to stick to the rules."

"I know," he said. "Doesn't it suck?"

She punched him again and laid her head on his chest.

28

January 15, 2010 – 9:02 a.m.

Orange Park, Florida

Friday morning loomed large with a massive cold front descending upon the First Coast bringing freezing temperatures into the upper teens at night.

The low on Saturday morning was supposed to hit fourteen degrees, and the news stations were all saying the freezing weather could last as long as ten days. North Florida had not seen a cold snap like this since the 1860s. People were staying indoors or bundling up in whatever they had that might fend off a bit of the biting cold.

The homeless shelters in the City of Jacksonville were filled to capacity with many being turned away to fend for themselves in the frigid temperatures. Two deaths had already been reported Friday morning. Both were being blamed on the temperatures.

More would probably follow.

Teri, Jake and Maddy were in the lab, going over some menial tasks. They had spent a little time searching cracks and crevices for bugs and video cameras they may have missed the previous day, but they did not find any.

Mid morning, Jake had to run to the printer's to have some paperwork copied and he left the two girls to tend shop. He returned to find a palpable tension in the air and Maddy clearly angry.

When he asked if everything was all right, both women said they were 'fine,' which meant they weren't, and Jake could get neither to comment about anything more. When Teri went to the ladies room, Jake eyed Maddy, but all Maddy said was, "She's a bitch!" and wouldn't talk any more about it. Jake hoped he hadn't created a monster. He decided it was time to talk with Teri.

When Teri returned from the ladies room, Jake said, "Teri, could I see you a moment in my office?"

She nodded and followed Jake to his office where he shut the door behind them. He sat on the corner of his desk while Teri stood looking at everything but Jake.

"Are you all right?" Jake asked.

Teri nodded and said, "I'm fine."

"You seem a little angry. Are you and Maddy getting along?"

She didn't answer right away. "To be honest, Jake, not really."

He nodded and said, "I may have made a mistake bringing in someone new without consulting you and I'm sorry for that, but I assumed it wouldn't be a problem. Has she done something to upset you?"

"I really wish you had asked me, Jake. We've been a team for a long time and then you throw a new person in the mix. One who has little or no experience in a lab such as this and you expect me to be all excited about it?"

"We needed the help. I know she's lacking in clinical expertise, but I hired her mainly for secretarial duties. Is she getting in the way of your work?"

"No."

"Then what's the problem?"

"She's a distraction."

"She's distracting you? I thought you said she wasn't getting in the way of your work."

"She's not distracting me," Teri said. "She's distracting you."

"I don't have a problem with her," Jake said, but he had a bad feeling about where this was going.

"I'm sure you don't," Teri said, sarcastically. "You two are bumping into the walls, falling all over each other. Making eyes and giggling. It's disgusting. She's been prancing around here in her short skirts and tight blouses while you and Bodey drool at her feet."

"You have a problem with the way she's dressed?"

"I have a problem with the way she does anything. Jake, we don't need her here. If you want to bang the first little girl who bats her eyes at you, be my guest, but don't drag it in here where we have a serious chance of destroying everything by losing our focus."

Jake was getting angry. He did not like the direction this conversation was taking.

"I say we do need her here. She's been nothing but beneficial since the day she arrived. Who suggested the sound anomaly was a kind of digital distortion which led to the discovery of the music in the NDE, along with the Life Review being cleared up by that discovery? She did. And last night, she made me realize that we had proven the existence of life after death with the recorded content of the Life Review. How can you say we don't need her here?"

"Did she tell you this before or after you took her clothes off?" Teri shouted.

"Teri, that's enough!"

"No! I want to know. Did the little whore wait a whole day before seducing you, or was it a couple of hours? Because if I were to bet on it, I'd put money on an hour."

"Dammit! Shut up! How dare you insult her like that. You know nothing about her. You've had it in for her since the day she came to us for help. You just can't stand to see me happy for a change."

"Are you sure she's made you happy? Or were you just horny and now you've gotten a little release. Because I could've made you hap…" She stopped, catching herself.

"Because you could've what?" Jake shouted. "You could've made me happy? Is that what you were going to say? Because I doubt it. You're a bitter, moody, angry girl and frankly, I'm not interested."

Jake stopped. He knew he had gone too far and the look on Teri's face told him so. She stared at him for a second, a look of such shock and pain, Jake immediately regretted what he said, and then a single tear tumbled down her cheek. She turned and stormed out of his office without another word.

Maddy must have heard the whole exchange and as Teri swept passed her in a rush she said, "Teri, I…"

Teri stopped and glared at Maddy. "You what? I don't want to hear it. Just keep your mouth shut you little tramp!" And she grabbed her purse and left without another word.

"Teri!" Jake yelled. "Wait!" But Teri was gone and the door closed with a hiss of empty air. "What have I done?"

Maddy went to him and held him as the quiet enveloped them both.

29

January 15, 2010 11:30 a.m.

Orange Park, Florida

Jake tried Teri's cell phone but she had either turned it off or was rejecting his calls. It went straight to voice mail.

He left a message. "Teri, please call me back. I went too far and I'm sorry. We can work this out."

But the message felt insincere and empty to Jake. Losing her now was going to be a huge setback for the program and a huge setback in his life. Teri was too good a friend to lose like this. He hoped she would cool down and they could talk this out.

"I'm so sorry, Jake," Maddy said after he tried to call Teri. "I know this is my fault."

"No, Maddy. This was going to happen eventually anyway. I just wish it hadn't happened now."

"She's right. I feel like a tramp." And her eyes welled up and she looked away.

"Hey," Jake said, coming to her, "she's wrong. How can you think that anything we have shared is cheap or trashy? Do you really believe that?"

"The way she puts it makes me feel cheap," Maddy said, softly crying.

"Have I made you feel that way?"

She looked into his eyes and without hesitating shook her head and said, "No."

"You know the little rules we made up that we keep playing games with?"

She nodded.

"Well, that's just what they are, games. It's never been just physical for me. I feel something when I'm with you. Something I didn't know how to feel anymore." He reached out and held her face softly in his hands. "You bring me to a place I haven't been to in a long time. A place I used to know so well, but in my pain I became disoriented and that place became something else, something dark and lonely. I was lost—lost and didn't know it. I thought by holding on to Beth as tight as I could, I could hold on to that place and keep her alive in my heart. If getting to know you means letting go, then I can do that now. I have to do that, because now that I know you, I can't go back to that dark and lonely place."

She reached up and touched his face and said, "Don't go back. I need you here."

"I'm not going anywhere," he said, and kissed her.

30

January 15, 2010 11:30 a.m.

Orange Park, Florida

Teri turned her cell off and walked angrily to the coffee shop, ordered a double mocha frappuccino, and sat feeling sorry for herself for the next hour.

The swiftness and intensity of the argument between Jake and herself had taken her by complete surprise and she was ashamed of how she had reacted. She kept going over and over in her mind how things had deteriorated to this point, and the only person that kept surfacing was Madison McClaughlin. The little bitch had practically ruined her life in a matter of days. Where had she come from? What the hell had happened?

Teri knew Jake cared about her. They had been friends so long and she had been the only one to help him when Beth died. She just didn't know if Jake felt the same for her as she did for him. She had kept those feelings buried deep inside for a long time in fear of him rejecting her. She had waited for Jake to come around. Waited for him to acknowledge her. But she had apparently waited too long and now Jake had found someone else.

Her pain was intense, and the thought of being completely without him put her in a panic. As she imagined going through her life, every day, without Jake, her breath came in short gasps and she found she was breaking out in a cold sweat.

The waitress came over and asked her if everything was ok. She got control of herself and nodded. She would have to swallow her pride and go back. Teri didn't know how she was going to do this, but she knew she must.

She turned her cell phone back on and tried to steel herself for what she would have to do. She saw she had five messages and as she listened to Jake's repeated pleas to come back and talk, she felt a little better. Maybe he had seen the little whore for what she was and kicked her to the curb.

She had a vision of herself walking back into the lab, Jake rushing to her apologizing and taking her into his strong arms, promising to love her always. A fantasy she knew, but it seemed to give her a little comfort.

She paid her tab and began walking back to the lab and Jake, her fantasy replaying in her mind as she walked.

31

January 15, 2010 1:00 p.m.

Orange Park, Florida

Jake was getting worried.

He had tried Teri's cell numerous times over the last hour and still nothing. He was about to call again when Teri walked back into the lab.

Jake hurried over to her and said, "Teri, I'm sorry. I never should have said those things and I want you to know I didn't mean them."

"I know. Me too. I feel like an idiot. You guys probably think I'm insane. I would if I were in your shoes."

"I don't want us to ever get that angry at each other again," Jake said, smiling. "Do you think we can get past this?"

"I'm already over it. No more personal attacks from me, I promise."

Jake smiled and gave her a hug. "Thanks, Teri. It's very important to me for you to be here."

Teri turned to Maddy and said, "I'm sorry I said those things to you. You didn't deserve that."

"It's ok, Teri. We're good."

Jake could tell Maddy was still upset, but he didn't know what to say, so he let it go.

Even though Teri had seemed sincere enough, he was worried the problem would rear its ugly head again, probably sooner rather than later. This whole situation seemed vaguely familiar and now that he knew Teri's feelings, memories came flooding back. Teri had gotten mad at him about Beth as well and made up some crazy story about how she was not the right girl for him and everything had happened too fast with her. He was an idiot for not seeing it. Too late now, he'd just have to try and keep things calm.

"Well, now that we've gotten that out of the way, let's get back to work," he said.

* * *

Jake and Teri began going through Sara's NDE again with the new software patch running.

Jake showed Teri the disc Bodey gave him and explained it needed to be in the drive for the software to function. The patch worked flawlessly and Sara's NDE was clear and glitch free. He liked what he was seeing and hearing.

"Let's look at Rachael Swanson's recordings," Teri said. "Hopefully they'll be as clear."

They punched up the file for Rachael's NDE and began playing it back. Where the distorted sound was supposed to start, a new musical chord played through the speakers instead.

"Wow!" Teri said. "That's really beautiful."

Jake nodded and said, "It's different though. The chord must have different notes."

Maddy came over and said, "That music is definitely different than my mom's. It's still beautiful, just different."

"Do you think everybody's chord is different?" Jake asked.

"There is only one way to find out," Teri said, and punched up another file.

It was an older one they hadn't looked at in a while. The musical chord was different for that one also. Jake wanted to be sure there wasn't a glitch in the new patch so he called Bodey in Chicago and told him what was going on.

"So, the music is different?" Bodey asked.

"Yes, each person's NDE appears to have a different sounding chord. The notes that make up the chord must be different."

"Have you looked at them through the tonal analyzer?"

"No, I didn't think of that."

"Do it and e-mail the file right now."

Jake loaded the files into the analyzer and then made a copy of the results and e-mailed it to Bodey.

"Got it yet?" asked Jake.

"No, not yet. It should—oh wait—here it is." He paused for a minute or so as he looked at the analysis and then said, "They are definitely different. Each one has its own pattern of tones and elements. Have you guys considered that they are different for a reason?"

"What do you mean?" Jake asked.

"What if this musical chord is like a signature or something? Each individual person has their own signature or fingerprint if you will. A key that fits only that unique human being."

When Bodey said the work 'key,' a light bulb went on in Jake's head and he yelled, "Bodey, you're a genius! It's a key. The music must be a key which unlocks each person's essence. This is what made these people different. The chord triggered the release of energy in their body and because the energy had to be called back, the trigger must not be able to be reset. It must stay open until they move on for good."

"That's an interesting theory," Bodey said, "but if the trigger stays open, how is their energy being contained? What keeps the energy from leaving their body?"

"I don't know," Jake said, perplexed now. "I'll have to think about it some more." He paused, thinking. "I still think the music has got to be some kind of trigger or key. Maybe, it toggles on and off as needed. I have an idea, but I won't be able to test it until Monday when our next test subject comes in. Thanks, Bodey. Once again you're a life saver. I'll call you on Monday and let you know what happens."

"All right, dude," Bodey said, "talk to you then." And he hung up.

Jake had a huge grin on his face and was doing his pacing thing.

"This is big," he said. "This has got to be what we've been looking for, I can feel it."

"What's the idea you have, Jake?" Maddy asked.

"Remember the other day with Rachael?"

"Yes."

"When we played back the segment of her NDE with the distorted musical chord, we affected her ability to read minds, remember?"

Teri and Maddy both nodded.

"After we record Frank Lucas's NDE, I want to play back his musical chord while he's hooked up to Andee. Now that we will have the complete chord instead of static and distortion, I think we'll see something amazing."

32

January 15, 2010 3:00 p.m.

Orange Park, Florida

The rest of the afternoon was spent building a database for each recorded NDE.

The life review segments were very long for most of them and the CRAY took an hour to catalogue about fifteen years worth of someone's life. Jake thought it kind of pathetic when you put it like that. Someone's life reduced to a computer database crunched into numbers in a fraction of the time it took to actually live it. He felt like an intruder.

Teri and Maddy were civil the rest of the day. At least Jake hadn't noticed any conflicts between them. The truth was they hardly said two words to each other.

At six thirty, they powered everything down and locked up. Teri left by herself, waving out her window as she drove out of the parking lot. Jake and Maddy decided to have dinner together and he said he would pick her up at her parents' in an hour.

"Bring something warm," Jake said.

The temperature had already dipped into the low thirties. It was going to be cold.

At Maddy's parents' house, Mike welcomed Jake with a beer and they sat and talked while Maddy finished getting ready. The house was warm with a roaring fire going in the family room. Mike said he couldn't remember the last time it had been so cold.

"Sir, may I ask you something about Vietnam?" Jake said.

Mike said, "Shoot."

"Did you ever know anyone who had a Near Death Experience during the war? Someone who had been seriously wounded and talked about seeing a tunnel or a bright light?"

Mike thought for a moment and then shook his head. "Nope, I can't recall anything like that. Most of the seriously wounded got a ticket home or died before I ever talked to them again. We had a few who had rotated stateside, recovered and shipped back, but they never talked about seeing anything like that. What's bothering ya' Jake?"

"When my wife died, she slipped away right there in my arms. She was talking nonsense, or so I thought, about white lights and her long dead mother being with her. I thought at first it was her brain malfunctioning from lack of oxygen, or she was confused from being knocked unconscious. Now I believe she was having a Near Death Experience, only she never came back from it to tell me about it."

"That must have been pretty hard on you. I don't know how I would have handled it myself."

Jake paused. "Have you ever felt like there was something you didn't get to tell one of your buddies who didn't make it over there? Or ask them something important you needed to know? What if you had that chance? Would you take it?"

Mike nodded, as if understanding where Jake was coming from.

"I have many unanswered questions and many things that were left unsaid, but I get through it because I know one day I will get my answers and I will get to tell my tales. I just have to be patient."

"But what if there had been something you needed to know, right then? Something that couldn't wait?"

"I'll answer that with a question. If you never get to find that answer, will your life be any different than it is now? Will it change the way you look at the world?"

"I don't know, sir."

"I know you don't. Live your life. Your answers will come one way or the other."

Jake nodded and swallowed the rest of his beer.

Mike clapped him hard on the back and said, "Want another one?"

"No, sir, thank you. I need to drive."

Maddy walked in looking beautiful. Her hair was pulled back behind her ears and held with a simple pale yellow ribbon. As she moved across the room toward him, the firelight reflected off the gold necklace she wore. Jake's smile must have betrayed his appreciation of her appearance because she blushed and smiled coyly.

Mike said, "I don't know if I should let you out like that," but smiled at his daughter as she came and gave him a kiss on the cheek.

"Daddy, stop," was all she said.

Maddy went to Jake and clasped his hand in hers.

They went to leave and Mike said, "Be good to my daughter, now. She's my baby."

"Sir," Jake said, "I couldn't imagine being anything other than good to her. She's too beautiful for anything else."

Maddy squeezed his hand and smiled so big, the dimple at the corner of her mouth smiled too. Mike nodded and waved goodbye.

They went to a local Japanese steak house in Fleming Island and sat at a large hibachi table with eight other people.

The food was good, the wine better and Maddy, beautiful. Jake found himself staring and smiling, watching Maddy laugh at some joke or antic performed by the chef, and when she caught him, she would smile and blush. He would laugh at her then, her eyes sparkling in the candlelight, and she would grab his arm, laying her head on his shoulder.

They tried feeding each other with chopsticks, but Jake missed, sticking a piece of shrimp up Maddy's nose. She threw it at him, laughing.

When the meal was finished one of the other diners said to everyone at the table, "Hey, I'm DJing at this club down the street starting at ten. Come hang with me and I can get everyone in free."

Maddy thought it would be fun, but Jake wasn't so sure.

"It's been a long time since I've been to a club," Jake said. "I don't know if I can dance."

"C'mon old man," Maddy said. "What are you afraid of? I'll protect you."

He laughed and said, "Hey! Thirty six isn't old."

Outside, the temperature had plummeted and Jake held Maddy close to keep her warm. She didn't seem to mind the cold.

The club was packed and around 11:30 the DJ who had been sitting at their table pointed at them and played the song *You are so*

Beautiful by Joe Cocker. They danced, holding each other tight as the whole room seemed to be smiling at them. Jake thought the song fit her perfectly.

Maddy stared into his eyes, her fingers running through the hair at the nape of his neck, a content little smile on her lips the whole time as the music enveloped them. She pressed her body so close to his they were almost one.

He whispered in her ear, "You're driving me crazy."

She smiled a sexy little smile and pressed her lower body harder into his.

The song ended and Maddy whispered in his ear, "Let's go. I don't want to share you with all these other people."

They waved to the DJ and left the club, Maddy clinging to him against the cold.

They jumped into his car and cranked the heat up, holding on to each other as the car warmed. When the car was comfortable, he went to put the transmission in reverse but she put her hand on his and said, "Let's play like we're teenagers," and climbed into the back.

He locked the doors and followed her, getting his shoe stuck between the console and the driver's seat. She giggled at him, pulling on his leg to free it. He kneed her in the forehead as it came loose and she laughed even harder.

"Oh shit, Maddy, I'm sorry! Are you all right?"

He could tell she was because she was giggling uncontrollably. He couldn't help himself. He started laughing too.

As the laughing settled to giggles, he held her face in his hands and said, "Let me see."

He looked close at her head, said "I'm sorry," again and then kissed her softly. It was just a kiss on the forehead, but to him, it looked like he had given her the world.

She softly kissed him, and then slowly ran the tip of her tongue along his lips. He placed a hand on her breast and caressed her until he could feel her nipple harden through the fabric. She took his hand and slipped it up underneath her sweater while she reached behind her with the other hand and unsnapped her bra. When his hand touched her bare breast she gasped and kissed him harder. The sweater came off as did Jake's shirt.

The windows had steamed over so they didn't see the police officer approach until a flashlight beam tried to penetrate the fogged windows.

The flashlight tapped on the glass and Jake said, "Shit!"

Maddy was laughing and trying to get her bra and sweater on while Jake fumbled into his shirt.

The flashlight tapped on the glass again and a voice said, "Open up, Police!"

Jake waited another minute until Maddy was decent, and then he rolled down the window. The police officer shined the flashlight directly in Jake's, then Maddy's eyes, and finally back to Jake's.

The police officer chuckled and said, "Everything all right, folks?"

"Yes sir," Jake said.

"Uh huh," was Maddy's response.

"Can I see some I.D., please?" the officer asked.

Jake and Maddy both fumbled around and produced their I.D.s, while the officer shone his light around inside Jake's car.

"What's going on in here?" the officer asked with a grin on his face.

Jake thought the officer knew exactly what was going on.

"Just getting some air, sir," Jake said, kicking himself for how lame it sounded.

"Getting some air, huh? In twenty degree weather?"

Jake started to speak, but Maddy interrupted.

"Sir, my friend and I were enjoying a little alone time since the heat in his house is broken and my house is full of little twelve year old girls having a slumber party. It's my niece's birthday." She smiled her radiant smile and looking at Jake said, "We were going crazy."

The officer's face softened and said, "Well—uh—Jacob and Madison, I sympathize with you, but I can't let you stay here. Why don't you get a room?" and he handed them back their I.D.s.

He turned off the flashlight, winked and said, "Goodnight."

"Thank you, sir," Maddy said, and the officer turned and left.

Jake rolled up the window and they cracked up laughing.

"Let's get out of here," Jake said. "Should we go to the house with no heat, or the screaming girlie party?"

"Neither," Maddy said. "Let's get a room."

They went back to Jake's place and rushed inside out of the cold. They were both naked before either of them said a word.

Afterwards, Maddy said, "I told my mom I wouldn't be home tonight."

Jake looked at her and said, "Are you sure?"

She nodded and said, "I don't want to be anywhere else but right here," and she snuggled up closer to him, laying her head on his chest.

He stroked her hair and said, "I can keep you?"

He could feel her smile against his skin. "You can keep me."

"Sweet," he said.

A moment passed in silence and then Maddy said, "Jake? What if we fall in love?"

"There's not a chance in hell that will happen," Jake said "You're too ugly."

She barked out a "Ha!" and pulled the hairs on his chest.

He feigned injury and said, "I need those."

"Seriously, Jake."

"We're not supposed to be serious," he said, still joking.

She lifted her head off of his chest and looked into his eyes. They were so green right then and beautiful. Sometimes she took his breath away.

"Do you feel it?" she asked.

His gaze never left hers and he simply said, "Yes."

She kissed him sweetly and lay her head back down on his chest.

Shortly, he fell fast asleep.

33

January 16, 2010 – 3:30 a.m.

Orange Park, Florida

The dream was bad.

Jake held Beth again as the blood seeped out of her onto the cold ground. The wind howled in tonight's dream and her mumblings were carried away with it. The loud thumps were thunderous and her visage, ghastly, when he looked down upon her in his arms. Black blood trickled from her bright red lips, streaking down her pale skin.

Her lips did not move tonight, but her eyes conveyed the meaning as "Stop!" was shouted while the howling wind ceased at that exact moment. It was deathly silent as she slowly rose up from his lap, towering over him.

Pointing and breaking the silence she said, "Stop the balance!"

His ears felt like they were going to bleed.

Out of the corner of his eye, another vehicle approached rapidly. As he watched, it lost control and began flipping, careening directly toward him and Beth. A body was flung from the vehicle and landed grotesquely twisted a few feet from him with the truck resting upside down to the right of the body. Jake watched as the male shape slowly began crawling toward him, reaching for a cell phone which had landed between Jake and the male figure.

The phone was ringing.

As his face came into view, Jake realized in horror it was Maddy's fiancé, Ryan. He was bleeding from wounds on his face and hands, but he was grinning, a macabre mask of pain and anger on his face.

He grasped the phone in his outstretched torn and bloody hand and said into it, "Jake…must not be…lost."

He awoke to screams as Maddy, her hands held near her face, a look of complete terror in her eyes, pointed to Jake's abdomen. He looked down, and Maddy's cell phone lay flipped open on his stomach. A number had been dialed and ringing could be heard through the tinny speaker. It was answered by a voice mail message from a long dead Ryan.

Jake repulsively flung the phone against the wall where it laid speaker up, a happy Ryan asking if the caller would like to leave a message at the beep.

Maddy, terrified, reached for Jake and clung to him shaking and sobbing.

34

January 16, 2010 4:01 a.m.

Orange Park, Florida

Sitting at Jake's kitchen table, sipping coffee, Maddy shuddered.

Jake went to her and rubbed her arms and shoulders trying to massage the fear from her.

A half hour had passed since they were both wrenched from their sleep by the horrible nightmares. Maddy had confirmed what Jake already knew. Her dream had also been horrifying and Beth had made an appearance at the end imparting her own words of wisdom into Maddy's world.

Maddy pulled Jake down to sit next to her and her haunted eyes seemed to search his for comfort. Unfortunately, Jake didn't have any to give. He was frightened himself and unsure how to proceed.

"Jake, I left my phone down here—in my purse," Maddy said. "How did it get upstairs with us?"

"I don't know. Could we have been sleep-walking?"

Maddy shook her head. "I woke up with my head still on your chest and that's when I saw the phone. It was dialing all by itself."

"Well, someone is trying to scare the shit out of us," Jake said, angrily. "I think they're doing a pretty good job."

Maddy started shivering again and took another sip of the warm coffee.

"What are they trying to tell us?" Jake asked.

"It's obvious, Jake. We're not supposed to use Andee. We're supposed to stop, now."

Jake wasn't ready to abandon his work just yet and he shook his head.

"I'm not sure. It could mean something else."

"What?" Maddy asked, frustrated. "What else could it be?"

"Maybe we're supposed to stop. Maybe we're not supposed to be together."

Maddy looked wounded. "Do you really believe that?"

"I don't know what to believe," Jake said, standing and pacing. "All I know is we're supposed to stop doing something."

"Jake, look at me."

He stopped pacing and sat down in front of her again.

"When I touch you," she said, reaching out and cupping his face in her hand, "what do you feel?"

He closed his eyes and reached up, placing his hand over hers. He said, "I feel peace."

She nodded, her eyes welling up with tears. "I feel the same."

Jake was amazed that they were so in sync.

"And I feel joy. How can this be a bad thing? How can anyone want us to stop this?" she asked, pleading.

"I don't know," he whispered. "I do know I can't give up Andee yet. She's too important. I need more time to decide what's really going on."

"Do you remember the other day I told you I trusted you?" she said.

He remembered.

"Jake, I'm scared, but I trust you with my life. Promise me you'll stop if it gets out of hand. Promise me you'll end it."

"I promise. I could never hurt you and I don't know what I would do if I lost you now."

She finally smiled. He touched her face and she kissed his fingers. Before she could stop it, she said, "I love you, Jake."

He searched her eyes and reaching his other hand up to hold her face, he gently kissed her. "I know you do," he said, "I can feel it. Can you feel me?"

She smiled and whispered, "Yes."

Her eyes were shining in the soft glow and he said, "I love you. I think I've known I could love you from that first night. I was just afraid to admit it."

She grabbed him and clung to him. He held her fiercely, the fear and anxiety of the dreams forgotten for the moment. He stood then, picked her up like a child and carried her to the couch where he lay her down and squeezed in next to her. She snuggled up with her head in her favorite spot on his chest and they eventually fell fast asleep.

35

January 16, 2010 10:00 a.m.

Orange Park, Florida

They slept late and woke together, the sun shining on their faces through a window.

She smiled a sleepy smile and he touched the dimple in the corner of her mouth and then kissed it.

"Morning," he said, enjoying the feeling of waking up with someone next to him. "You are very cute when you wake up."

"I like your spiky hair," she said, playfully running her hands through it. "Can you get it to do this during the day?"

"Only with tons of gel."

She laughed at him and tried to flatten the spikes with her palm. They refused to succumb. She rested her chin on his chest and looked into his eyes. "Was last night real?"

"The bad part or the good part?"

"The good part," she said, smiling. "The part where we said we loved each other."

"That was very real. It just felt like a dream."

He made her breakfast and then they showered together where they immediately made love and then had to shower again. He didn't mind.

Maddy said she needed to go home to get some fresh clothes so they ventured out into the cold day and arrived at Maddy's place at one thirty in the afternoon. It was a little awkward at first, but as Mike and Sara picked up on the change in their daughter, everything seemed fine with them.

Maddy pulled her mother aside before they left and whispered something in her ear. Her mother smiled and hugged her and eyed Jake with a knowing look that only succeeded in embarrassing him. Mike tried to get Jake to stay for a bit and have a couple of beers, but Jake told him they were heading down south for the evening and he would have to take a rain check.

Mike clapped him on the back and said, "I'll hold you to it."

Before she left, Maddy gave her parents Jake's cell phone number in case they needed to get in touch with her.

"What's wrong with yours, honey?" Sara asked.

Maddy looked at Jake and then said, "I broke it. I'll have to get a new one."

Sara nodded, a funny look on her face. She hugged them both goodbye and Jake and Maddy headed to Orlando for the weekend. It would be good to get away for a bit. Jake kept trying to convince himself they could outrun their nightmares. At least for a little while.

36

January 17, 2010 - 3:47 a.m.

Orange Park, Florida

Peter met the female operative at Wal-Mart, then they left together in his rental car. Her loaner would remain in the parking lot until someone noticed it, called the police and the police in turn called Alamo.

They drove the few miles in silence, concentrating on the job at hand and parked the car a few blocks from the lab. They walked the remaining distance.

It was 3:47 a.m. on Sunday and they had one hour to get in and out.

The freezing temperatures were bothersome and the woman struggled with the biometric cipher lock, her own fingers numb from the cold. She was able to bypass it but not before three minutes had passed which was two minutes too long for Peter's liking. He cursed, scowling at her. She glared at him.

The alarm system proved much easier and they were in the lab with the door shut within four minutes.

She worked on placing listening devices while he installed the one video feed. The eraser tip sized camera was placed within a feature of the decorative trim surrounding a picture which faced the main part of the test area. It was virtually invisible and would hopefully remain undetected for the remainder of the lab experiments.

He was glad to see her finding places less conspicuous then he had used while playing the part of Peter Vargas. The bugs had been difficult to hide while he had been watched. Her placements were virtually invisible.

The last piece of equipment Peter used was a listening device which would send him data directly from the CRAY system. It required the woman's technical expertise and skill to install. It also took twenty precious minutes to finish. Peter was growing very impatient as the clock ticked, increasing their risk of exposure exponentially with each passing minute.

When she had finished, they quickly re-checked their work and verified they were receiving feeds from every device.

Satisfied everything was working correctly, they re-armed the alarm system and then attempted to engage the biometric lock, thus leaving everything as they had found it. Unfortunately, the lock was proving stubborn and she once again wasted five minutes engaging it. Peter was livid and berated her when they returned to the car.

The mission had been a success even with the delays the woman had incurred and the only evidence they had been there laid in the biometric cipher logs. They couldn't defeat the computerized logging system, but they could confuse it. If anyone bothered to check, they would find that the system had been locked and unlocked fifteen hundred and eighty three times between the hours of 3:54 a.m. and 5:03 a.m. Sunday. It should create doubt in the mind of whoever was looking at the data, as to the integrity of the computer log. Peter hoped it would be dismissed as a glitch.

He drove the woman operative to her motel and when he suggested he could keep her company for the rest of the night she glared at him, opened the car door and slammed it shut in his face.

What a bitch, he thought as he drove off. He'd find other suitable entertainment on his own.

37

January 18, 2010 – 8:30 a.m.

Orange Park, Florida

Frank Lucas buzzed the lab entrance at 8:30 in the morning.

Jake shivered as a freezing draft blew in through the door. He hadn't been this cold since his school days at Johns Hopkins University.

The day was gray and cold with a nor'easter blowing the temperatures into the teens. Most of the northerners had seen days like this, just not this far south. It smelled like snow. He half expected to see a blizzard blowing drifts against cars and storefronts, but of course that didn't happen in Florida.

Frank, a short heavy set man of about sixty five, wore a worn blue coat and stocking hat with denim jeans and cowboy boots. His plaid flannel shirt was new and still had a tag he apparently could not see. His balding head had a ring of grey hair, with patches of a darker color showing through here and there. His blue eyes twinkled as he greeted everyone and his smile showed a set of cheap but white dentures. To Jake, he seemed jolly, for lack of a better word.

After introductions were made, Frank said, "Doc, how can you concentrate with all these pretty ladies around?"

Maddy smiled and Teri blushed, but Jake said, "It's not easy. You'll help keep them off of me, won't you?"

"You bet," Frank said with a grin. "You won't even have to pay me." And he winked.

Teri said, "Please, follow me, Mr. Lucas. I'll be prepping you for your session today."

"Lead on young lady, lead on. Time's a wastin'."

Teri began the process of placing the leads and connections onto Frank's skin and scalp and she explained what would be happening today for him as they progressed. Maddy came over about half way through and went through the interview she had conducted over the phone with him the other day. She asked if there was anything else he wanted to add but he could think of nothing. He said it was still very fresh in his mind since he had died less than two weeks earlier.

Maddy explained to him Andee would pick up anything they missed, but for the most part, people who had had experiences such as his, had an almost photographic recall of the event.

"Damn right," Frank said. "It made quite an impression on me."

"My mother also," Maddy said, smiling. "She still recalls every detail of hers and she was eleven at the time she drowned. She's in her fifties now."

Jake stepped up and said, "Mr. Lucas, we're going to start today using an older body mold, which is this device here." Jake indicated the body mold hanging from the ceiling next to them. "If it proves unsatisfactory, we'll measure you for your own, but it will save us quite a bit of money if we're able to utilize this one. The process of recording your Near Death Experience usually takes between ten to thirty minutes per session. Do you have any problems lying supine for that length of time?"

"Supine?" Frank asked.

"That means on your back," Jake said.

"Oh—ok—no, sir."

"Great. We usually try to do two or three sessions in a day, but we can accommodate anything and always keep your best interests in mind. Don't hesitate to let us know if you are tired or uncomfortable. We'll make it right. We'll be starting in a few minutes, so try and relax while we get you hooked up."

"Yes, sir," Frank said.

Teri finished hooking the leads up and Frank was now in the chair, resting comfortably and ready to go. Jake had Bodey's disc in the drive and the system was online and ready to record.

"Mr. Lucas, this is very easy on your part," Jake said, talking through the two way intercom. "We're going to ask you to visualize a few specific items in your mind to help calibrate the system to your specific body mechanics and then we will begin the actual Near Death Experience."

"Sounds good," Frank said, a little muffled. "I'm ready."

Jake went through the process of having Frank visualize the blank room and then the ball in the room, along with a few other tests. Everything looked good, so he moved on to the actual NDE.

"Now Mr. Lucas," Jake said, "we want you to relax as much as you can and try to empty your mind of everything but your experience. All you will need to do is relive it in your mind and the machine will capture the whole event. Are you ready?"

"Yes," Frank said.

"Great, sir. Begin anytime you would like."

Jake, Maddy and Teri watched the events unfold on the monitors starting with Frank rising above the scene as he left his body, floating overhead. The picture and sound quality were excellent as expected, but Jake was waiting to see how Andee dealt with the musical chord and Life Review.

A figure which could only be Frank's father appeared and outstretched his hand toward Frank who in turn reached for the offered hand. As their fingers touched, a brilliant light formed to the right side of the display and the fullest and most beautiful musical chord Jake had heard suddenly filled the lab with its vibrant sound. The music seemed to come from all around them, filling every void with its sound and texture. Jake gasped at the magnificence of the notes, as he not only heard the sound, but felt it all the way to his core.

He turned and saw Maddy weeping, clutching her hand to her heart as she laughed. On her face, the most glorious smile Jake had ever seen.

Along with the music, a wave of comfort swept over him and he stood in awe of what he was experiencing.

The Life Review had started and the images, though crystal clear, were racing by at a speed which did not allow him to see anything but brief glimpses of Frank's life. Suddenly the life review slowed and Jake watched a scene unfold before him. A woman was being raped and Jake watched Frank try to stop it. Jake could feel the horror and anger Frank was feeling as a man with dead eyes attacked him and they fought. It ended with the man's hair on fire and Frank stabbing him in the throat with a knife. The Life Review moved on. Jake didn't understand what had just happened but he knew it was something very important in Frank's life.

Jake had to pull himself away from the experience and monitor the systems he knew would begin ramping up as the NDE progressed toward its conclusion. He was shocked to see the cooling system already at ninety percent and watched it very closely. He could not hear the pumps running because the music dominated the sounds of the lab.

Just then, a loud sucking sound, followed by a huge thump shook the room and caused a coffee mug to fall off the console onto the floor. It shattered and spread its contents in a widening circle on the floor. Jake ignored it.

Teri was trying to get his attention, pointing at the gauges of the cooling system as they approached the ninety seven percent mark. She had a hand poised over the abort button and a questioning look on her face, but Jake shook his head no. He wanted to see how far he could push the system. Teri shrugged and removed her hand from over the button.

As a second defibrillator jolt shocked Frank's heart back to life, another larger sucking sound overcame the music, followed by a thundering clap which shattered one of the glass room dividers that separated the console from the chair.

Maddy screamed in surprise and Jake shouted, "Are you all right?!" She nodded, but looked shaken up a bit.

The NDE ended and silence returned to the room as everyone looked at one another and then surveyed any damage which may have occurred. Other than the broken glass divider and shattered coffee mug, Jake could see no other damage except maybe some papers shuffled to the floor.

Jake smiled at Maddy and said, "What a ride!"

She nodded, catching her breath. It was then Jake heard a sound. It was coming from the intercom system. A soft whimpering could be heard. They all rushed to the chair and raised the body mold to find Frank crying. His face was happy, but tears streamed from both eyes.

"It was beautiful," he cried. "How did you do that? It was like I was there all over again. I didn't want to come back." And he sobbed into his hands, overcome with emotion.

Jake, Maddy and Teri looked at each other, shock and disbelief in their eyes. Jake wondered what other surprises lay in store for them this day.

38

January 18, 2010 9:45 a.m.

Orange Park, Florida

Teri let Frank out of the chair to take a break and he relaxed, sipping a soda. He said very little and Jake could tell he was overcome by the experience. Jake, Maddy, and Teri gathered at the console to talk about what had just happened.

"Maybe we should send him home for the day, Jake," Teri said. "He's seems pretty shook up. Hell, I'm shook up."

Maddy nodded.

"I'll talk to him in a minute, but I agree," Jake said. "I don't want to stress him this close to his recovery."

"Jake," Maddy said, "What was so different about today than from the others? Why was everything that much more powerful?"

"It must be the music," Jake said. "Now that we can hear the whole thing, it's having an effect on the system. It really must be some kind of key or signature and now we have the ability to unlock some of those effects."

"I don't like some of those effects," Maddy said. "What else could we unlock?"

"The music was beautiful, though," Teri said. "I felt so calm and peaceful. How could that be?"

"It must be having some residual effect on our surroundings," Jake said. "This is all new to me, guys. I'm trying to figure this out as we go."

"Maybe we shouldn't go any further," Maddy said, a worried look in her eyes.

Jake looked intensely at them both and then over at Frank and said, "Let me talk to him. Let's see what he's feeling, now."

They all walked over and Jake said, "How are you Mr. Lucas?"

"It's Frank. Please call me Frank. I'm fine. Just a little confused about all this. I'm not quite sure how to feel."

"Of course, Frank," Jake said, "I wouldn't know how to feel either. What happened today has never happened before. We weren't expecting this and I want to apologize to you."

"No need, I'm in awe of what you can do here. I wish you three could have felt what I felt. You might understand a little better."

"Try and explain it to us Frank," Teri said.

He thought for a minute. "When it was over, I was disappointed. Disappointed because I was still here. I felt exactly like I had when I first experienced the heart attack. I can honestly say, it felt like I just had another Near Death Experience and I'm ashamed to say I wish I hadn't come back from it. Is that wrong?"

Jake smiled. "I can't answer that for you, but I can say from our experience with other survivors like yourself, it would be unusual for you not to feel this way. Whoever created us must have engineered this process to happen for a reason. To ease our transition from this life to whatever awaits us beyond it. The peace and comfort you feel only helps alleviate the fears everyone experiences, naturally, with death."

"Your explanation makes sense," Frank said, "but it does little to change the fact I still feel regret about being alive."

"Hopefully it will pass with time," Jake said. "Because you did not move on, your mind, or soul if you want to call it that, has to deal with the effects of being prepared to move on, while still being in this realm. I'm sure it's very confusing and upsetting."

Frank nodded.

"I think we'll call it a day if that's ok with you?" Jake said. "We've put you through enough."

"No! I want to stay and help. I can't stop now. I'm fine—let's get me hooked up again and fire this thing up."

"I don't think that's a good idea, Frank. I don't want to overstress your body so soon after your heart attack."

"Nonsense, I'm fine."

Jake looked at Maddy and Teri, but neither offered any support one way or the other.

Jake stood and paced a few steps. "All right, we'll do one more session and see how you are, but if I feel it's getting too tough on you, I'm pulling the plug and we'll start again another day. Ok?"

Frank nodded. "Fair enough."

They had him hooked up and after a preliminary check of the computer system, everything was ready to go.

Jake pressed the intercom and said to Frank, "Before we start, there is something I want to check in the last session. Relax, and we'll start up again in a moment."

Jake said to Teri, "Bring up his session and let's look and see where the music starts. I want to be sure we know where all the extra effects begin."

Teri loaded the file and began playing the recording. Jake watched as the playback began and then out of the corner if his eye, he saw Maddy's head jerk up from her notes as panic spread across her face.

"Jake! Stop! He's hooked up to Andee and...!"

As the music began to play, a low rumbling began from somewhere below them. It rapidly grew to a tearing, ripping roar as the floor shook and items began breaking all over the lab.

Jake yelled, "Teri! Shut it down! Turn it off!" But Teri was mesmerized by what was happening over the chair Frank was in.

A pinpoint of light appeared above the body mold and then exploded into a gash of purple and brilliant white streaks all as a horrible tearing sound pierced the room. A hole formed in thin air where the light had appeared and Jake could see through it into what appeared to be a whole other area or room. It was as if a jagged door had opened up into another dimension. A roaring sound permeated the room and Maddy's cries could barely be heard above the noise as a wind kicked up inside the lab.

Papers whirled in circles over the chair and were sucked into the hole floating over Frank. Jake watched as an office chair was drawn up into, and through, the hole.

Maddy grabbed his shoulders, shaking him and shouting into his face, "Jake! Shut it off! Hurry!"

Jake, his attention now fully on what was happening, jumped over and hit the abort button, shutting the system down and stopping the playback of the recording. The roaring peaked and then a huge sucking sound followed as the hole collapsed upon itself with an explosive 'whoosh!'

The papers and chair which had been pulled into the vortex, shot outward from it as it collapsed, the chair shattering into pieces as it hit the wall opposite the console. Papers fluttered to the ground as the machinery spooled down, silence returning to the lab once again, with the exception of Teri who quietly cried.

Jake rushed over to Frank in the chair and Maddy joined him as they pulled the body mold up to reveal a very still Frank Lucas.

Jake shouted, "Frank! Can you hear me? Mr. Lucas! Wake up!"

Jake shook him and put his ear next to his mouth but could hear no breath. He felt for a pulse on his wrist and then his neck, but nothing was there. He turned with a shocked look on his face as Maddy held a shaking hand to her mouth, tears forming at the corners of her eyes.

"He's gone," Jake said, and reached for Maddy as she fell into his arms.

39

January 18, 2010 10:47 a.m.

Mandarin, Florida

Peter had been monitoring the lab with all the new sensors and video equipment installed, when the incident happened at exactly 10:47 a.m. on Monday, January 18, 2010.

When the hole opened up above their test subject and it seemed the entire world was going to be sucked into it, he stood up, shocked and said, "What the hell!?"

As the hole closed and a great deal of energy was released with it, the video and audio feeds abruptly came to a halt. They did not return for twenty minutes. During that time, Peter had been on the phone with the General explaining what he had seen. The General was demanding more information which Peter was unable to supply. His equipment was disabled.

"Well then get your butt down there and find out what the hell is going on!" the General shouted into the phone. "Take charge and start some damage control. If this accident has caused destruction to the surrounding structures, we need to be on top of it. We don't want this leaking out to the press. Keep a lid on it. I'll be there in two hours."

Peter looked at the disconnected phone in his hand and said, "Shit!"

Part 2

40

January 18, 2010 – 11:37 a.m.

Orange Park, Florida

Peter arrived at the lab as an ambulance pulled out of the parking lot, its siren wailing and lights flashing. Peter wondered who was inside. The last thing he had seen on the monitors was the gaping hole over the body of their test subject, Frank.

He didn't see any noticeable damage to the outside of the structure and the only emergency vehicle that had responded had been the ambulance. It looked to Peter like his job would be easy. He walked to the front entrance of the lab and, since the door was standing wide open, strolled right in.

Jake was on the phone. The lab assistant, Teri, was sweeping up what looked like broken glass and the new girl, Maddy, was hovering by Jake listening to one side of the conversation.

"Yes, Mrs. Lucas," Jake was saying into the phone, "they've taken him to St. Vincent's Medical Center." He nodded in response to something the person on the other line said. "Yes…in Riverside…No, he wasn't awake. They had to perform CPR on him when they arrived. They got his heart beating again, but he was still unconscious when they left."

Jake turned and saw Peter standing in the entranceway. A look of shock, and then anger spread across his face, but he turned back to continue his telephone conversation.

"I'm very sorry, Mrs. Lucas, I don't know what happened...Yes ma'am...No ma'am...I will. And please let us know how he is...Ok...Bye," and Jake hung up.

He whipped around and strode briskly toward Peter. "What the hell are you doing here?"

"I'm here to assist you with damage control," Peter said.

"Damage control? What the hell are you talking...?" He paused, a knowing look crossed his face and then he continued, "You've been spying on us again. We didn't find all the bugs did we?"

Peter kept his face stoic, and chose to ignore Jake's questions. "The General will be here in about two hours. I'm to detain all of you here until his arrival."

"We're not staying. We're leaving for the hospital. Now."

"My orders are to keep you here."

"I don't care what your orders are," Jake yelled. "I just had a man's heart stop in my lab and I'm concerned about his condition. I'm going to the hospital, and Teri and Maddy are coming with me."

Peter looked at Jake and was about to say something, but thought better of it. He was supposed to be in damage control mode, as the General ordered, so forcing these three to do something they didn't want to do might make things worse. It wasn't that he was worried about being outnumbered, or in physical danger, he just felt a different way might be better. He decided to try a more tactful approach.

Peter held up his hand in a placating gesture and said, "Calm down, let's think about this for a moment. Has there been any major damage to the building or surrounding structures?"

"What? No!" Jake said.

"Have the police or media been alerted to the situation?"

"No."

"Has the lab and any of the equipment been damaged?"

"I haven't had time to do any diagnostics on the equipment and I'm not going to do them now. We're wasting time!"

Peter nodded. "All right—we'll all go to the hospital, but we need to be back here in ninety minutes."

Jake looked at Teri and Maddy and said, "Fine, we can do that."

"Good," Peter said. "I'll drive."

Teri looked at Jake and said, "I'm not riding with him. I don't trust him."

"You don't have a choice, Miss Newton," Peter said. "Either we all stay here, or we all go to the hospital. I cannot allow you to be separated from the group."

"You can't tell me what to do," Teri said. "If I don't want to go, I won't."

Peter became very quiet.

"I've offered you three what I considered an amicable solution to our problems. You want to take care of your client. I'm required to keep you under wraps. You three can either choose to do it my way or you can be forced to do it my way." Peter put on his best smile. "Choose now."

"It doesn't sound like much of a choice," Teri said.

"Stay or go," Peter said. "I will not offer it again."

Jake looked at Teri, "It'll be fine, Teri. He can't hurt us at the hospital."

Teri hesitated and then nodded.

"Let's go," Jake said.

Peter stepped to the side and gestured for them to lead the way.

St. Vincent's Medical Center was a sprawling 528 bed hospital complete with two Intensive Care Units, one Cardiac Care Unit, and five Intermediate Intensive Care Units along with Emergency Room, Neonatal Intensive Care Unit, and a large Open Heart Surgery wing.

It took them twenty minutes to find a parking place and the entrance. Another ten minutes were spent locating Frank and then making the trek to the Cardiac Care Unit on the third floor.

Since the Unit only permitted two visitors at a time, Jake and Maddy were the only ones allowed in to see Frank. Teri sat fuming in the waiting area with Peter after she lost the argument to go in. Peter heard her call him the Dickhead during the heated conversation.

"Teri," Peter said when they were alone, "I enjoyed our sessions together back when I was a test subject. Very stimulating having your hands on me while you stuck the leads to my skin."

She gave him a disgusted look and said, "What are you?"

"I'm just a man."

"That's funny, I could've sworn you were a pig."

He chuckled. "So hostile. And you like obscene gestures, too. Not very ladylike."

Peter enjoyed watching her squirm as she realized he was talking about the hidden camera she had found in the lab.

"No really, what are you? Are you like General Breckenridge's pet? His little patsy? Too afraid to do anything on your own?"

His hand shot out and grabbed her wrist, twisting it until he saw the pain and fear in her eyes.

"I'm not afraid of anything, especially a conniving little bitch like you. And you don't want to know what I am."

He let her go, but continued glaring at her. He watched her rub her wrist and the fear stayed in her eyes. *That ought to shut her up,* he thought.

They sat in silence for a few more minutes and then Jake and Maddy walked out of the CCU and headed their way. Jake looked like he'd seen a ghost and Maddy kept glancing over at him like she was worried he would bolt and run. *This ought to be good,* Peter thought.

"How is he?" Teri asked.

Jake still looked dazed but said, "Not good. He's on a ventilator and his blood pressure keeps bottoming out."

"Did something happen while you were in there?" Teri asked.

Jake nodded and then looked at Maddy.

Maddy said, "The nurse told us he had been unresponsive and his pupils were fixed and dilated, which she said meant his brain was not functioning. When we first walked in, his eyes were wide open but staring at nothing. One eye even looked in a different direction than the other."

"He looked empty," Jake said. "Like a shell with nothing inside."

He paused and looked around uncomfortably. Peter could tell there was something else he wanted to say.

"And?" Teri asked.

"And then he looked straight at me," Jake said. "His eyes focused and turned to me—and they looked angry. They seemed to bore right through me. His lips moved, but because he was on the ventilator, I couldn't tell what he was saying. It didn't look nice. I turned to the nurse who was making some adjustment to his I.V. and said, 'He seems awake now,' but when I turned back to Frank, his eyes were vacant again and his mouth slack. The shell had returned. I thought I had imagined it, but Maddy said she saw it too."

"The nurse thought we were grasping," Maddy said, "and said he didn't look any different than when he came in."

Peter laughed and said, "You people are amazing. Is Freddie Kruger going to pop out of one of these rooms and attack us with his finger knives? Or maybe aliens from another planet? Come on. We need to get back to the lab before the General gets there."

They rode in silence and Peter was thankful. They had run into Frank's wife as they were leaving and Jake spent a few minutes talking with her. Peter didn't hear what was said, but he could see it was a very tense conversation. She was crying when they left. Peter really didn't want to hear anything about it, so the silence in the car was golden.

Arriving back at the lab, Jake, Teri, and Maddy busied themselves with some menial tasks as they awaited the arrival of the General. Peter sat and watched. He couldn't believe he had wasted his time in this place, playing 'Peter Vargas,' Desert Storm veteran and Near Death Experience survivor. What a crock. He was having a hard time believing these clowns were going to provide the General and The Organization with anything remotely useable.

The General arrived alone, and Maddy buzzed him in through the front entrance. Peter strode over and briefed him on all that had transpired since the incident.

"So—no police or media?" the General asked.

"No. Just the ambulance and no one seemed to be paying attention or caring."

"All right. Good. I need to speak with Dr. Townsend for a few minutes. Keep everyone here until I say so, got it?"

"Yes sir."

The General took Jake into his office and Peter resumed his position reclining in a chair.

After fifteen minutes, the General and Jake came out of his office and went straight to the computer console where Jake booted up the system and loaded a file.

The General watched for a few minutes and said, "Everything? Every scrap of memory however small or trivial?"

"Yes, sir," Jake said. "At least up to the time of their Near Death Experience."

The General thought for a moment and said, "How long will it take the computer to prepare a database of the information?"

"It averaged an hour for every fifteen years, but that's a preliminary estimate. We haven't had a chance to have Andee crunch the numbers on more than a few files. It could be more or less, depending upon the individual."

Peter watched as the General smiled, something Peter had never seen him do.

The system continued to play back the video and something caught Peter's eye. He stood slowly, mesmerized, and walked toward the console. He interrupted the conversation.

"Play that back," Peter said.

"What?" Jake asked.

"Rewind it. Play that part back."

"Smith, we're busy here," the General said.

Peter ignored him. "Play it back. Now!"

Jake shrugged. "All right." He pressed a few buttons and the sequence Peter first saw started over again. He watched, enthralled.

"I remember this," Jake said. "During Mr. Lucas's testing, this part of the review slowed all on its own. It was strange. It must be something very important in his life."

Peter watched, and when the dead man's eyes were shown as Frank stabbed him in the throat, he sat down, hard.

"Sonofabitch," he whispered.

"What is it?" Jake asked.

Peter sat, stunned. He would never have believed it. Ever.

"Smith!" The General yelled. "What's gotten into you? We don't have time for this!"

Peter snapped back to the present and stood.

"Yes, sir! Sorry, sir. I thought I saw something, but I was mistaken."

"Keep working Dr. Townsend," The General said, "I'll be in touch."

The General marched toward the exit.

"Whose Near Death Experience is this?" Peter asked Jake when the General was out of earshot.

"It's our latest subject. Frank Lucas. Why?"

"Just curious."

"Smith!" The General yelled. "Move out. You're with me," and he strode out through the main entrance.

"What the hell," Peter whispered to himself as he hurried after the General, leaving Jake and the lab behind.

41

January 18, 2010 – 3:00 p.m.

Orange Park, Florida

Jake sat at the console and put his face in his hands.

The pace of the last eight days was taking its toll on him and he badly needed rest. Maddy walked over and placed a hand on his shoulder. He looked up and smiled.

"Are you ok?" she asked.

He nodded. "Just tired. How are you holding up?"

She slid onto his lap, wrapped her arms around his shoulders and rested her head against his. "Better, now."

She felt good to him despite the fact his body ached all over.

"I could really use a nap," he said.

"Mmm—sounds good," she said, running her fingers along the back of his neck and in his hair.

He laughed. "You know, even as tired as I am, you can get me going. I'll make a deal with you," he said.

"What?"

"Let me finish running these diagnostics and we'll close up early and head to my place."

"You sure you don't want me right now?" she said, straddling him in the chair and wiggling against him. "Teri's gone."

171

He kissed her softly and said, "If you don't mind performing for the hidden cameras, let's go."

She stopped, then giggled leaning against him, "Shoot! I forgot about those. Ok—finish up. Can I help?"

"Sure—stay right here on my lap and that will help me a lot."

She turned and sat across his lap again and he pressed a few keys initiating a diagnostic program on Andee. The computer worked for thirty seconds or so and the results showed everything working properly.

"I need to check the video file of Frank that we got today, and then we can go."

She rested her head on his shoulder and hummed an acknowledgement.

Jake started the video and it played for a bit without any surprises. He was relieved. His concern that the events of the morning may have damaged some of the components of the computer system was unfounded. He let it run a little longer and was about to hit stop when the video changed.

As Frank's NDE was ending, static appeared and the sound became distorted. The whole file seemed to stutter, like someone was trying to tune in a channel on an old TV or shortwave. Suddenly it cleared up and a view of the lab appeared with Frank in the chair, the body mold over him. Jake sat forward and Maddy lifted her head off of his shoulder.

"What happened?" Maddy asked.

"This is different," Jake said.

As they watched, the events of the morning unfolded again in front of them with the hole opening over Frank. Paper whirled around the lab and a chair was sucked into the cavity. Suddenly, Frank sat up, looked toward the camera view, got to his feet and walked closer to whatever was filming the video. As he approached, he looked very angry. He glared straight into the camera but pointed at the hole over the chair.

"Stop! Jake!" Frank said, "The balance must be restored!"

Jake flinched as if he'd been struck.

As they both watched, fear spread across Frank's face and his features started to smear. It was like his visage was made up of sand and the separate grains were being blown or sucked toward the chair. The upper half of his body leaned toward the gaping hole and tendrils of sand led away from him into the opening over the chair.

The features of his face became unrecognizable as the vortex pulled particles of Frank toward it.

In the video, Jake was reaching for the abort button and both he and Maddy, watching this, shouted "No!" but of course the Jake in the video couldn't be stopped. As the button was pushed, the opening over the chair snapped shut, the paper and office chair spewing out from it, but the part of Frank that had been sucked in was not ejected like the smashed chair.

The remaining part of Frank that was still on the lab side of the opening stuttered and then fell to the floor like so many grains of sand. Nothing was left to hold him together. A very faint wailing could be heard that faded away to nothingness. The playback stopped.

42

January 18, 2010 4:40 p.m.

Orlando, Florida

Peter stood on the other side of General Breckenridge's desk.

The General spoke, but Peter was trying to absorb what he had just finished telling him.

"...we'll fly him in tomorrow. I'll want you there to escort him to Orange Park," The General said. "Soldier! Are you listening!?"

Peter's attention snapped back to the General and he said, "Yes sir! Sorry, sir! I'll escort the prisoner to Orange Park tomorrow."

"Very good. I'll have Colonel Davis give you the itinerary."

Peter paused and then said, "Permission to speak freely, sir?"

The General eyed him and Peter thought he would deny the request, but The General said, "Permission granted."

"Sir, I'm not at all comfortable with all this—uh—supernatural stuff and it surprises me that you would buy into it. The prisoner is quite valuable and I don't see how any of this will benefit us."

"If you had been paying attention, you would know how. Our usual tactics are not working. This prisoner holds considerable information and we now have a means of obtaining it."

"But sir, if I understood correctly, these files that Jake Townsend showed you, I don't have any hard evidence they are genuine. He could have manufactured the video to keep you off of his back."

"Well, if you had better intel like I wanted, we wouldn't be having this conversation would we? We'll find out tomorrow if Townsend is telling the truth or not. Personally, I think he is. Dismissed."

Peter came to attention, saluted and exited the office.

As he made his way to his room, he couldn't help but wonder if all he had gone through, ten months earlier in Afghanistan, would be wasted in one swift day. The memory of the mission was still fresh in his mind.

After being inserted into Kandahar from the air, he had met with a local who would assist him with the mission. Forook Bandahar had been somewhat less than Peter was used to, but it had all turned out. Peter still wondered if the man had survived afterward.

After surprising him in the dark as Forook waited across from the Taliban safe house, Forook scolded him for being late. "You are late," he said. "I was about to leave."

Peter said nothing.

"Our mutual friend is a half a kilometer north of here," Forook said. "We must hurry if we are to prevent him from soiling the girl."

The 'mutual friend' was Qayum Omar, a particularly gruesome Al Qaida operative utilizing the local Taliban insurgents as his personal body guards. He normally stayed at the safe house across the street, but because of his fondness for young girls, was currently at another location close by. The girl Forook spoke of was his cousin's fifteen year old daughter.

Peter nodded and pointed north indicating Forook was to lead.

They headed out through the streets and shortly arrived at a secluded house set back off the main path. A single window was illuminated by a weak light from a candle or lantern. A man stood guard at the front entrance to the house. They crouched behind a low wall across the path and waited.

Peter watched as the single guard smoked a cigarette and stared into the night, bored. As Peter assessed the situation, Forook sniffled loudly next to him and shuffled his feet. Peter's noisy guide smelled, and he would be glad to be rid of him.

"Is there anyone else in the house besides our friend and the girl," Peter whispered.

"No," Forook said, "they are alone. Please hurry. He will do horrible things to her and I fear he has already been in with her too long."

Peter nodded. "Remain here. Stay quiet and out of sight."

"Yes. I will wait."

Peter worked his way along the low wall to the south and crossed the path out of sight of the guard and the door. He crept around the back of the house and came up behind the guard quietly. Peter needed to dispatch this man silently, if he alerted Omar inside, things would get messy.

His favorite stealth method involved using his knife to sever the spinal column just below the base of the skull. But with the robes and headdress the Taliban soldier wore, his anatomy was not immediately visible and Peter couldn't risk misjudging the entry point of the knife possibly missing the spinal nerve altogether. He quickly and silently moved to within arm's length of the man and grabbed his robe at the neck, yanking him backwards causing him to lose his balance.

As the human body begins to fall backwards, the head has a tendency to move forward in anticipation of a strike to the back of the skull upon landing. Peter used this reflex and forced the man's head further forward in a quick jabbing motion and then twisted it violently to the right. Performed correctly and with enough strength, the vertebrae will snap at the base of the skull and cause instant death.

The crack of the man's neck breaking seemed very loud in the quiet night as Peter caught the slack body and eased it silently to the ground. He moved quickly to the door and waited in the shadows until he was sure no one had been alerted inside.

Peter could hear a young female pleading in Arabic.

"Please—do not make me do this," she begged.

"You will do as I command!" a gruff voice answered, followed by a sharp slap as someone struck the girl.

Time to move.

Peter checked the door silently to make sure it was not locked. Finding it open, he rapidly turned the handle and was through before anyone could react. He found Omar standing over a kneeling young girl, his small erection standing straight out, the girl's hand being forced toward it. Movement to his right caused Peter to instinctively pivot to his left. Whipping his left fist violently in an arc behind him, he connected with the unknown man's throat, crushing his larynx in a painful and brutal blow. He followed through in a complete circle and was upon Omar before the first man had hit the floor.

Omar was dropping his robes and reaching for something inside them when Peter brought his right foot down upon Omar's right leg just below and to the side of the knee, snapping the weak joint like a brittle twig. Omar briefly cried out as he went down.

Peter's momentum carried his left leg over the falling Omar and as he straddled the terrorist's body from behind, he bent, wrapped his right arm around Omar's neck in a sleeper hold, and squeezed until the man went slack, unconscious.

Peter looked over to see the other man thrashing around on the floor, his hands at his throat and wet choking sounds emanating from his smashed windpipe. The man's struggles quickly subsided as he died of asphyxiation.

The young girl had fallen back as she tried to get out of the way of the violence all around her. She now lay curled in a fetal position under a small table against the near wall, shaking and mumbling in Arabic. Peter went to her and tried to calm her, but she shrank from his touch seeming not to hear his words.

"It's ok," he said in Arabic, "I won't hurt you. He won't hurt you anymore. It's over."

Peter stepped outside and beckoned to Forook who scrambled across the path and entered the house. He stared at the dead man on the floor and Qayum Omar lying a short distance from him. Forook saw his relative and went to her, speaking in a soothing tone and cradling her in his arms. She clung to him fiercely when she recognized him and sobbed into his shoulder.

In English Peter said, "He was trying to get her to touch him when I entered. I don't think anything else had happened."

Forook glared at the unconscious Omar and spat in his direction. "Is he dead?" Forook asked.

Peter shook his head, no. "This one and the one outside are. We must leave quickly. Can she move with us? I need you to help carry our friend to the rendezvous."

Forook spoke to her briefly in Arabic and Peter understood her to say she would try.

Peter grabbed Omar's shoulders and Forook, his legs, and they carried him outside and over to the low wall which had hidden them only a few moments before. The girl scurried along beside Forook, her haunted eyes searching the darkness.

Peter said, "We must carry him a quarter kilometer to the north, can you manage?"

"I will try," Forook said, and they picked him up again and began moving north along the street. Forook struggled and the girl helped him as they made their way slowly north. They had to pause frequently for Forook to catch his breath.

No one else was on the street and the houses were dark and quiet. At one point Omar stirred and moaned, and as they set him down, Peter prepared to render him unconscious. The terrorist never woke and soon became silent and still once again. They resumed the trek and arrived at a spot Peter knew to be the rendezvous.

Lights came on in the distance and a vehicle's engine could be heard as the lights slowly approached their position.

Peter asked Forook, "What is her name?"

"Kessa."

Peter had a soft spot for children and despised anyone who would do them harm. He hated to see them suffer. He knelt in front of Kessa and spoke to her in Arabic.

"You are a brave girl, Kessa. You did not deserve what this man was going to do to you, but I need you to be braver still."

She looked at him with wary eyes and nodded slowly.

"Men will come and ask you what happened. You can tell them about me, but you must not tell them about Forook. They will kill you and Forook, along with your family, if you tell these men the truth about tonight. Can you lie?"

She nodded. The vehicle was close.

Peter turned and watched it approach for a moment and then turned back to Kessa.

"Remember, Forook was not here. A man dressed in black came and killed the two men and took the third man away. You ran home through the streets when the man in black left you alone. Repeat it to yourself many times tonight until you believe it."

He smiled at the girl and touched her head.

The vehicle arrived and two men jumped out, taking Omar and placing him in the back of the beat up Toyota Four Runner. They handed Peter a package and Peter in turn gave the package to Forook.

He shook Forook's hand and said, "Be safe."

Forook nodded.

Peter climbed into the back of the small SUV and it drove away. He watched as Forook and Kessa turned and walked up the street. He never knew if they survived or not.

As Peter lay in his bed, the mission replaying over and over in his mind, he couldn't help thinking that if Kessa hadn't survived, she would have been sacrificed for nothing. Tomorrow they would risk everything on the hocus pocus of some crackpot scientist.

43

January 18, 2010 4:42 p.m.

Orange Park, Florida

When the video was finished, Teri turned her back to the screens, sat on the console and folded her arms across her chest. Jake couldn't read her.

When he and Maddy had called her at home, she didn't want to come all the way back over the bridge, but Jake had insisted, saying it was important. Jake could tell she had been angry. She had stormed into the lab a half an hour later and said, "What!?"

He showed her the video.

"What did Bodey have to say?" Teri finally said.

Jake looked at Maddy and then back at Teri. "I haven't talked to him yet."

"We should probably talk to him, don't you think? What if this is some kind of computer glitch?"

"Do you really think this could be a malfunction?" Jake asked.

"I don't know what to think," Teri said, moving away from the console. "You call me back here to watch this—this—I don't even know what to call it, and then you expect me to have some kind of answer for you?"

"Teri, I didn't ask you for an answer. I wanted you to see this because I think it's important."

"All right—I saw it. Can I go now?"

"That's all you're going to say? 'Can I go now?' I was hoping for a little more input from you."

"Ok. Here's my input. I think you need to stop this before you do something catastrophic. Maybe we've already done something we can't fix. According to Frank, we've knocked something out of balance and you have to restore it, whatever that is."

"Teri, I know you're upset,..." Jake started.

"Upset? Upset!? Dammit, Jake. I'm terrified! What the hell have we done? Have we created some 'Twilight Zone' rip in the space-time continuum? Torn open a hole into our own continued existence? What if we can't set it right? Have we doomed ourselves or even mankind to extinction?"

"I don't know!" Jake shouted, trying to get a word in.

"What about Frank? He's lying in a hospital bed, a shell of a man. Is part of him trapped over there while the rest is here? Maybe we've denied him his afterlife because his soul has been torn in two, one half stuck here and the other in limbo on the other side of that hole we opened up and then slammed shut."

"I don't know!" Jake shouted, the frustration building. "That's why I need your help! Help me, Teri! I need you to help me."

"Whoa—guys," Maddy said, putting a hand on Jake's shoulder and one on Teri's. "We're all a little frazzled here. Let's just try and stay calm."

"You try and stay calm," Teri snapped at Maddy, "I'm out of here," and she turned to leave.

"Teri—wait," Jake said, softly. He saw the tone of his voice cause her to stop.

She turned back, waiting.

"I'll stop."

She said nothing, but her eyes welled up and a tear rolled down her cheek.

"I'll stop this madness, but I need your help to fix this. We need to fix this."

She walked over to him, fell against him and held him tight. He was shocked at first, but took her in his arms and held her tight as she cried. Maddy was looking at him and tears were falling down her face. He gave her a look that said 'I love you' and she nodded.

Teri said, "I know what all this means to you. All this for Beth. But I'm scared. Scared for you." She got herself under control and pulled away.

Wiping her face with her hands she said, "I'll help."

44

January 18, 2010 5:10 p.m.

Orange Park, Florida

"Can you come?" Jake asked.

"I just left," Bodey said. "What's up?"

"We have an issue. Can I e-mail you a large file? It's a video."

"Yeah dude. Shoot it my way."

"Watch it and call me back. You'll understand. Oh—and don't let anyone else see it."

"No problem," Bodey said. "Top secret—got it. Call ya' in a few." And he hung up.

Jake had the file ready, and sent it to Bodey. It took ten minutes to upload. While they waited, Teri wanted to know more about their dreams, so they spent the time filling her in on what had been happening.

"So in your dream," Teri pointed to Jake, "you hear Beth telling you to 'Stop the balance?'"

Jake nodded.

"What do you think that means, now?" Teri asked.

"That's what's so confusing," Jake said. "At first, she was just saying 'Stop!' and I thought she wanted me to stop trying to hear what she was mumbling. I mean for the last two years, I've been trying to figure out what she's saying in the dream. Remember, she said to be good to Madison and Lucas, but she also said something I couldn't hear."

"You said at first, what about now?"

"In a later dream, she says, 'Stop the balance,' which makes no sense. I can't seem to read anything into 'Stop the balance.'"

"Jake and I have gone over and over our dreams and still come up empty," Maddy said. "It's very frustrating. Jake even thought at one point, Beth was telling him to stop being with me."

"In yours," Teri said, pointing to Maddy, "Ryan says 'Jake must not be lost.' What do you think that means?"

"I felt like it meant I wasn't supposed to lose him," Maddy said. "That he and I were meant to find each other and be together. That's why it didn't make sense to me that Beth would be telling Jake to stop seeing me and Ryan was telling me not to lose Jake."

Teri stood up and started pacing. Jake could tell she was working something out.

"Frank says in the video, 'Stop Jake, the balance must be restored.'" Teri was looking right at Jake now. "Almost the same words as in your dreams. Maybe you guys were thrust together because you were getting parts of the message separately? Combine your dreams and what do you get?"

"Stop the balance, Jake must not be lost?" Maddy asked, confused.

"No." Jake said, understanding now. "Put them in order from the first message to the last. Mine and then yours. My first message was 'Stop!'"

"And mine was 'Jake,'" Maddy said.

"So, 'Stop Jake! The balance must not be lost' is what we would get," Jake said.

"Exactly!" Teri said excited. "You guys never could put it together until now so you didn't get the message. Maddy, you were supposed to stop Jake, so the balance wouldn't be lost."

"Well, we screwed that up," Maddy said.

"We better make sure we don't screw up the next part," Jake said.

The phone rang and Jake answered it. "Encephalographic Systems."

"Dude," Bodey said, "you guys got some major shit going on down there. What the hell was that?"

"Bodey, Teri and Maddy are here and I'm going to put you on speaker."

Jake pressed the speaker button so everyone could hear and talk.

"We're not sure what it was, but if I had to guess, I would say we opened up a hole between this plane of existence and the afterlife."

"No shit," Bodey said. "That dude in the video looked messed up."

"Bodey, this is Teri. Could this in any way be some kind of computer glitch or artifact?"

"Not a chance. Why do you ask? You guys didn't see this live?"

"No," Jake said. "Well, not all of it. The rift opened up but the part with Frank in it showed up in the playback afterwards. I was checking the system out after things had calmed down and that part at the end was there."

"What happened to the guy?"

"He's in the hospital," Maddy said, "on life support. His heart stopped in the chair and the paramedics got him back—or what's left of him back."

"Don't tell me he's like cut in half or something."

"No—no," Jake said, "he's whole. He's just not all in there. He's a shell of a man or something—all body and no soul."

"You guys have to get him whole again."

"Yeah—we figured. That's the problem. I'm not sure how. Can you come?"

"I'm already working on it. Cheryl is booking the flight as we speak. It won't be until tomorrow afternoon, your time. That ok?"

"It'll have to be."

"All right, you guys be cool. I'll see you tomorrow."

"Ok—tomorrow."

"Oh! And make sure that dude doesn't die," Bodey said. "I have a feeling we may need him."

45

January 19, 2010 3:31 a.m.

Orange Park, Florida

Jake was in the dream again.

Beth was in his arms but there was no blood. He knew the accident had happened, but she seemed uninjured, eyes closed, a small smile on her perfect lips, as if she were sleeping. He stared at her face and his heart ached for her.

A faint rumbling could be heard in the distance and Jake watched as Beth's eyes opened and she looked at him like he had been lost from her, and then found again. The love pouring forth from her eyes made his heart break and tears fell freely onto her perfect face. She reached up and touched his cheek and he gasped at the feel of her.

"Oh God, Beth, I miss you so."

"I'm right here," she said. "I always have been."

Movement to his right caught his eye and he looked up to find Maddy and Ryan walking toward them holding hands.

"Jake, I don't have much time," Beth said. "We have come together because it is very important you understand."

"You must make us whole," Ryan said. "We are all here so you will see."

Ryan turned and nodded at Maddy, giving her some kind of signal. She reached out and touched Jake.

Brilliant white light burst from Beth and Ryan, encompassing everything.

Maddy now stood next to him and he looked into her shining, green eyes. They were the only things visible within the light and Jake held her gaze for fear of losing all sense of direction. Her eyes grew in brightness and intensity and he knew he had never seen them so beautiful.

"Oh Jake," Maddy said. "Do you see? Close your eyes."

Jake closed his eyes and saw everything.

* * *

Jake and Maddy woke together, face to face, her hand touching his cheek from the dream.

As they both became fully awake, a shuddering ripple of energy passed through them and a powerful vibration shook the house all the way to the foundation. It was as if the house lifted up and then settled again. The bed came up off the floor slightly and then came back down quickly as thunder trailed off into the distance.

"You were there," Jake said softly, caressing her face.

She smiled and nodded. "I was there."

"I know what to do."

"Yes," and she kissed him.

46

January 19, 2010 0600

Over The Atlantic Ocean

Qayum Omar sat shackled to the seat of a Cessna Citation 500, heading south.

He knew this not because he had been told, but because the sun was peaking over the horizon to his left. He wore a drab gray jumpsuit with no markings or insignia, shoes which were two sizes too big, and his face and head had been shaved.

Two men in suits sat close to him with one in the seat in front and the other to the right. He had seen their pistols holstered beneath their coats as they moved around getting settled before the flight departed. Neither spoke. The Americans were all business and this suited Omar perfectly since he had nothing to say to these pigs anyway.

They had pulled him from his cell at 3:30 in the morning and made him dress. Since he refused to shave his face, they held him down and shaved it for him. The Americans knew the importance of his beard and because of that, they had taken a razor to it immediately after his capture and twice a week since. He made them hold him down every time.

His leg had healed for the most part and he no longer needed the brace. It had taken two surgeries to repair the torn ligaments in his knee from the kick so accurately placed by the American pig who had disrupted his life. The American would one day pay for that mistake.

The aircraft began a rapid descent and Omar closed his eyes trying to relax. He calculated distance and speed of the aircraft in an attempt to calm his nerves and after a few minutes determined they were somewhere in Florida. His hosts seemed to go out of their way to keep their guest in the dark as to his location and destination, but Omar had studied many things in his life, and after catching brief glimpses of landmarks upon his arrival in the U.S., he knew they had been keeping him somewhere in Northern Virginia.

Having knowledge of aircraft and their individual performance characteristics he was able to easily determine the general area over which they were currently flying. If he had to guess his destination, he would say Central Florida. Perhaps Orlando. They would not have begun their descent if they were to travel further south.

His flight training had prepared him for a role in the attacks of September 11, but since he was to be in the second wave, he never had the opportunity for martyrdom.

The U.S. Federal Aviation Administration had denied him paradise by landing every single aircraft in the air as soon as the motives of the terrorists were realized. He was able to escape detection in the mass exodus of passengers and then secured other means of transportation through Canada and eventually to Afghanistan. He had been very busy since.

His last operation, prior to his capture, had also involved aircraft, but of a different type and size.

It was possible to purchase through the internet most of the materials necessary to construct a rudimentary 'smart bomb.' The tools necessary included a radio control aircraft, basically a fancy toy, a telemetry device with a very small camera and transmitter, and virtual reality goggles commonly used for computer gaming. Semtex, a very light and powerful explosive was also used, but of course, that could not be obtained through the internet.

The radio controlled aircraft was fitted with the camera mounted onto a gimbal. This gimbal was controlled by the same type of servo motors the control surfaces of the model used for its flight controls. The gimbal responded to sensors mounted on the virtual reality goggles so that whatever direction the helmet was turned, the gimbal would respond likewise, enabling the pilot to have a cockpit view from the aircraft. The telemetry unit the camera attached to fed live video in real time to the virtual reality goggles and since the aircraft had a range of up to six miles from the transmitter it could be flown beyond visual range of the pilot.

The first use of the system became Omar's responsibility and he chose what he considered a lucrative target. The Americans were using Kandahar Airfield as a base of operations in the south, finding its close proximity to the mountain passes to the north and Pakistan to the east perfectly suited for operations against the Taliban and its Al Qaeda affiliations. Overcrowded and difficult to defend, the base was irresistible to Omar. Since the radio controlled aircraft was electric and smaller than two meters, it was impossible to detect via radar and nearly silent.

Omar brought the aircraft into the mountains just to the north of the airfield and from behind an outcropping hidden from view of the base, launched the aircraft by hand and flew it the mile south, over the fence without detection, and in to the open doors of a mess hall at lunch time, detonating the Semtex just inside the doorway killing anyone within fifteen meters. Thirty four of the American Marines had been killed and another twenty-two injured.

It had worked with deadly precision.

The Citation touched down as full dawn broke over the horizon and when the agent to his right closed his window shade, Omar caught a glimpse of the word 'McCoy' on the main terminal building before his view was completely blocked.

He grinned to himself. Orlando International Airport. His calculations had been correct.

They removed the shackles from the seat, then secured the chains binding his wrists to his ankles and with one agent in front and the other behind, marched him through the cabin and down the short steps of the aircraft.

A nondescript van sat idling five meters away and they guided him toward it as the side doors of the vehicle opened. He was helped inside, seated on an uncomfortable bench, his shackles removed again from the chains and attached to secure rings mounted to the wall of the van. It was then he noticed the man sitting in the rear of the compartment, his face obscured by gloom. As the van pulled away from the tarmac, the rising sun shone through the window, illuminating the man's face for an instant.

"You!" Omar spoke for the first time all morning.

The man chuckled.

47

January 19, 2010 9:45 a.m.

Orange Park, Florida

Jake and Maddy were discussing their illuminating night with Teri in the lab at 9:45 a.m. when the front door buzzer sounded and Jake said, "Yes? May I help you?"

"General Breckenridge," is all the voice said, and Jake looked at Teri who shrugged.

"Come in, sir," Teri said and she buzzed the lock, allowing The General to enter.

He strode in with a contingent of personnel, some in uniform and others in civilian attire. Eleven men total and one woman. Jake's good mood turned foul in an instant.

"General, what's going on?" Jake asked.

"Time for you to put our generous funding to work, Doctor," The General said. "We need some information and I believe your equipment will provide us with it."

"What information?"

"That is classified and I suspect one of your new employees is lacking a security clearance. I cannot discuss it with her present. Would you ask her to leave or give her the day off. She will not be needed."

"General, there is nothing in this computer system she has not seen and I can't imagine what you would need in the files. Exactly what information would warrant all this?" Jake asked, indicating the scattered personnel in his lab.

"The information is not in your computer system," the General said. "Yet."

"Yet? What do you mean by that?"

"Just what it sounds like. We will be using your machine to gather information and then we will need to form a database of that information."

Jake was about to ask another question when one of the civilians approached and, listening to something being said in the earpiece the man wore, told the General, "He's here."

"Tell them to wait, the area is not secure yet. Doctor Townsend, either ask the young lady to leave or we will escort her out."

"You have no right to tell me…" Jake started, but Maddy said, "It's all right, Jake. I'll go."

"No—it's not all right," he protested. "I need you here, today. We have major problems to work out, and I need all my employees."

"What problems?" the General asked, concerned.

"Well, for one, the sensors were damaged during the incident yesterday and I haven't been able to evaluate how badly yet. We were in the process of doing that before you arrived."

"And the other?"

"The cooling system may have been damaged," Jake lied, "and we have not had a chance to evaluate that either."

"Anything else?" the General asked, sarcastically. "Yesterday, when you demonstrated the capability of this—machine, I was under the impression it was fully functional."

"Well, sir, it was fully functional. Until yesterday. I explained the incident we had to you, I was under the impression you understood the situation. And may I also add you have a tendency to barge in here whenever you feel like it, unannounced. May I suggest that in the future, you make your plans clear to me so that I may adjust my schedule accordingly. We might be able to avoid inconveniencing each other."

Jake thought the General was going to shoot him right there.

"How long?" the General asked.

"A day, maybe two. I won't be able to tell until I actually get into it."

"You have two days."

"Two days or what?" Jake asked.

"You have two days to get this system up and running or I will come in here and shut you down."

The General signaled his people, turned and walked out with his little posse following on his heels.

As soon as the door closed behind them, Jake motioned for Maddy and Teri to follow him into the women's restroom.

"I would bet my life there are more bugs in this building," Jake whispered.

Teri nodded.

"We need to find them. Now. Especially any video cameras. Audio bugs we can fool, but video will be difficult. I don't want them to see Andee is fully functional. I'll start on the console. Maddy you take the chair and the area around it. Teri, I don't think they'll be in here or the kitchen. They need to be able to view the work area so concentrate on the perimeter walls and duct work around the main lab. Don't discuss anything about our plans for the day while we are in here. Got it?"

Teri and Maddy nodded and they set out.

Jake found a listening device within fifteen minutes and Teri located the video camera in the frame of the picture shortly after that. Maddy was not having any luck. Jake came over to help her and they both found another listening device, seeing it at the same time. It had been attached to one of the sensors on the chair.

They searched for another hour, but found nothing else.

"Let's get lunch and get out of here for a while," Jake said.

At the Mexican restaurant, Jake and Maddy told Teri what needed to be done and surprisingly she took it all in stride.

"I think we should stick together today as much as practical," Jake said. "If they went to such great lengths to keep an eye on us at the lab, I can pretty much guarantee our cell phones are tapped along with our houses and landlines. If you need to use your cell phone, try and remember that someone is probably listening, ok?"

Teri and Maddy nodded.

"What should we do about Mrs. Lucas?" Teri asked.

"I was thinking about her too," Jake said, "and this is what I came up with."

He told them both his plan and they smiled in agreement.

Jake said, "We need to pick up Bodey soon, so let's go to my place on the way to the airport. I need to grab a few things for later."

Jake paid the tab, tipped the waitress, and they drove in Maddy's car to Jake's house where they picked up a few things then went straight to Jacksonville International Airport and waited for Bodey to arrive.

48

January 19, 2010 1:00 p.m.

Orange Park, Florida

Peter had never seen the General so angry.

He was glad some of the heat was off him, but it was very uncharacteristic for the General to lose it. Peter kept looking back on this whole mission with Encephalographic Systems and couldn't help thinking one thing after another had gone wrong. He wasn't superstitious, but if he didn't think too hard about it, he could see how someone would believe the whole thing was jinxed.

"What the hell are we going to do with the prisoner?" the General raged. "I've got to have a place to keep him under wraps until the day after tomorrow. Any of you have any suggestions?"

Peter watched the group and he could tell they all felt like he did. The General was not a well liked man. He also rarely made such a mistake as the one he made today and frankly, Peter could tell the General didn't know how to handle it. No one in the room was willing to offer any suggestions at this point, at least not until they were sure the General wasn't going to try and blame this mess on someone other than himself.

As if on cue the General said, "Nobody has any ideas? All right, since I messed this up, I guess I'll have to fix it."

"General, if I may," Peter said.

General Breckenridge nodded.

"The way I see it is we have three options. First, we can drive him back to Orlando and house him in the facility there until we know Andee is operational. Second, we can find a secluded motel and keep him sequestered in a room while we wait. Or third, we can keep him under wraps at my apartment, which has three bedrooms and would be fairly easy to secure with the contingent of assets we have present. I'm leaning toward the third option myself, since this seems to be the least problematic."

"All right, Smith, let's get him moved to your place and secured before I change my mind and send him back to Virginia. Make sure this goes smoothly. I'm putting him in your hands."

"Yes sir."

49

January 19, 2010 1:45 p.m.

Orange Park, Florida

Bodey's flight arrived on time and Jake felt a little luck was on their side for a change.

During the forty five minute ride from the airport to the lab, they briefed Bodey on everything that had happened. He listened without saying a word which was unusual for Bodey, and Jake asked if he was ok.

"Just in awe, my brother, just in awe. I would definitely classify these events as life changing."

When they arrived at the lab, Bodey removed a gadget from his duffle bag, turned it on and began walking around the lab pointing it at things.

"What are you doing?" Jake asked, but Bodey put a finger to his lips, silencing him.

After a moment the small device made a beeping noise and Bodey crouched down beside a counter top and removed another listening device. He crushed it under his shoe. He searched the rest of the lab and was almost satisfied it was clean when the beeping noise started up again. Bodey looked around the computers and was having a hard time finding anything. He finally pulled out a screwdriver, removed a cover from the back of the CRAY and after a moment, pulled out another device much larger than anything they had seen.

"Those bastards," he said. He put it on the console and drove the screwdriver threw the center of it, shorting it out. "All right, we're clean."

"What is this?" Jake said picking up the black box Bodey had destroyed with the screwdriver.

"This was sending every bit of data the CRAY was processing to whoever planted it. They were eavesdropping on the computer system. What bothers me is the fact they were fiddling around inside my baby. Now I'm mad."

"Any damage to Andee?" Jake asked.

"Not anything I can see, but I'll check her out along with everything else while you guys are gone."

"All right—we've got to move if we're going to make it," Jake said. "Everybody know their part?"

Nods all around and Teri had a small smile on her face. Maddy looked happy, but a little nervous.

"Let's go. Teri, you drive your car and Maddy, you're with me. Wish us luck, Bodey."

"You won't need it. Somebody's looking out for you guys."

Jake smiled and herded the girls out.

They arrived at St. Vincent's Medical Center twenty minutes later.

Teri was up first.

While Jake and Maddy waited in Jake's car, Teri donned her lab coat from school and hung Jake's stethoscope around her neck.

"How do I look?" Teri asked.

"Like you belong," Jake said.

Jake and Maddy watched her head for the elevators and waited for their turn.

50

January 19, 2010 2:32 p.m.

Jacksonville, Florida

Teri entered the hospital through the Dillon building and worked her way straight to the second floor.

Having done a rotation in the Radiology Department during her post graduate studies with Jake, she knew as long as she looked like she fit in, no one would even give her a second glance. With her white lab jacket and the stethoscope hanging around her neck, she looked the part she was about to play. The only thing missing was a hospital employee badge, but she had a way around that if asked.

She approached the nurse's station of Two West, and without hesitation, began opening drawers and leafing through files and forms. She pretended to be looking for something and after a few seconds of searching, sighed and closed the drawer she currently had open, moving on to another one.

The receptionist noticed her and said, "What ya' need honey?"

"Respiratory order forms?" Teri said. "Hi, I'm Cassandra. I'm new in respiratory. Sorry—I thought I could find them without bothering you."

"No problem, honey. I'm Veronica, but call me Nicky," the receptionist said.

"Ok, Nicky. God, I feel so lost. This place is huge. I'm used to smaller hospitals."

"I know what you mean. It took me a week to find my way to this floor without having to ask someone for directions. It seemed like during my first week, I would have to park in a different parking garage every day, and then find my way here from across the world, all while trying not to be late."

"I know," Teri whispered, "I keep having to ask for directions. One doctor didn't even talk. He just glared at me and pointed. Sometimes they can be such assholes."

"Tell me about it, girlfriend. You don't have to sit here all day and take it like I do. Dr. Blemish, that man is impossible. He and I go round and round sometimes. If only he would learn how to write legibly, I wouldn't have to call him all the time. I swear."

The phone rang and Nicky picked it up, "Two West?" She held up a finger and rolled her eyes at Teri. Teri smiled back at her.

"Hold on, sir," Nicky said into the phone as she spun in her chair and pulled a chart out of the rack. "No…Mrs. Hancock is scheduled for dialysis today. That's right…uh…looks like five o'clock. Yep…uh huh…thank you," and she hung up. "Now, what were we doing?"

"Respiratory order forms?"

"Right, they're in that drawer."

Nicky pointed to a set of drawers right behind Teri that read 'Order Forms J – Z.'

Teri slapped her forehead and said, "Duh?" and walked over and opened it. "Thanks."

"Anytime, sugar, anytime." Nicky picked up the phone, dialed an extension and was soon requesting some test for another patient.

Teri thumbed through the folders and found Respiratory and pulled out a single order form. What she really wanted was in the folder just in front of Respiratory and glancing quickly over her shoulder at Nicky, who was still on the phone, she pulled out the Radiology folder and grabbing an order form, slipped it under the Respiratory one she already had. Quickly, she put the Radiology folder back in and closed the drawer.

As she turned to leave, Nicky hung up and said to Teri, "Who's getting the therapy? I don't remember seeing any orders for a new Respiratory treatment."

"Uh—well," Teri fumbled over her words for a second, "the order is for a patient in Two East, but they didn't have any forms left." She held up the two pieces of paper in her hand and added, "Can I take two?"

Nicky looked a little irritated and said, "You tell Jeanette in Two East she had better get her butt down to supply and get her own damn order forms. She's always borrowing mine."

"I will," Teri said. "Is it ok?" she asked again, holding up the forms.

Nicky smiled and said, "Yes, it's fine."

"Thanks!" Teri said and turned to go.

"You better find your badge, girl," Nicky said to Teri's back. "If security sees you without it, they will have your butt."

Teri feigned surprise and looked around at herself saying, "I had it earlier—what the heck happened to it? Oh—I bet I know. Mr. Leese in 2217 was out of his head and all grabby. He kept reaching for me while I was giving him his treatment. I kept swatting his hands away, but I guess he got a hold of it. I'll go check."

"Hopefully he didn't put it somewhere the sun doesn't shine," Nicky laughed.

"Really," Teri said. She turned and headed for Two East, the forms clutched in her sweating hands.

At Two East she turned left past the nurse's station, out of sight of Nicky, and headed straight for the elevators to the first floor and the parking garage.

Back in the car with Jake and Maddy, she said, "Thought I was going down for second. One of the receptionists made a remark about my missing badge and if security caught me without it, they would have my ass."

"What did you say?" asked Maddy, an anxious look on her face.

"I told them a patient must have grabbed it off of my jacket and I would go back to his room and look for it. She seemed to buy it."

"Ok," Jake said. "We're on. Let's go."

Teri gave Maddy her lab coat while Jake slipped his on. Jake took the radiology order form and quickly wrote an order for a C.T. scan of the head for Frank Lucas in room 2427. He scribbled a signature that could be anything, but looked very much like a doctor's hurried John Hancock. Teri thought it looked great.

"Good luck," she said, and Jake and Maddy walked off together for the elevators.

Teri hoped it would work. That Nicky girl was on her game and definitely in control of her realm. Jake needed to be calm and confident. She sat back in the car and waited for the signal.

51

January 19, 2010 3:00 p.m.

Jacksonville, Florida

Jake had called the hospital earlier in the day and learned Frank had been weaned from the ventilator and then transferred to room 2427 at around noon.

His condition had improved, but he still remained catatonic. Since it was now approaching three o'clock, the nurses were full into shift change and the confusion that often came with it. Jake was hoping it would give him and Maddy the edge they needed to pull off what they had planned.

First, they stopped at another wing on the second floor and got a wheelchair out of Two East's equipment closet.

Jake noticed Maddy glancing around nervously and he whispered to her, "Relax. It will be fine." She nodded, but didn't look any better.

They pushed the wheelchair up to Two West and straight in to room 2427, which was right across from the nurse's station. The nurses were busy giving the new shift a report on each patient they had been responsible for during the day. A lot of people were in the area, but no one paid attention.

Entering Frank's room, Jake saw him sitting up in his bed with the head cranked up, but staring blankly at the wall in front of him.

As Jake and Maddy approached, his head turned toward them and his eyes focused on Jake and he grinned.

Jake smiled back and said, "It's time Frank."

Frank nodded imperceptibly and then he was gone again, replaced by the empty shell he had been only a moment before.

It took all their strength to get him in the wheelchair.

They almost dropped him but Frank ended up sitting in the wheelchair, a blanket across his lap and drool running down his chin. Jake had to rest for a second and catch his breath.

They wheeled him out of the room and as they were passing the nurse's station a voice called out, "Hey! Where are you guys taking Mr. Lucas? Hey! You two—hold it!"

A bulky nurse with bright orange hair and dark blue scrubs caught up to them. "I said where are you guys taking him?"

"C.T.," Jake said.

The nurse turned back to the nurse's station and yelled, "Nicky, is Mr. Lucas scheduled for a Cat scan?"

Jake watched the receptionist look at something on her desk and then say, "Not that I can see, but he just got here from ICU a little while ago."

Jake held up the radiology order form saying, "Here's the order."

The nurse snatched it out of Jake's hands and scowled as she looked at it.

Jake said, "We went to ICU to get him, but they said they transferred him here. I'll bet they forgot to note it in the chart."

"Dianne," another nurse yelled from the nurse's station. "Come on! I want to go home."

"Hold on Jen, just a sec'." To Jake and Maddy she said, "How long will he be gone?"

Jake took the order back from the nurse, looked at it and said, "C.T. scan of the head—about an hour. Shouldn't take more than that."

"All right, but he has some medication due at that time, so you guys make sure he's back by then or else I'll hunt you down."

"No problem," Jake said.

"Dianne…!" the other nurse yelled again.

"All right, all right—coming," and Dianne, the orange-haired nurse went back to the station and continued her briefing.

Jake and Maddy wheeled Frank out of Two West and turned right, heading past the bank of elevators on their left. A security guard rounded a corner on Jake's right and almost ran straight into the wheelchair.

"Whoa! Sorry guys," the guard said.

Jake nodded and kept moving.

The guard let them pass, and then called back to them, "Hey! You two! Hold it!"

Jake ignored him and pushed Frank faster down the hall.

The guard jogged after them and grabbed Jake's shoulder stopping him, "Hold up guys," he said, looking them up and down. "Where are your badges?"

Jake looked over his uniform, acting surprised and said, "I don't know. I had it a minute it ago." He looked through the blanket over Frank's lap and then turned back looking the way they had come as if searching for the badge. "Maybe I dropped it in his room."

"Well, you need to go back and get it," the guard said. "You know you're supposed to have it on at all times." He turned to Maddy and said, "What about you?"

Jake said, "She's new. She doesn't have hers yet."

"They didn't give you a temporary badge?"

Maddy shook her head no and said, "They were out."

"What?" the guard asked. "Those idiots! All right, well let's get you fixed up. Follow me."

The guard turned and headed back the way he had come.

Jake said, "We don't have time for that now."

The guard turned and said, "You'll have to make time."

"You don't understand," Jake said, forcefully. "This man needs to go to C.T. right now. There was some confusion when they transferred him from ICU and the nurse is going to kill me if I don't have him back in an hour. We'll come to Security right away after we drop him off. I promise."

The guard frowned looking Jake and Maddy up and down. "All right—but you find your badge and get her a temporary one right after. Don't make me come find you. What's your name?"

Jake said, "Ben Worthington. And she's Sarah Mills."

The guard scribbled the names on his notepad and said, "All right—get it done."

"Thanks," Jake said, and pushed Frank past him down the hall.

They had gone about forty yards when Maddy turned around and said, "He's still watching us and talking into his walky-talky."

"Hey!" came a shout from behind them and Maddy said, "Shit! Here he comes."

Jake pushed Frank faster and took a hard left almost toppling the wheelchair over. An elevator door opened up to their left and Jake steered the chair quickly into it, barely missing a lab tech.

"Hey!" the lab tech said, "Watch it!" and glared at Jake and Maddy.

They could hear the guard's footsteps chasing them down the hall while Jake pressed the close button repeatedly, but the doors remained open.

"Come on!" Jake said frantically, "Close!" The doors finally started closing just as the guard rounded the corner.

"Hey! Stop!" But the guard couldn't keep them from shutting and Jake watched him talk into his radio as they came together.

Jake pressed four.

They rode the elevator up two flights and bolted out of it as soon as the doors opened.

Turning right and then immediately left, they headed for the walkway to the DePaul parking garage. Jake knew they only had seconds to get out of the hospital as the whole security force was probably alerted by now.

They took a hard left and then right, past a sign that said DePaul Medical Building and Jake heard a radio chattering behind them.

"Call Teri," Jake said to Maddy, "tell her change of plans. Meet us in the DePaul parking garage on the fifth floor."

Jake picked up speed and sprinted down the hall with Frank while Maddy called Teri and told her the new plan.

They got to the elevators for the DePaul building and Jake pressed the up button. The doors opened immediately and they rode it up one flight to the fifth floor.

Jake pushed Frank through the exit and they waited for Teri inside the doorway, trying to stay out of sight. Right before Teri got there, a security guard in a golf cart whizzed by heading down the ramp for the fourth floor, his radio chattering away, but he didn't see them.

Teri pulled up after the golf cart passed and all three of them got Frank into the back seat.

Jake ripped off his lab coat and threw it in the back, grabbed a baseball cap from the rear seat and put it on.

"Maddy, take your coat off," Jake said, "and put your hair up in a pony tail. You two walk back to the Dillon garage and take Teri's car to Mrs. Lucas's house. I'll take Frank to the lab. Remember, act like you're visitors now. Stay outside of the hospital and take the sidewalks to the Dillon garage. You should be fine. I'll see you back at the lab."

Maddy kissed Jake and said, "Be careful."

"You too, both of you," and Jake smiled, getting into the driver's seat.

52

January 19, 2010 3:35 p.m.

Jacksonville, Florida

Jake made it out of the parking garage easily and as he turned right onto Shircliff Way, he watched Security scramble around the front entrance of the hospital.

He scanned the street and walkways along it and was thankful to see they hadn't expanded their search outside yet. Maddy and Teri should be fine.

Jake drove Frank straight to the lab and pulled around to the back entrance. He and Bodey struggled with the dead weight, but managed to get Frank into a rolling office chair and maneuver him inside. They picked him up and sat him in Andee's chair, trying to make him look comfortable.

"How did it go?" Bodey asked.

"As well as could be expected. I haven't heard from the girls yet and that worries me a little. I'm going to call them now."

Jake pulled out his cell and called Teri's number. She picked up on the fourth ring.

"Hey," she said, the connection breaking up a bit.

"Everything ok?" he asked.

"We're here, but she's not cooperating. I think we scared her. She's threatening to call the police."

"Let me talk to her."

"Ok—I'll put her on."

Jake heard Teri telling Mrs. Lucas that Jake was on the phone and after a second she said, "Hello?"

"Mrs. Lucas? This is Jake Townsend, I…"

"I know who this is," she said, a little distortion causing her voice to sound tinny. "Just what do you people think you're doing? You've kidnapped my husband from the hospital and now you want to hook him up to that machine of yours again? I think not! I expect…" static. "…to take…" garbled, "…police!"

"Mrs. Lucas, I'm losing you. Can you hear me? Hello?"

"I can –ear you fine. You bring him back…" static, "hospital, now!"

Jake felt frustrated. He was getting nowhere with her and regretted involving her at this point.

"Mrs. Lucas, please—just come down here. It's very important. I know you don't know what's going on, but if you come to the lab with Teri and Maddy, everything will be explained."

Jake knew the phone conversation was being monitored, but he felt he had no other choice at this point. She had to be convinced to come down.

"I'll do no –uch thing. I'm calling the pol…" garbled, "now!"

Jake made a decision. He never liked threatening anybody, but he felt he had no choice.

"Mrs. Lucas, if you want to see your husband alive again, you'll come down to the lab, now."

Silence for a moment and then Jake heard a very different Eve Lucas say, "Please. Don't hurt him."

Jake hated himself at that moment.

All the pain he had caused, the hardships he had put others through for his selfishness, it all hit him in that instant and the blow was palpable. He had to sit down for fear of toppling over. He hung his head, his resolve failing and could think of nothing to say. What could he tell this woman that would make any difference? He had taken her happiness away and now threatened to cast her even further into despair.

"I'll come," Eve Lucas said through the tinny connection, "just don't hurt my Frank."

"I won't," was all Jake could get out.

He ended the call.

53

January 19, 2010 4:15 p.m.

Mandarin, Florida

After Peter and four of the General's men got Omar settled into the second bedroom of the apartment, Peter checked on the monitoring equipment being used to keep track of Jake and his clan.

He was not surprised to see they had found everything. Disappointed, but not surprised. This little group was relentless and he wondered what they were up to and why they had spent over an hour scouring the lab to make sure what they were doing was not seen.

He punched a few keys on his computer and a log of the cell phone activity came up. He scanned it quickly and since they had used the phones so little over the last twenty four hours, the activity on Jake and Teri's phones during the last hour stuck out like a sore thumb. He downloaded the audio file and listened to the conversation. He immediately called the General.

"They're up to something, sir." And he explained what he had just heard.

"What do you think they're going to do?" the General asked.

"I can't even guess, but they went to great lengths to get this man back to the lab. The wife mentions kidnapping during the conversation."

"Great. We need to find out what's going on. Can you get down there?"

"I'll have to leave our package with the four you supplied me. Do you trust them?"

"Yes, but I'll send two more to help. Get down there and find out if that machine is functional and what they're up to. If he lied to me and that equipment's fine, I don't want him doing anything else and damaging it."

"How should I handle it sir, if they won't listen to reason?"

"Use whatever it takes, but do not harm Townsend. He's too valuable at the moment. No one else knows that system like he does. I'm sure you can think of other ways to be persuasive."

"Yes, sir."

54

January 19, 2010 4:15 p.m.

Orange Park, Florida

Jake watched Eve Lucas as she walked into the lab.

She looked anxious and a little angry, but as her eyes fell upon her husband in the chair, relief spread across her features and she hurried over to him, making sure he was all right. Jake took a deep breath and walked over to the couple.

Eve looked up, a scowl forming on her face as she saw him, and said, "You had no right to do this to him."

Jake wasn't sure if she was talking about the fact they had kidnapped him from the hospital, or the catatonic state they had put him in when Andee had gone berserk. He realized it didn't really matter which.

In the gentlest voice he could summon, he said, "You're right, Mrs. Lucas, I had no right whatsoever, but I needed him here now so we can fix him."

"Fix him? You've almost killed him. How do you expect to fix him?"

"I need to show you something."

She searched his eyes, and seemed to arrive at some decision, but reached down and caressed her husband's face, as if just the act of touching him could revive him and everything would be all right.

When her hand failed to evoke a response from Frank, a little of the light went out of her eyes, replaced with blame that she now directed toward Jake.

"There is nothing you can show me that will bring him back."

Jake smiled, gestured toward the console area and said, "He'll be ok. What I want to show you will take just a moment."

Teri and Bodey worked to load Frank's file into the system and Maddy brought a chair over for Eve to sit in. She accepted the seat, but looked at Maddy like she was so much trash. Jake thought if Eve had a handkerchief, she would have probably wiped the seat with it before sitting down. He looked into Maddy's eyes, trying to reassure her everything would be all right. She smiled at him, but looked tense.

"Mrs. Lucas, let me start by saying the threat I made on the phone to harm your husband was not genuine. I have never, nor would I ever, intentionally harm Frank or anyone else for that matter."

She looked skeptical and said, "Why would you say those things?"

"I had to find a way to get you here."

"I'm here. And you've already hurt him. All you've succeeded in doing is frightening me to death."

"I'm truly sorry and I know you don't believe me right now, but I'm going to do my best to make things right."

"How?"

"Let me show you what happened first."

Jake nodded to Teri who started the playback of Frank's NDE.

As Eve watched her husband's Near Death Experience unfold in front of her, the features of her face slowly softened. Her eyes widened in astonishment as the film-like quality of the playback continued. She began gently weeping, the power of the experience overwhelming her.

Jake stopped the playback before the segment where everything went bad.

"I need to stop for a moment and explain something before we continue," Jake said. "What you just watched was a representation of your husband's Near Death Experience as interpreted by this system. For the most part, we believe it to be extremely accurate as verified by the people who have experienced them. Just like your husband."

"It was beautiful," Eve said.

Jake smiled. "Very much so. They all have their own individual beauty, but, as we have found out, a danger also. The music you hear is unique to Frank. It's the music of his soul—his essence. Think of it as a signature or fingerprint, matching only the individual to whom it belongs. If we had time, I would let you watch others' experiences and you would hear what I'm talking about, but that will have to wait for another day."

Eve nodded, fully attentive now.

"During our testing, we found that if the person's Near Death Experience is replayed while they are still hooked up to the system, a very powerful and amazing response is evoked. And very dangerous. This may be a little upsetting for you."

Eve looked concerned and a little frightened, but she nodded once and Jake hit the playback button again.

On the video screens, the static disrupted the scene and then cleaned up, showing the view of the chair with Frank in it. As the hole opened up over her husband, Eve sat forward and watched intently as her husband angrily told Jake to 'Stop! The balance must be restored.'

Her hand flew to her open mouth as the hole sucked the fine grains of sand composing her husband's body, and then she flinched, as if slapped, when the hole slammed shut and the remaining part of Frank fell to the floor. The video stopped.

"Oh my God."

Eve scanned all of them, her hand at her mouth, tears forming again in her eyes, a look of panic on her face, as she struggled to catch her breath.

Jake went and knelt in front of her, "Mrs. Lucas. It's all right— I'm sorry you had to see, but you needed to know what happened. Mrs. Lucas—look at me."

Her frightened eyes turned to Jake's and he held her hand trying to calm her.

"Do you see? He's only a shell. Some part of him is lost, or trapped, and we need to make him whole again. Do you understand?"

She nodded.

"We think we know how to do that, but there is some risk." Jake looked at Teri, Maddy and Bodey.

They all nodded encouragement.

"We need to put him back in the machine and turn it on. We think we interrupted a process we never should have witnessed in the first place, but we have been given a vision of how that process will conclude and we now know what must be done."

"What will happen?" Eve asked.

Jake looked at the others again, turned back to Eve and said, "I know he will be made whole again." Jake stood, but still held her hand. "What I don't know is if he will be whole on this side of the opening or the other."

She looked away from him, considering what he'd said.

"So, what you're saying is this may kill him? He may be gone from me for good?"

"Yes. But he will no longer be in limbo."

In the dream Jake shared with Maddy, Frank had been made whole again after they hooked him up to Andee and played the music. It had been powerful and beautiful all at the same time. Frank had been so happy, and Beth and Ryan, peaceful. They had not been given a vision of Frank afterwards, so Jake and Maddy had no idea if Frank would still be with them.

"Will there be pain for him?" Eve asked.

"No. It should be a very happy experience." Jake turned away and paced a few steps, then turned back to face her. "I want you to understand that I will not do this without your blessing. I cannot make this decision for you or him. I know it's hard and you've had little time to digest all of this, but I feel we must hurry if we are to try this."

Without hesitating she said, "We must do it. I cannot leave him like this."

Jake nodded and took her hand. "I feel the same and I hoped you would too."

He knelt in front of her again, looked at the ground and when he looked back up at her, tears were in his eyes.

"I am truly sorry my selfishness has caused you and your family this terrible pain. I hope you can forgive me one day."

He rose, turned to Teri and said, "Let's hook him up."

They worked quickly to make all the necessary connections and twenty minutes later, Frank lay reclined in the chair, and Andee, ready to proceed.

Bodey had prepared the lab environment as best he could by stowing any loose items lying around and securing keyboards, mice, and other essentials so they would not be sucked into the vortex. Bodey told Jake he expected it to be worse this time and Jake agreed.

"We don't know how powerful the effects will be," Jake said, "so I want everyone to remain behind the console glass and watch out for debris. Mrs. Lucas, I would feel more comfortable if you would wait in my office, just to be safe."

She shook her head. "No—I want to be here."

He looked into her eyes and nodded. "Here we go."

Jake pressed play.

55

January 19, 2010 5:00 p.m.

Orange Park, Florida

Peter arrived at Encephalographic Systems forty five minutes after he'd hung up with the General.

It had taken twenty five minutes for the two other assets to show up and be briefed. He hoped Omar would still be there when he got back.

He pressed the buzzer for the front door but after half a minute, when no one responded, he pressed it again. Nothing.

He pushed his face up against the glass trying to peer through the black tinting, but could see nothing. He heard something faintly through the window, so he knew they were in there. He pressed the buzzer again and held it down for a full minute and still no one acknowledged his presence.

The noise he heard was getting louder. He could hear it coming through the door while he was standing a foot away.

Something was happening.

He looked around the area and finding no one else around, pulled his gun and fired two rounds around the locking mechanism on the door. The glass fragmented but did not shatter.

He kicked at the door but it didn't budge. He fired three more rounds into the door, breaking small pieces of the bullet proof glass from around the lock. He kicked again. The door gave a little. He kicked it three more times in a row and on the last, the door gave way and flew open.

He rushed inside and found himself in a maelstrom.

* * *

Jake watched and listened as the music grew in intensity, filling the room with full and rich sound.

A low rumble grew from beneath the floor and a tearing sound could be heard over the music as the conduit between worlds began to grow. Bright white light burst from above Frank and purple streaks shot outwards from within the light. The jagged hole opened up above him and a wind began to blow inside the lab. Jake could see dust and dirt picked up by the wind and a few scraps of loose paper Bodey had missed joined the dust in a swirling vortex that was sucked into the gaping hole.

The wind grew to a roaring rush of sound as the music was drowned out by it.

Jake felt like he wanted to hold on to something. Teri gestured toward the monitors and as Jake turned and watched, the Frank on the screen rose up from the chair. Jake quickly looked over at the Frank in the chair and was not surprised to see his body still lying in it, unmoving.

He turned back to the screen and watched as a smiling Frank dissolved into a fine powdery dust and then was drawn away into the opening above his body.

Movement out of the corner of Jake's eye caused him to turn as Peter came rushing at him, a gun at his side and fire in his eyes.

Peter yelled, trying to be heard above the wind. "Shut it down!"

Jake shook his head and smiled.

Peter raised his gun, pointed it at Jake's head and repeated the command.

"Shut it down—Now!"

Jake turned and glanced at the monitor. Frank was halfway gone. Jake needed to keep the machine on a little longer.

He turned back to Peter and shouted, "Not yet, just a little longer."

Peter moved forward and pressed the muzzle of the pistol against Jake's forehead, "Do it—now!"

"I can't, if I stop it now, Frank will be lost."

"I don't care about Frank. Do not make me shoot you."

"You won't. You need me."

Jake calmly took a step back, turned and looked at the monitor. Frank was almost gone.

Jake turned and yelled to Peter who had lowered the gun in defeat, "Almost there."

Just then, the music became a deafening blast and rays of white light shot out of the hole above Frank.

The light looked like it had form and substance, and as it lost momentum, seemed to bend and fall to the floor where it rapidly dissipated. The wind had stopped. The music peaked as everyone covered their ears and one final burst of light came as the hole expelled the paper, dust and light, snapping shut with a palpable clap.

Silence returned and everyone looked around at everyone else, making sure they were all ok. Jake thought Peter looked the most shocked.

Eve rushed over to Frank, but yelled at Jake frustrated, because she could not get past the body mold over top of him.

"Jake, hurry!"

Jake and Maddy rushed over and started unhooking leads and wires, but Frank had not moved. They finally cleared enough wires as everyone gathered around in silence, waiting. Jake lifted the mold from over Frank and Eve rushed to him.

"Frank—Frank! Can you hear me?"

He did not move.

Jake dropped his head. He felt destroyed. He was so sure they were going to be able to bring him back. Maddy put an arm around him and started to cry.

"Eve?"

Jake's head snapped up as Frank opened his eyes, saw his wife, and smiled.

56

January 19, 2010 5:35 p.m.

Orange Park, Florida

Frank was sitting up and drinking a soda. He seemed weak, but happy. Jake was relieved.

"My chest is so sore," Frank said.

"It's from the CPR we had to do on you," Jake said. "You might even have some broken ribs. It's not uncommon to break a few during CPR."

"When did Eve get here?"

Everyone looked at each other and Eve said, "Honey, do you know what happened to you?"

"Yes, I came in this morning so they could run some tests on me and let them record my experience. I remember going through it once and how it felt so real—like I was reliving it. I must have fallen asleep when we started again because the next thing I know you're here and everyone is standing around me."

"He doesn't remember a thing," Maddy said.

"Should I?" Frank asked. "What happened to me?"

"Honey, you came to this lab *yesterday*," Eve said. "Something went wrong and Jake and his girls had to call an ambulance. Your heart stopped again and you spent the night on a ventilator. You've been in the hospital, kidnapped, and then brought back here."

"Kidnapped? Why?"

"It was the only way to get you back in here," Jake said.

"What the hell happened to me?"

"It's a long story," Jake said. "You rest a bit and Eve will tell you everything. I'm glad you're back."

Jake motioned for everyone to follow him over to the other side of the barrier out of sight and earshot of Eve and Frank so they could have some time alone. Peter was by the front entrance, on a cell phone, presumably talking to the General.

"How did Andee hold up?" Jake asked Bodey.

"The systems seem fine. All of that energy in the room and Andee didn't even flinch. Teri and I will check the sensors as soon as Frank and Eve leave."

"We did well, people," Jake said. "I'm proud of all of you."

"Aw shucks, Dad," Bodey said. "Do I get a lollipop?"

"Seriously, I could have imagined this going a bunch of ways where we didn't have such a positive outcome," Jake said.

"I told you," Bodey said. "Someone's watching out for you."

Jake realized that on some level, he believed Bodey was right.

Someone had been watching out for them or else they had been extremely lucky. The dreams, the hospital, and now Andee performing flawlessly, everything had clicked. He hoped the good karma would continue.

"Do you think the dreams will stop now?" Maddy whispered into Jake's ear.

"I was wondering the same thing. I hope so."

"Me too. I would like to spend more than one whole night with you without being terrified or sent on a mission."

"What are you talking about? You didn't like those nights?"

She jabbed him in the side and leaned against him. "I love you."

"I love you, too."

Teri was talking to Bodey about the weird light at the end. "Did you notice how it seemed solid?" Teri asked. "I mean, it looked like thick water, or syrup."

"It must have been some kind of energy matter. I could never imagine anything like it much less find a way to produce it. It was cool."

Peter walked over and closed his phone. "The General wants all of you to remain in this building. He will be here shortly. Everyone that is, except the old man and woman."

"What now, Peter?" Jake asked. "We're exhausted and Frank may not be ready to get up and walk out of here. You saw what he went through."

"He and the wife must leave. Help him if he needs it."

"You're an asshole, and I'm tired of your shit." Teri picked up the phone and started dialing.

"Put the phone down," Peter said. When she did not comply, he drew his gun, chambered a round and pointed it at her head. "Now!"

Teri slowly replaced the handset in its cradle.

"You people fail to appreciate the seriousness and resolve of my mission. Every one of you is expendable. You will do as I say or I will kill you right where you stand. Do I make myself clear?"

They all nodded.

"Peter, you don't have to point the gun," Jake said. "We'll do whatever you want. Please, put it down."

Peter lowered the gun and holstered it.

"Help the old man and woman on their way."

Jake and Bodey went to help Eve with Frank. He was still weak, but managed to stand and walk with help from them both. Maddy went and stood by Teri.

Frank said, "That guy scares me. Do you want me to call the police when we get out of the building?"

"No," Jake shook his head. "We'll be fine. He won't hurt us. He's all talk."

Frank paused and leaned close to Jake.

"You be careful. I've seen eyes like his before and even though I regret it more than anything in my life, I had to kill the owner of those eyes or die myself. He will not hesitate when it comes to taking life. You'd better not either."

Jake looked at Frank and saw the sincerity in his eyes. "I'll be careful," he said, and helped him the rest of the way to the car.

Jake didn't think he could make good on Frank's advice. Taking a life would be something very hard for him to do. He would have to make sure it never came to that.

Eve and Frank drove off and before Jake and Bodey walked back inside, Bodey said, "What's going on? What does this General want?"

"I have a hunch, but I'm not sure. He mentioned something about having Andee retrieve information for him and building a database. He must have a NDE he wants us to hook up."

"This Peter guy is unstable. We need to be extra careful or have some kind of back-up plan. I can't tell if he's bluffing or not."

"I know what you mean. I was pretty confident he wouldn't hurt us, but I'm not so sure now. Just do what he says and we'll go from there."

Bodey nodded and they went back inside.

Jake went up to Peter, "Can I talk to you for a minute?"

Peter followed Jake into his office and shut the door.

"What is wrong with you?" Jake asked. "You can't go around threatening anyone you want with a gun. We have rights just like anybody else."

Peter smiled. "This is a whole different game, Jake. I don't have time to waste explaining myself or my actions. I expect you to do exactly what is asked of you without any questions. Is that going to be a problem?"

"Did you not see what just happened in there?" Jake asked. "Or did you have your eyes closed? This is beyond you and me. This is bigger and more important than anything you and your organization are doing. Don't you see that?"

"I saw a newly discovered energy source for which I'm sure someone will find a use, but if you're trying to hint at something more mystical or religious in nature, I fail to see any connection. Amazing? Yes. Miraculous? No."

Jake stared at Peter and shook his head. "What are you? What are you so afraid of?"

Peter became very still. Then, with a speed Jake never expected, Peter was across the desk and holding Jake's throat in one hand.

"I'm afraid of nothing," he said through clenched teeth.

Jake's eyes felt like they would pop out of his skull, not only from the pressure being applied to his neck, but from the fear he was feeling, staring into the unfeeling and lifeless eyes of this madman. Frank's words came back now, and Jake understood what the old man was talking about.

Peter smiled suddenly, let go of Jake's neck, and stood up straight in front of the desk.

"Anything else Doctor Townsend?"

Jake shook his head, afraid to speak for fear of how his voice would sound.

"Good. Let's go. You have work to do."

Peter opened the office door and gestured for Jake to walk through it.

He obeyed, somewhat shakily, and walked through the door, ashamed, into another chapter in his life.

Part 3

57

January 19, 2010 5:55 p.m.

Orange Park, Florida

When the General and his entourage entered the lab from the rear delivery door, Jake knew this was not going to be pleasant.

Two of his men carried submachine guns at the ready and marched a shaven and shackled man of Middle Eastern heritage between them.

As the unknown prisoner shuffled into the room, he looked decidedly calm, but curious, while he took in the equipment and the chair. But as his eyes found Peter, they locked onto him and Jake could see the anger seething beneath the calm exterior.

Maddy whispered to him, "Who is that?"

Jake shrugged. "I would guess he is our next test subject. Maybe you should go."

"I'm not leaving you."

"Please, Maddy. The General will ask you to leave anyway. Remember?"

"I don't want to leave you here. What if you need me?"

Jake, still a little shaken up from the run in with Peter, tried to smile, but his face felt tight.

"I'll always need you. I just don't want you hurt if something goes wrong."

"I'll be fine. I'm staying." She turned and wandered over to Bodey.

The General marched over.

"We have some additional equipment we will be using. Do you have any folding tables or rolling carts available?"

Jake nodded, watching a man and woman wearing white lab coats roll two hard aluminum travel cases into the lab.

"We have two folding tables. They're not very strong, just folding tables you would find in any Wal-Mart or Target. Will they do?"

"Yes—perfect. My crew will be setting up and should be ready in thirty minutes. Your people can relax for a few. How long does it take to prepare a test subject?"

"About twenty to thirty minutes to connect all the leads and sensors. We normally need to take measurements for the mold you see there, but since we won't have that opportunity, we'll just hope it fits him. He looks about the same size as Peter, so we'll use his mold."

"Great. We did some background checks on Madison Ann McClaughlin and she'll be fine. I just need to have her sign a top secret clearance form. Can I borrow her for a few minutes?"

Jake hesitated, trying to come up with an excuse to keep her from signing the document, but nothing came to him.

"Yes. That's fine."

The General walked over and began talking with Maddy as Jake watched the man and woman in the white lab coats unpack their equipment. Teri walked over.

"They have EKG and pulse-ox monitors," she said, "along with an automatic blood pressure monitor, I.V.'s and a crash cart. What do they need all that for?"

"I'm not sure, but I'm getting a bad vibe from all of this. When the General is done with Maddy, I'll find out more."

"What's he doing with her?"

"Security clearance—he apparently did a background check on her."

"That was quick."

"I know. He's pretty serious about what's going to happen today. Listen, I have to get the folding tables from the storage closet. Wanna help?"

"Sure."

As they moved boxes and other items, Teri said, "Jake? I know I've been a total bitch lately. I wanted to say I'm sorry."

"It's ok. We've all been under a lot of strain. I don't blame you for being a little grumpy."

"I was more than a little grumpy. I was jealous."

Jake's face must have conveyed his shock at hearing those words come from Teri's lips, because Teri smiled. "I know I caught you off guard. What I really need to say is I've seen you and Maddy together, and I can tell she really cares for you. I haven't seen you this happy in a long time. I'll stop being an ass. I kind of like her now anyway. She's pretty cool."

Jake's face felt hot and flushed, but he smiled.

"Thanks, Teri. You've been my friend for a long time. I can't imagine you being gone from my life. I was worried for a while that's exactly what was going to happen. You won't leave will you?"

"You'd have to drag me away."

He dropped what he was doing, went to her and took her in his arms.

Bodey walked up and said, "Whoa—can I get in on this action?"

Jake and Teri laughed.

"Sure. Take over for me," Jake said, and let Teri go.

"They're looking for the tables," Bodey said, hugging Teri hard. "You'd better get 'em over there. I've got Teri."

Jake chuckled, shook his head and grabbed one end of a table.

"Come on Bodey. Give me a hand with this."

"Man…" But he grabbed the other end, grinning, and they carried it over to the mysterious lab coats.

"Where do you guys want these?" Jake asked.

The woman indicated the spot, saying, "Here will be fine. Can we use these electrical outlets?"

"Yes. Use all you like. What do you need all this medical equipment for?"

The woman looked at the man and then back at Jake.

"General Breckenridge can answer all your questions. We've really got to keep working."

She turned back to one of the monitors, ignoring Jake and Bodey.

"Friendly, huh?" Bodey said as they went back for the other table.

"I don't like this," Jake said. "I need to find out what's going on. Can you and Teri grab the other table?"

"Yep—no problem."

Jake went up to the General who was having Maddy sign a form. She looked a little pissed.

"General, what exactly are your intentions today?" Jake asked.

Looking over the form Maddy had signed and nodding to her, satisfied, he turned to Jake.

"We're going to put our friend there into your machine and pull some much needed intel from his brain."

"Will he cooperate?" Jake asked.

"We will be sedating him."

Jake shook his head.

"General, I need the test subjects alert and oriented. We need to record his Near Death Experience first before we can begin building a database. If he's out, I can't ask him to relive his experience."

"He hasn't had one."

"He hasn't had one, what?" asked Maddy.

"We're going to be recording his Near Death Experience live," the General said.

"What?" Jake said, loudly.

"Quiet!" the General said. "I don't want him any more difficult to work with then he already is. We will be inducing a Near Death Experience and then recording the results."

"Inducing? You're going to kill this man?"

"We will bring him back," the General said, bluntly.

Jake and Maddy looked at each other, their mouths hanging open. Jake had seen and heard some pretty crazy things in the last two weeks, but this revelation was a total shock. He started to speak but Maddy beat him to it.

"No! That's impossible."

"General," Jake said, "I can't condone this. This isn't something I or my staff are comfortable with or even prepared to handle. I won't allow it."

"You don't have a choice in the matter."

"Bullshit I don't! I won't help you kill a man, just to gain access to his memories."

The General glanced over at the prisoner and Jake could see his words having an effect on him. Apparently the man had no idea what they intended to do to him.

Teri had walked over and asked, "What's going on?"

"They want us to help them kill this man so they can record his Near Death Experience live."

"What?!" Teri said. "You're kidding, right?"

"Do I look like I'm kidding?" the General said. "This man has killed countless U.S. soldiers and citizens and if we don't retrieve the information contained in that head of his, many more will die. Hundreds, maybe even thousands. Do you understand?"

Jake watched as the prisoner grew restless, his eyes darting back and forth like a caged animal. Peter had apparently noticed the same thing. As Jake watched, he gave some signal to the two men with the machine guns and they tightened the distance between themselves and the prisoner. Peter walked over to the group.

"Problem, sir?" he said.

"Maybe," the General said. "Our little group of scientists here is having an attack of conscience."

Jake said, "I don't care what this man has done, I won't participate in the killing of some prisoner. I'm not playing judge, jury, and executioner."

"I'm not asking you to," the General said. "You'll connect this man to the machine, we'll induce the necessary physiologic effect and you'll record the activity as it happens. Simple enough?"

Teri said, "I won't have any part of this, Jake. I refuse to assist them in any way."

"Teri, it's ok. I won't do it either. As a matter of fact, General, I need to ask you to leave."

Peter chuckled. "You people just don't understand, do you? The General isn't making a request. He is ordering you. You have no choice."

Jake stared at Peter—then turned, "Bodey, call the police."

Bodey, who had been watching the whole thing from the console, nodded, reaching for the phone. Peter drew his pistol, aimed, and fired a single shot which hit Bodey in the lower arm. Maddy screamed and Teri ducked.

Jake had had enough.

He lunged at Peter, knocking the gun from his hand and tackling the man, pinning him briefly beneath him. Peter reacted by elbowing Jake in the side of the head, slipping out from beneath him and then pinning his arm behind his back as he drove his knee into Jake's kidney.

"Don't move or I'll crush your kidney! Believe me, it'll be a very painful death."

Multiple guns were now drawn and all of them were trained on Jake.

"Enough!" shouted the General. "All of you! Stand down! Smith, let him up."

Suddenly, a voice with a thick accent said, "Nobody move or the General dies!"

Somehow, during the confusion, the prisoner had managed to surprise one of the guards and now held his machine gun pointed at the General's head.

All the weapons in the room immediately turned and drew a bead on the shackled prisoner. Peter let Jake up, but his weapon was on the floor a few feet away.

"You have three seconds to place all of your weapons at your feet or I kill the General first, and take as many of the rest of you as I can. One…"

The General nodded and everyone dropped their weapons at their feet.

"Good," the prisoner said. "Now, kick them to the center of the room."

As all the operatives in the room did as he asked, he shuffled closer to the General, distancing himself from any other person near him.

Jake looked at Maddy who stood three feet away from him between Peter and the General. Bodey cradled his arm and tried to keep still as the blood poured out between his fingers. Teri stood between Jake and the General.

As the prisoner shuffled to within two feet of General Breckenridge, he shouted, "You! Woman! Get the keys for these locks and unchain me."

Female lab coat pointed to herself.

"Yes! You—stupid woman—now!"

"I don't have them," she said.

"Find them you ignorant bitch! Who has the keys?"

No one moved.

The prisoner quickly turned to his left and opened fire on the nearest operative. A short burst of three rounds cut him down and he was dead before he hit the ground.

"Who has the keys?!" he shouted.

"I do, Omar," Peter said, calmly.

Omar glared at Peter. "Remove them slowly, and place them on the floor."

Peter did as he was told.

"Now kick them to me."

Peter kicked them to him, hard, and they slid past him, but Omar did not chase them. Peter shrugged nonchalantly and inched a little closer to his gun on the floor. Jake had noticed Peter was ever so slowly edging his way toward his gun. As much as he despised the man, Jake hoped Peter would reach it before this Omar character hurt anyone else.

"Woman! Get the keys and unlock me!"

Lab coat scurried over, snatched the keys from the floor and unlocked Omar's shackles. Jake saw Peter inch a little closer to his gun. Apparently so did Omar.

"Move another step," Omar said, "and I will kill you and your pathetic General."

The chains were off now and lying in a heap at Omar's feet. He shooed the woman back to her place.

"Everyone, on your knees!"

Peter took the opportunity to fall to his knees in the direction of his gun, which now lay three feet from him.

"Not you!" Omar pulled the General up. "You are coming with me."

On some unseen signal Jake could not detect, the General suddenly dropped and rolled toward Omar as Peter dived for his pistol, retrieved it and brought it up to fire at Omar as he slid across the floor. The General had caused Omar to lose his balance as he rolled into his legs and Peter fired as the prisoner fell. Omar's gun went off as he tried to regain his balance, but then spun to his left as one of Peter's bullets hit him in the shoulder.

"Don't kill him!" the General shouted.

But maybe that's what Peter should have done, Jake thought.

Even though Omar was hit, he focused on the General picking himself up off the floor, raised his gun and fired point blank into the General's chest. He went down hard and lay still.

"Son of a bitch!" Peter said and dived for cover behind the console as Omar swung his gun to the right searching for Peter.

Omar fired a burst after Peter, just missing him but spraying the console and the computer with bullets. Sparks flew and smoke rose from one of the consoles.

Omar got to his feet and bolted for the front door.

Even with his shoulder injured, he was still very fast. Peter stuck his head up just as he was passing through the broken door and fired four shots, hitting nothing but air.

Omar was gone.

58

January 19, 2010 6:25 p.m.

Orange Park, Florida

Omar, his shoulder on fire, ran out the door and turned right.

There was another building in front of him that had a small parking area between it and the building from which he had run. He turned right again and ran between the buildings toward an area thick with foliage and trees at the rear of the complex. He could see glimpses of a fence between the thick bushes and brambles.

A neighborhood.

Perfect, Omar thought, as he ran. *There would be lots of places to hide in there.*

Surprisingly, he could hear no one following him, so he dived into the thick bushes and slammed against the old wooden fence. Three of the pickets gave way from his weight and he crawled through the gap into a large yard with a gazebo on his right and a swimming pool directly in front of him. He glanced back through the hole. He could not see through the thick foliage and he was sure no one had seen him come through it.

Pushing himself up with his good arm, he made his way through the yard, avoiding the dirty black pool to his left, and finding the gate on the other side of the gazebo. Lifting the latch and passing through it, he found himself in a little alleyway between the house whose yard he just passed through and the house on his right.

Kneeling behind a bush, he stopped and assessed his wound.

The bullet had passed through his deltoid cleanly, just below his shoulder. The bleeding had slowed, but his whole left arm felt like it was on fire. He worked the strap loose from the machine gun and cinched it around the wound with a piece of shirtsleeve he had torn off as a bandage.

He checked the ammunition remaining in the gun and found the clip held twenty one more rounds. Slapping it back in, he stood, swayed a little, and after supporting himself against the house until the vertigo passed, moved through the small alleyway, stopping at the edge of the house to check the street.

It appeared deserted.

He could see a kind of drainage ditch across, and to the right of the road. Looking left and right, he ran across the street and down into the depression. It was filled with water which moved off perpendicular to the roadway. The backs of houses flanked it on either side, their fenced yards sloping down into it. The small stream of water moved away toward a destination he could not see. Staying low, he followed the creek bed as it snaked its way through the quiet neighborhood.

So far, no one pursued him, but he knew that would change.

He had to get as far away as he could while he had the time. If only he had been able to kill the man who put him here. The more he thought about it, the more he knew he would get another chance. He was sure his pursuers would include the man they called Peter.

59

January 19, 2010 6:25 p.m.

Orange Park, Florida

Jake watched Peter fire at the retreating prisoner, and then turned to see Maddy kneeling next to a figure on the floor. She looked up, anguish on her face, as Jake's heart sank.

"Jake—Teri!" she said.

Jake rushed over as the General's men grabbed guns and followed Omar out the front door in pursuit. Jake knelt next to Maddy as Teri bled onto the floor from a wound at the center of her chest. Her face ashen, blood oozing from the corner of her mouth, eyes going in and out of focus, she gasped for breath.

"Teri—it's Jake. Hold on, we're getting you some help!"

Jake looked frantically around for one of the lab coats and seeing the woman yelled, "Hey! Help us over here! She's been shot!"

The woman rushed over and took one look at Teri and the wound and Jake could see in the woman's eyes it was hopeless. The woman slowly shook her head, but began cutting away Teri's shirt so she could get a better look at the damage.

"How bad?" Maddy asked.

"It's bad," the woman said, and kept working.

Teri coughed up a large clot of dark blood, grabbed at the air in front of her and as Jake took hold of her hand, she focused her eyes and saw him.

"Jake," she whispered, "I…"

"Shh," Jake said softly, clinging to her hand. "Don't talk. We're going to get you fixed up."

Tears formed in her eyes and Jake knew she didn't believe him. She was taking shallow wet breaths and more blood trickled out of the corner of her mouth as she struggled to breathe.

"Jake—I'm sorry for what I've been these past weeks. I couldn't help myself." She coughed wetly and moaned in pain.

"You don't have to be sorry for anything," Jake said. "Don't talk like that. Save your strength."

"No—I have to tell you."

"Teri—please!"

She turned to Maddy, "I'm sorry for what I did to you. You didn't deserve it. Take care of him." And she smiled weakly.

To Jake she said, "I love you. I always have. Don't bl…"

Her hand went slack in his and her eyes became vacant and blank as she slipped away.

"Teri! No! Stay with us! Teri!"

But she was gone.

The woman slowly closed Teri's shirt, trying to give her some dignity and said, "I'm sorry."

Jake looked around the room as if lost. He couldn't understand why this was happening. Teri, his friend, his partner, the only one to stand by him when Beth had died, was gone. How could he have let this happen? This was his fault. He never should have let things get this bad.

She had tried to tell him—tried to warn him that he had gone too far. He didn't listen and now Teri was gone. Gone in the blink of an eye. Killed by some crazed lunatic who didn't know anything about her, or for that matter, didn't even care.

He clenched his hands and squeezed his eyes shut at the vision of her lying there. Thrusting his fists in the air, a sound came from deep inside him that was animal like. Pure rage and sorrow spewed forth in a cry so painful everyone in the room stopped and felt his anguish.

Jake opened his eyes and saw Peter staring. Something snapped.

"You! You did this, you son of a bitch!"

Peter came over and said, "I'm sorry, Jake."

Jake jumped up and swung at Peter, connecting with a fierceness he didn't know he possessed.

Peter went down on one knee, looked up at Jake. "That one was free. Don't make me hurt you."

Jake lunged at Peter again, but Peter leaned to his left, brought his knee up into Jake's exposed abdomen, and pushed his backside, sending him sprawling onto the floor, doubled over in pain.

"I don't have time for this shit!" Peter stood and went to check on the General.

Maddy went to Jake and cradled his head in her hands "Jake, please stop. He will kill you."

Bodey came over cradling his wounded arm and knelt next to Teri. Jake looked at him and all the rage he felt left him. Bodey was crying.

"What have we done, Jake?" Bodey said.

Jake did not have an answer for him.

He looked down at the ground, his eyes on fire, tears flowing now as the full impact of Teri's death sank in. Maddy leaned her head against his and she caressed the back of his neck, trying to comfort him.

"I saw her go down," she said. "I didn't believe it at first and then I didn't know what to do. I'm so sorry."

"There was nothing any of you could do. This is my fault. I might as well have pulled the trigger myself."

"You can't think that way," Maddy said. "She was here of her own free will. She wanted to help. Remember?"

"But she kept questioning me and the decisions I was making. She thought I was going too far, and now she was right. Only she was the one who suffered. I did this to her."

"She told me while we were driving from the hospital to Eve's, she believed in what you were doing and felt guilty about the crap she'd been giving you—her words."

Jake looked into her compassionate eyes and she nodded.

"Please stop blaming yourself. Teri knew what she was doing."

Jake turned to Bodey who was nodding in agreement. "Now we know she's in a better place," Bodey said. "Remember? We're the ones who proved it."

Just then Peter walked up.

"The General's dead. I'm in charge at the moment and I need your help."

Jake and Maddy stood and both looked over at the General lying on the floor. Both lab coats were standing over him talking and gesturing about something.

"Bodey needs some attention," Jake said. "Can one of your people take a look at him since you shot him."

"Pierce! Take a look at this man's arm, will you."

"Yes, sir!" The man in the lab coat jogged over to Bodey.

"I need someone who knows the area," Peter said. "Since I'm not from around here, it would help to have some local expertise. You two both grew up here, right?"

Jake and Maddy both nodded.

Most of the other operatives were returning now with one yelling, "No sign of him. Morris and Johnson are still searching the complex, but he could be anywhere."

"Call them back," Peter said. "We'll track him enroute. I'll need everyone together, ready to take him down when we corner him."

The man nodded and then spoke into his cuff on his left wrist.

"Track him?" Jake said.

"Omar doesn't know it, but he has a chip implanted in his leg which allows us to track him to within twenty five feet of his position. During his capture, I shattered his right knee and when the surgeons repaired it here, we had them implant the chip."

"Why should we help you?" Jake asked. "You people have killed my friend and colleague, shot my computer expert, and every time I turn around you're either threatening me or beating me up. You can go to hell."

"I can understand your position, Jake, and in a lot of ways, I sympathize with you. But this man is bigger than you or me. We are expendable. He possesses information which could save thousands of U.S. lives. Do you know who Qayum Omar is?"

All three of them shook their heads.

"For starters, he was one of the masterminds of 9/11 and was actually supposed to pilot an aircraft into the capitol during the second wave, but his flight was forced to land before he could succeed. Most recently, he was the one responsible for the attack on the base in Kandahar, Afghanistan. Do you remember that?"

All three nodded.

"He knows things about their operations and the locations of certain individuals. What's in his head is very important to our national security. If he gets away, Teri and the General will have died for nothing."

Jake looked at Maddy, then Bodey, who gave a slight nod, and finally at Teri lying dead on the ground a few feet away. He knew he was being fed a bunch of bullshit, but he also could not allow Teri's death to amount to nothing.

"Did you shoot Teri?" Jake asked.

"No."

"How are you so sure?"

"I fired once and hit Omar in the shoulder. I then fired four more shots as he fled through the door. Teri wasn't in trajectory of any of those bullets. Omar hit her as he was firing at me."

Jake stared hard at Peter, but he never flinched or looked away.

"What are you going to do with him when you catch him?"

"We're going to bring him back here and finish what we came here to do."

Jake thought hard about this.

He couldn't make himself feel good one way or the other, but if Qayum Omar got a little taste of his own medicine, maybe that wouldn't be such a bad thing. The bastard had shot Teri and killed who knows how many others. A little payback for her just might be in order.

Jake turned slowly, still feeling the effects of being kneed in the stomach by Peter, and said, "All right—let's do this, but Maddy stays here. I don't want her in any danger."

Peter looked at Maddy and then back at Jake and nodded. He turned and went to give some instructions to one of the men who had returned from outside.

When he was out of earshot, Maddy said, "Jake, what are you doing? Are you really going to help these people?"

"That bastard killed Teri, and I won't stand by and watch him get away. If I can help capture him, I will."

"But they're going to bring him back here and put him in the machine. You're going to help them kill him?"

"I'm not going to stop them."

Maddy shook her head.

"I can't believe you're saying this. I know you're upset, but do you really think this is what Teri would want? I mean she stood there a few minutes ago and told the General she refused to help them and now you're all gung ho about it? Jake, maybe you should slow down and think about this."

"All I know is I'm going to help them catch that piece of shit. As to what I'm going to do afterwards—I'll have to think hard about it."

She reached out and took his hand.

"Are you sure you don't want me to go along with you?"

"No, I'd be worried the whole time."

"What do you think I'm going to be doing while you're gone?"

60

January 19, 2010 7:03 p.m.

Orange Park, Florida

Shivering, Omar watched the sun go down and the temperature drop with it.

The thin, grey jumpsuit was the only thing between him and the elements. His body, coupled with the shock of being shot, could not keep up. He needed to find shelter or additional clothing, and he needed to find it soon.

He had followed the creek until it entered a culvert that passed under a street, and since he could not fit inside, he was back in the open moving from yard to yard. It would be easier to remain hidden once it was fully dark.

He noticed some trash bags stuffed full and piled on top of each other just inside the front stoop of the house whose yard he was passing through and decided to see if there was anything useful in them he could use for warmth.

Surprisingly, they were full of clothes. He found a couple of long sleeve shirts and a sweater and though a little tight, they were wearable. His left shoulder ached and it was difficult to get the clothes on, but he felt better once he was warmer.

The movement caused the wound to open up again and he was bleeding more heavily now. The blood soaked through the shirts and sweater in a matter of minutes. If it didn't stop soon, he would have to remove the clothing and adjust the makeshift bandage.

The neighborhood had remained deserted except for an occasional car passing by on the street or a dog barking at him from the other side of a fence. No one had noticed him.

Up ahead, he could see the street he was following was actually a cul-de-sac and the road ended with a fence directly ahead. Omar thought he might have to break a hole in it since his wounded arm prevented him from scaling the eight foot picket fence, but as he got closer, he could see an opening in the gloom and realized it was a pedestrian entrance to the neighborhood. He passed through the fence and found himself on a path that ran alongside a two lane roadway traveling perpendicular to his current track. A car approached from his left.

He sprinted across the road and entered the small wooded area on the other side just before the car's headlights illuminated him. He trampled through the thick underbrush and emerged into an open area with a sharp incline in front of him. He climbed the slope and realized it was a set of railroad tracks. Crossing the tracks, he slipped down the other side into another wooded area.

He stopped to rest.

The bleeding had slowed again, but his sleeve was dark and sticky in the fading light. He didn't know how much blood he had lost, but his energy was waning and he thought the blood loss had something to do with it. He couldn't rest for long, though, and as he stood, he could hear a car passing by in front of him.

He pushed through the remaining wooded area and found another roadway. Cars approached from both directions, so he waited inside the foliage until he could safely cross without being seen. Three sets of headlights passed before the road was dark again.

He emerged from the bushes at a jog and ran smack into a woman walking her dog along the bike path. The noise of the passing cars had apparently masked her approach. He stumbled when he collided with the woman, and the gun clattered to the pavement, skidding out of reach. The dog, a large Rottweiler breed, growled and then attacked him, its owner screaming in surprise as she fell down.

The dog had his left forearm in its mouth and shook him furiously, pain shooting into his shoulder as the gunshot wound reopened.

The dog would not let go.

Omar used his good right arm, found the dog's eyes and attempted to insert his thumb into the socket, but the dog kept shaking its head back and forth making it impossible. He could not gain any advantage.

He used all his strength and lunged to his left, toward where he thought the gun had fallen. He tripped over the woman's legs and went down. The dog immediately let go of his arm and went for his throat.

Gritting his teeth through the pain, he kept his injured arm up, blocking the dog from his neck and reached out with his right hand trying to find the gun. After a few frantic seconds of pawing empty ground, his hand struck metal. He grasped the gun, brought it up and fired it point blank into the animal's chest. The sound was deafening in the cold night air. The woman screamed again, trying to get up.

Omar pushed the dead dog off of his chest and scrambled to his feet.

The woman was crawling away from him, sobbing, trying to get her feet under her. Omar strode over to her and raised the weapon, bringing it down hard onto her exposed head and she collapsed to the pavement, unconscious.

"Stupid bitch!"

Omar was shaking.

He looked around wildly, expecting another attack but nothing came at him out of the gloom. He heard a car approaching and saw the headlights in the distance. Regaining his bearings, he ran across the road and crouched in the ditch on the other side as he waited for the car to pass. As the headlights illuminated the street, he realized the unconscious woman's body was lying half in the road. He cursed himself and waited to see if the car would stop.

The woman remained unmoving as the headlights brought her fully into view. The car carried some speed and Omar thought the driver was going to run right over her, but at the last possible second, the driver saw the woman, swerved and slammed on the brakes, skidding sideways but missing the woman.

The car idled there for a moment and then the door opened.

A man of small build slowly got out and warily walked around his door to the front of his car. He saw the woman lying on the pavement, pulled his cell phone out and then crossed in front of his car and knelt next to her. Omar could no longer see the man as the car blocked his view of him and the woman. He could hear him talking into his cell phone, but could not tell what he was saying.

Omar realized that the altercation with the woman and the dog just might be a good thing. He stood, quickly crossed to the idling car, slid into the driver's seat, put the car in drive and accelerated rapidly away as the owner of the car jumped up in disbelief and watched his car drive off.

Omar grinned to himself despite the pain in his left arm, and followed the road into the night.

61

January 19, 2010 6:55 p.m.

Orange Park, Florida

Jake, Peter, and three of the other men who had been in the lab, were crammed into a van that Jake presumed was used to transport prisoners.

There were shackles and chains hanging from the wall and the windows had wire mesh embedded inside the glass. One of the men drove while Peter sat next to Jake in the back with a laptop open and a mapping program running.

Jake shivered in the damp cold. He couldn't understand why they hadn't turned the heat on.

Omar's microchip implant was working and they were getting a good signal from some government spy satellite showing his location about a mile to the south of their current position.

"Are you familiar with this neighborhood?" Peter asked Jake.

"Yes. That's Foxwood. I lived in there for a couple of years as a kid. Right here—Epsilon Court." Jake indicated a small cul-de-sac off the main roadway about midway through the neighborhood. His finger shook and Peter looked at him.

On the map, a red blip blinked on and off about three blocks to the north of Epsilon, moving ever so slowly northwesterly.

"It looks like he's heading toward this area," Peter said. "Is this a main roadway?"

"Not really. I mean it's a two lane road, and it gives access to a number of neighborhoods along it, but it's fairly quiet. It's called Moody Avenue and this is Doctor's Lake Drive just on the other side of these railroad tracks."

"All right, let's head into the neighborhood and see if we can cut him off."

"If you can get to him fast enough," Jake said. "If you don't, and he finds this opening in the fence here at the back of the neighborhood, we'll have to drive all the way around to get to Moody or Doctor's Lake."

"There's no way out of the neighborhood in the back?" Peter asked.

"Nope, only one way in and out—right here," Jake pointed to the entrance. "At least for a car."

"Morris, punch it! Take the first right after we get out of the parking lot and follow it around and then take the first left after that. We've got to move if we're going to cut him off."

"Got it," Morris said, and accelerated onto Kingsley, cutting off a Honda Pilot, its horn blaring at them.

Peter and Jake watched the red blip move toward the back of the cul-de-sac at the rear of the neighborhood.

"He's making a bee-line for that opening," Jake said.

They were flying through the narrow roads, but had to slow down every hundred yards or so because the builder thought it would look better if there were little islands built into the middle of the roadways to act as a deterrent for speeders instead of the usual speed bumps.

Jake thought it was working.

They were coming up on a fork about four hundred yards from the blip and Peter yelled, "Turn right here!"

Morris yanked the wheel to the right and Jake held on as the van leaned to the left. They took a shallow bend back to the left and then accelerated as the road straightened out for a few hundred yards. Another right turn, then left and the back fence of the neighborhood came into view.

"He's through," Peter said. "Dammit!"

There was no one in sight as they pulled up to the fence opening.

As the van sat idling, Morris asked, "What now, boss? Should we go around?"

Peter looked at the moving map and Jake saw that the red blip was crossing over the railroad tracks and heading for Doctor's Lake.

"Johnson," Peter said, "I want you to follow him on foot while we make the end run around. Look at the map here—he's heading this way across this road on the other side of the fence, over these railroad tracks and toward the road on the other side. If you see him, stay on his tail until we get into position."

"Yes, sir, got it," Johnson said, sliding the van door open.

"Remember, he's got Davis's MP5. Keep in touch with the two-way."

Johnson nodded and jumped out, shutting the door behind him.

"Morris, get us out of here!"

"On it!"

Morris turned the van around and headed back the way they came.

Jake pointed to the map and said, "Here—Orange Avenue—that will be the quickest way to both Moody and Doctor's Lake. We can make the decision to take either one at this intersection."

"Morris, exit the neighborhood to the right and we'll go down—uh—two streets and take that right. It's Orange Avenue," Peter said.

Morris nodded, concentrating hard on missing the islands in the road. Peter and Jake watched the red blip on the screen as it paused for a few minutes just before Doctor's Lake Drive.

"What's he doing?" Jake said.

"Probably resting," Peter said. "He's hurt and cold and he's been moving at a pretty good clip since he ran out of the lab. There! He's on the move again."

They watched him move close to the road and then he stopped again. About a minute later they saw the blip cross the road and then stop on the other side. The radio crackled to life.

"Alpha, this is bravo, gunshots fired, I repeat gunshots fired!"

"Stay down and do not return fire, bravo, copy?" Peter said.

"Bravo, copy." Johnson said. "He's not firing at me. I can see now through the trees. He's killed a dog, and a woman is lying on the ground. I can't tell if she's moving or not. Suspect is not in sight."

"He's directly across the road from you, not moving. Stay put!"

"Roger."

The van made the turn onto Orange Avenue and was trying to go around a slow moving Accord, but oncoming traffic prevented it.

"We'll be to your position in four minutes, bravo," Peter said.

"Roger, car approaching rapidly—shit! I thought the guy was going to run over the woman, but he's stopped now and getting out of the car. We may have trouble. He's calling someone on his cell. Shit! Suspect is moving! He's just climbed into the vehicle and is driving off to the—uh—north! Repeat, suspect is in a vehicle, moving north."

"Dammit!" Peter said, pounding his fist into the bench.

"What now?" Jake said.

"I'm thinking. Give me a sec."

"Do you think that guy called the police?" Jake asked. "You don't want the cops involved with this do you?"

"Johnson!" Peter said.

"Go"

"Subdue that guy with the cell! We don't want the police alerted. Hurry!"

A double click of the mike was the response from Johnson as they turned onto Moody Avenue about a minute away.

"Morris, turn left here and then right onto Doctor's Lake. Johnson is just up ahead."

"Right," Morris said.

They watched the red blip pull rapidly away down Doctor's Lake and then they were stopping as Morris pulled up to where Johnson stood next to two bodies and a dog.

Peter slid the van door open and Johnson said, "The woman is alive, the man is out cold and I checked the called numbers on his cell. This looks like a private number, maybe a friend, but definitely not 911 or the police. I think we're good for now, unless the friend calls the police for him."

"All right, good work Johnson. Let's get these people and the dog hidden in the bushes and then we've got to move."

Jake and Johnson carried the man to the side of the road and unceremoniously deposited him in the bushes while Peter and the other agent grabbed the woman and did the same. Morris pulled the dog off to the side of the road and left him on the bike path. They all jumped back in and accelerated north hoping they could catch up to Omar before he got too far away.

62

January 19, 2010 7:10 p.m.

Orange Park, Florida

Omar drove the speed limit.

It had taken him a minute to find the volume on the radio to turn it off. The music, or whatever they called it here, was full of bass and the vocalists all sounded like they were shouting at each other. Another reason the stupid infidels needed to die. Their music drove people to madness.

Omar calculated he had maybe thirty minutes in the car before the police were alerted and then he would have to leave it on the side of the road and continue on foot. His mind worked feverishly trying to figure a way out of this.

He did not know his way around this small town, and his contacts in America were limited and located in the New York and Miami areas. He needed to be free of his pursuers first, before he began actively seeking help.

He figured he would stay on this two lane road for as long as it would take him north. The streets passing by on his right were probably more neighborhoods and had names like, Woodland and Birchwood. He did not want to risk turning into a bottle neck where he would have to back track and lose time and distance.

Headlights appeared in his rear view mirror and he glanced up at it, concerned. *The police wouldn't have responded this quickly, would they?*

Headlights appeared in front of him and he made sure he was centered in the lane as the car approached from the opposite direction.

Omar glanced into the rear view mirror again. The headlights behind were now catching him quickly. The vehicle was moving rapidly. He was concentrating so hard on the lights coming up from behind, he had wandered into the other lane. As the oncoming car passed, it had to swerve to miss him and the driver angrily honked its horn. Omar jerked the wheel to the right, overcorrecting and then back left as he drove onto, and then off, the shoulder of the roadway. He had to slow to regain control.

The lights at his rear came right up on his bumper and stayed there for a half a kilometer or so, and then moved to his left and accelerated, passing him. Omar glanced over as a van passed and at first he thought it an overzealous driver late for dinner, but taking a second glance he recognized it as the vehicle the Americans had driven him in from Orlando.

Too late.

As it passed in front, it turned hard right into a skid. Omar slammed on the brakes and swerved right onto the shoulder again. His car crashed into the side of the van and came to a stop with its hood pressed against the sliding door.

He grabbed the MP5 with his good arm, fired it through the windshield, shattering the glass, and peppered the side of the van with bullets. Throwing the car in reverse, he backed away, grimacing, the pain from using the injured arm almost unbearable. Slamming the shifter into drive, he swerved left as he went around the back of the van, hitting the rear bumper and causing it to spin further to its right.

He pulled away into the night, his headlights smashed, windshield shattered, steering blindly down the dark road.

63

January 19, 2010 7:22 p.m.

Orange Park, Florida

Jake had been thrown to the rear of the van during the violent maneuver Morris had performed. His hip had banged painfully off of the bench and he ended up on his ass on the floor. Peter had somehow held on to the computer and maintained his seat, but now yelled at Morris.

"What the hell, Morris! Are you trying to kill us?"

Morris said nothing and then they were all diving for cover as bullets sprayed the van. Flat on the floor, Jake heard the car back up and pull away, slamming into the rear bumper of the van and spinning them sideways. The laptop, which Peter had dropped, slid into Jake's head painfully, but he reached out and held onto it, trying to keep it from banging into something else.

"Anybody hit?" Peter yelled.

"No's," all around as the five of them picked themselves up off the van floor.

"Morris, can we follow? Any damage?" Peter asked.

He didn't answer, just put the van in drive and spun around, accelerating after Omar.

Jake grabbed hold of the bench and hung on until the vehicle stabilized. Peter took the laptop from Jake and looked relieved to see it was still functioning. The blip was not too far ahead.

"Can you see him, Morris?" Peter said.

"Tail lights ahead. It looks like his headlights are out so he's driving blind."

"That'll slow him down. This time, try to run him off the road from behind without killing us."

Morris grunted.

Jake looked around the van and saw that Johnson was bleeding from the head. He didn't seem to care. Jake took inventory of his own aches and pains and was relieved to find there were nothing but bumps and bruises.

If Peter were to ask him again to come along and act as guide, he would say no. He was in real danger here and didn't like it.

It was one thing to be tailing someone in the night, but the violence of a car crash, even one intended, and being shot at, was taking its toll on him. He kept thinking of Teri, trying to feed his fear with anger. It didn't seem to be working.

Peter handed the laptop to Jake who took it with shaking hands. "Hold on to this for a moment. I need to ride up front with Morris for a bit."

Peter slid into the front passenger seat and took out his pistol, checked the clip and then slid it back in.

"How many bullets do you think he has in that clip?" Peter asked no one in particular. "We need to make him waste the rest of it."

"He fired a three round burst that killed Davis in the lab," Johnson said. "Another single shot into the General and then maybe five rounds at you in the lab."

"Ok, nine rounds. How many to kill the dog?" Peter asked.

"Three rounds into the dog."

"Twelve. Anyone able to estimate how many he fired into the van? I want to say nine."

"That sounds about right," Johnson said.

"So he's fired about twenty one rounds of a thirty round clip. Let's see if we can get him to blow the remaining nine. Morris, get close and I'll see if I can draw his fire."

* * *

Omar could barely make out the road.

There was scarcely enough light between the widely spaced street lamps for him to navigate, but he kept the accelerator pressed as the cold wind whipped at his face through the missing windshield. He shivered uncontrollably.

Headlights approached rapidly from the rear. He cursed loudly in the wind.

Letting go of the steering wheel for a second, he secured the seatbelt. It pressed against the wounded shoulder but he would just have to bear it. This was probably going to get nasty

The van came up on his rear and then slid to his left, but did not pass. Gunfire—and a bullet ricocheted off of the hood. He ducked and swerved into the van, but they were ready and easily fell back behind him. More gunshots as bullets missed him but one broke the left rear window and then his rear windshield was shot out.

He grabbed the MP5, gritting his teeth against the pain from having to steer with his injured arm, and turned left in his seat, firing a three round burst at the van. It swerved behind him just in time and he missed wide.

He watched it slide left again as more gunshots rang out. A bullet whizzed past his left ear. He turned again and fired another short burst anticipating the van's move. He caught the left headlight, before it moved out of position. He turned the other way and fired through the shattered rear windshield and watched as the right headlight blew out and two bullet holes appeared in the windshield of the van. The van swerved back to the left out of his line of fire.

Turning back to his left, he pointed the MP5 at the driver and pulled the trigger.

Nothing happened.

He squeezed again, but the gun was empty. Cursing, he dropped the gun and switched hands on the steering wheel. He swerved left into the van, trying to force it off the road, but it slowed and stayed behind him, keeping pace with his speed.

He was out of options.

* * *

"All right! That's it! He's empty. Use the bumper and spin him out. It's time to end this," Peter said. "Hold on everyone!"

Using a technique popular with law enforcement called PIT, Morris moved to the left lane and sped up just enough so his right front fender was even with the left rear fender of Omar's vehicle. He then brought the van back right, connecting with the left back fender, causing the rear end of Omar's car to fishtail and spin out.

At fifty miles per hour, the effect was spectacular.

The car slowly spun sideways, the tires screaming as Omar tried to regain control. It wandered into the right median and struck a rut in the turf as it slid sideways. It began to flip.

The momentum carried the car through three complete revolutions and then it settled back down on its tires, right side up.

Morris slowed the van to stay behind the out-of-control car and as it came to a stop, everyone but Jake jumped out and surrounded the car.

Jake heard shouting, but no gunfire.

After the wild ride, Jake was glad the gunplay was over. He wasn't sure if Omar had survived the horrible crash, but at this point, he really didn't care. He just wanted this night to be over.

64

January 19, 2010 – 7:45 p.m.

Orange Park, Florida

Maddy couldn't seem to sit still.

Jake had been gone for over forty five minutes and no one had heard a thing. She knew she should have gone with them. She walked over to the one called Pierce and asked again for the third time in fifteen minutes if he had heard any news. He shook his head.

Bodey sat in an office chair inside the console area with his arm bandaged in a sling. She wandered over, sitting down on the stool next to him.

"He'll be all right," Bodey said.

"I know. I can't help worrying. I should have gone with them."

"I'm not worried at all. I still think he has something else to do and nothing can happen to him until he finishes it."

"I don't know. The last dream we had seemed kind of final to me, as if there was nothing else to fix once we made Frank whole. That's why I'm so worried I guess. Nobody is looking out for him."

"That Peter guy is looking out for him and he's pretty badass. Hell, he shot me in the arm. Pretty good shot."

"I don't think Peter cares for anybody but himself. He'd shoot Jake if he got in the way."

Commotion in the back of the lab made Maddy stand and Bodey turn. Two of the men who had left with Jake came in carrying the terrorist through the back door. Peter followed behind and shouted for Pierce and the woman who both ran right over. Jake came in behind the last operative. Maddy rushed over and threw her arms around him.

"No one knew what was happening," she said against his chest. "I was going crazy!"

"I'm all right," he said. "It was probably good you didn't come. It got kind of rough. Gunfire and car wrecks. It was pretty hairy!"

She looked over at Omar. "Is he alive?"

"Yeah, but unconscious. We caused his car to lose control and he flipped three times. He's been out since."

Maddy could see dried blood on Omar's shoulder and arm, and his head appeared wounded. They put him in Andee's chair and the two medical people looked him over.

"How is Bodey?" Jake asked.

"Good. They gave him a mild pain killer after cleaning him up. He's sitting over behind the console. Want to go see him?"

Jake nodded, kissed the top of her head and smiled. "First, I need a drink or something. I'm dying of thirst, but I'm glad to be back."

"I'm glad too. Come on, I'll get you a soda while you talk to Bodey."

* * *

Jake and Maddy walked over to the console and as soon as Bodey saw him, he smiled and said, "See! He's perfectly fine. I knew he'd be all right."

"You look a little better," Jake said.

"Doin' ok. They gave me something for pain and it's working pretty good. If I had a beer, I'd probably be passed out."

"I'll get your soda." Maddy walked to the kitchen.

"What's the verdict on the arm?" Jake asked.

"In and out. No major blood vessels involved. Just meat. I should be fine. It just hurt like hell."

"I'm sorry I got you into this, man."

Bodey waved his hand at him like it was nothing.

Jake looked around the room, trying not to look too hard, but not being able to help himself.

"They took her away," Bodey said. "Her, the general, and that other guy. I don't know where. Maybe in the back."

Jake nodded.

Three people dead in his lab in one afternoon. One of them his best friend.

It was hard thinking about her in some plastic bag, unceremoniously shuffled to some back room so the living didn't have to contemplate the dead.

Death. It had been a part of Jake's life for what seemed an eternity now. His life traded for the secrets of death. He wasn't sure who had made out in the exchange.

His world was in such turmoil, swinging from one extreme to the next, sometimes in just a matter of seconds: Marrying Beth, burying Beth; finding Maddy, losing Teri; seeing the afterlife, and being blinded by it. He was surprised that he wasn't in some insane asylum, playing checkers with a guy who urinated on his hands because he liked the smell. Maybe he was in the asylum and this was all a dream. Some drug induced state where he would never be able to tell reality from hallucination.

Thinking like this made the world seem to tilt. A strong sense of vertigo grabbed him and he had to steady himself against the counter for fear of falling over. Maddy came up with his soda, saw him stagger a little, and took his arm, steadying him.

"Are you all right?" she said.

"Yeah," he said, looking around a little dazed. "I guess I was feeling a little overwhelmed by all this. It feels like a dream to me. I can't believe Teri's dead."

"I know," Maddy said. "I keep trying to stay positive, but it's difficult. So much good has happened to me in the last few weeks and then so much bad. You know, we've spent all this time trying to either keep the balance, or bring it back from chaos, that we haven't seen our own lives. Is something trying to keep us balanced? Not too much good, or too much bad?"

"Life has always been this way," Bodey said, "just not this intense."

Peter walked over. "Good job out there, we would've had a much harder time getting to him without your help."

"How is he?" Jake asked.

"The docs say mild concussion. And of course the gunshot wound and the dog bite. He's still unconscious and that's fine. It will make him much easier to deal with while you hook him up."

"I said I would help you catch him," Jake said. "I'm still not comfortable with what you people want to do to him."

"And I explained to you before, it doesn't matter what you're comfortable with. We need the information in his head and we're going to get it no matter what your concerns or morals."

"Yeah, and this is the same argument that got us here," Jake snapped. "You shot my friend and then got my partner killed. What if I refuse?"

Peter started to reach for his gun.

Before Peter could get it all the way out, Jake said, "I know what comes next. You've pointed the gun at my head before. It didn't do any good then and it won't now."

Peter held the gun in his hand, looking at it like it was something curious or foreign to him.

He looked up, said "Fine," with a smile on his face, and pointed the barrel at Maddy's head. "How about now?"

Maddy froze and Jake put his hands up trying to calm Peter down. "All right," Jake said, "just don't hurt anyone else, please. I'll do whatever you want."

"I knew you'd see things my way," Peter said, lowering the gun. "I'm out of bullets anyway."

He removed the clip, dropped it in his pocket, pulled another out and rammed it home, chambering a round.

"Well—I was." He smiled again, tightly, and then became serious. "Hook him up." And he turned and walked away.

65

January 19, 2010 8:30 p.m.

Orange Park, Florida

Jake had finished connecting all the leads to Omar. The terrorist was still unconscious and that had made his job a lot easier.

He and Maddy were at the console booting up the system, getting ready to test the connections, when Bodey said out of nowhere, "We don't have to do this."

"I'm not risking anyone else's life," Jake said. "I'll do what he says and then we'll be done with it."

"Do you think it's going to end with this one?" asked Bodey, grimacing a little as he shifted in his chair. "This is just the beginning."

"Doesn't matter, I can't take the chance of him killing Maddy or you. I couldn't live with it. He wins."

"He doesn't have to win."

Jake turned, looked at Bodey and was about to say something, but saw that he was smiling.

"Do you think he knows about the disc?" Bodey asked.

Jake thought hard for a moment, trying to line up everything in his head. It was difficult keeping the days straight.

"He might not," Jake said. "I know I've never said anything to any of them, but he may have some video of us using it. Whether or not he knows what he's looking at on the video, I don't know."

"Take the disc out of the drive and put it in your pocket. At least we won't have all the fireworks, like with Frank."

"I'm not sure what we'll get," Jake said, ejecting the disc and slipping it into his lab coat pocket. "We were still getting some mild effects and energy spikes without the software upgrade, remember?"

"I don't think that conduit will open up though," Bodey said. "And that's the main thing."

"I'm not positive it won't. They're going to induce this NDE and that's got to be some pretty powerful stuff. Let's keep our fingers crossed."

"Want me to keep the disc in my purse?" Maddy said. "It's right here under the counter."

Jake slipped it into her hands. "Yeah, that would be better."

Maddy grabbed her purse, put the disc in and then pulled out some makeup and pretended to freshen up. Jake glanced around. No one seemed to be paying attention to them.

"Whenever this happens, I want all of you to be ready to duck and run," Jake said. "If we get anything at all like what we had with Frank, it could be dangerous."

Maddy and Bodey nodded.

The system had booted up now and Jake started the software that calibrated the connections. The body mold they were using was a little bit small, but there were only very minor losses of data and they were all in the acceptable range. Jake didn't think it would make a noticeable difference in the quality of the playback. He didn't care anyway.

Peter's medical team had been setting up their equipment while Jake had been making the connections and calibrating the system. They looked about ready. Jake walked over to them.

"I'm ready whenever your people are," Jake said to Peter.

Pierce nodded and said, "All set."

"Just curious," Jake said, "how is this going to happen?"

"We're going to give him two drugs: morphine and pavulon. The pavulon will paralyze him, and the morphine will sedate him."

"If you sedate him," Jake said, "I can't guarantee the results will be what you want. His brain may produce hallucinations associated with the medication and we don't have enough experience with drugs to tell the difference. In all our previous cases we made sure no other types of drugs were in their systems so we wouldn't have to deal with any questions later. Is the morphine necessary?"

"Uh, no—but it will be extremely uncomfortable for him. Basically, it will be like suffocation to him. He will not be able to move or breathe and this will lead to hypoxia and then myocardial infarction. A heart attack. It can be quite painful and frightening."

"Good," Peter said. "The son of a bitch deserves some pain. Don't give him the morphine."

Pierce nodded slowly and started to turn back to his work when Jake said, "How will you bring him back?"

"What difference does it make?" Peter said. "You just do your part and you let us worry about the rest."

"Fine, just tell me when to push record." Jake returned to the console area.

Maddy saw his face and said, "What's wrong?"

"They're basically going to torture him is what's wrong. Dammit, I wish I could stop this!"

"What's going to happen?" Bodey said.

"Part of this is my fault," Jake said. "They were going to sedate him and then paralyze him so he couldn't move or breathe, inducing a heart attack. I told them the morphine they wanted to use would interfere with his reality and asked if they had to use it. Pierce told me it would be painful and frightening for Omar if they didn't."

"Let me guess," Maddy said, "Peter told him not to use the morphine."

"Yeah. He thought he deserved a little pain. This just keeps getting better and better."

Nobody had anything else to say.

Jake couldn't risk anyone else being shot or killed and he couldn't think of any other way to stop the test. Sure, he could sabotage the system, or fake a malfunction, but that would only delay the inevitable.

He kept asking himself why he was having such a problem with this.

The bastard had killed Teri. Why should he care what happens? He had been angry enough at the man to help capture him, why couldn't he harden his heart enough to see this through without feeling so guilty?

Because you're not an animal, a voice kept saying in his head. *You're not an animal.*

"Well," Jake said, "let's see what he's dreaming about."

"It's probably in Arabic," Bodey said, and that broke the tension a bit, causing Jake to smile and Maddy to giggle.

Jake turned the system on and watched the monitors. At first he wasn't sure what he was seeing, but as the screen cleared up, Jake understood. He went to get Peter.

"I need you to see this," he said to Peter, and led him back to the console.

Jake pointed at the screens and said, "I turned the system on to see what we'd get, and this is what's going on in his mind."

"What am I looking at?" Peter said.

"It's a view of the underside of the body mold over him—through slitted eyelids," Jake said.

"He's awake?"

"Yes."

Peter actually smiled, turned and instructed his people to restrain him in the chair. Omar immediately began to struggle, but they were able to keep him from loosening the leads as they secured him in the chair.

Pierce told Jane (the woman in the lab coat) to start the I.V. She had to have Morris hold his arm steady because he kept squirming, even in the restraints, and she was having a hard time hitting a vein. Finally, the catheter had good blood return and the I.V. was dripping into his arm with a solution of normal saline to keep it open until they were ready for the drugs.

"Let's do this," Peter said, and then to Omar, "I hope they can't bring you back."

This only made him fight more and Peter laughed. "All right," he said, "hit record."

Jake started the software and they all watched the screens.

* * *

Omar had been feigning unconsciousness ever since they put him in the chair.

His arm and shoulder ached, his head hurt, and he was having a hard time thinking clearly. His plan had been to wait for the right moment and ambush one of them, but the opportune time had come and gone. He was now at the mercy of whatever contraption they had him strapped to.

He had overheard them talking about the drugs they were going to give him and this terrified Omar more than anything he had ever been through in his life. The fear was like a clawing, living thing.

His body hummed like a thousand angry bees and the panic he felt took his breath away. He thrashed and bucked, but could not break the grip of the restraints holding him to the chair. A needle pierced his right arm and thinking this was the drug being injected into his body, he twisted and shook his arm trying to keep the needle away. Strong hands grasped his upper and lower arm and pinned it so that no matter what he did, he could not wriggle away. The needle found its mark and he waited for death to come.

* * *

As Pierce administered the Pavulon into Omar's I.V., Jake watched his struggles quickly grow weaker and then completely stop. On the screens, Omar panicked and Jake could feel this as he watched.

"Start the timer now," Pierce said.

Jane pressed a button and a large LED clock began counting down from four minutes. Jake presumed they would begin reviving him after this time.

Peter wandered over to the console area and watched the screens intently, seeming to enjoy the discomfort Omar exhibited as the oxygen levels dropped in his blood stream.

"I can't breathe! I can't breathe!" Omar's mind shouted in Arabic as Peter translated with a whining sarcasm.

Jake looked over at Omar's body and saw that it was completely still and all his facial features were slack. Respirations had stopped, blinking had ceased, nothing on him moved.

"O2 Sat dropping," Jane said. "89%, 88%..."

The timer showed 2:51 left.

Omar's Arabic had changed and Peter continued to translate. "I must breathe! The pain! My chest will burst! I must breathe!"

"O2 Sat 78%. Heart rate dropping," Jane said as Pierce bent to check some other gauge.

"When will he start having his Near Death Experience?" Peter asked. "I thought this is what you people did?"

"We've never recorded one happening live," Jake said. "I have no idea what to expect. For all I know, it could happen in a split second, and we wouldn't even know it. From what we understand, time doesn't elapse at the same rate it does here."

"Great," Peter said. "How will we know?"

"I guess when we play it back."

The timer was down to 1:02.

Omar's Arabic had deteriorated to a continuous, mumbling, ramble that Peter didn't bother to translate. The visions on the screens were graying out, starting at the edges and slowly collapsing in, like tunnel vision.

"O2 Sat at 50%! Heart rate 23—no—flat line! Heart rate is flat line!"

The EKG and O2 Sat monitors began alarming and then all hell broke loose.

Andee's monitors had closed into a pinpoint of light and then sprang back open showing a view from above as Omar's Near Death Experience began.

Music poured out of the speakers and then split the air as the sound seemed to come from everywhere.

Discordant notes clashed together as an ear splitting noise. It caused everyone to cover their ears and involuntarily duck, trying to avoid the cacophony that permeated the room. Jake likened it more to the angry bellow of some animal or prehistoric beast, than music.

The room reverberated with the sound and the glass panels separating the console area from the chair began shattering. On the monitors, an orangish hue emanated from the top right corner and images of Omar's life began flying past him into the strange light, slowly changing it into a blood red ball of pulsing luminosity. The images were blurry and passed by so rapidly they were indistinguishable from one another.

The ground beneath them began to tremble and shake violently, as if an earthquake were somehow happening in the sandy soil of Florida. An earthquake only targeted at this building. The floor suddenly shifted to one side and then quickly back in place and Maddy fell to her knees while Jake and Peter steadied themselves on the console. The trembling stopped.

"Fifteen seconds!" Jane yelled, trying to be heard above the noise.

Pierce nodded, sweat breaking out on his brow as his eyes darted around frantically.

Jake helped Maddy back up. "Are you ok?"

She nodded her head up and down and Jake went back to the monitors. The coolant system was pegging the needle at 95%. He looked up at Bodey and their eyes met for a moment, and then Bodey shrugged, as if to say, *Keep going.*

Jake looked up at Omar's body and noticed Pierce and Jane trying to take in all that was happening. Apparently someone had forgotten to brief them on what to expect. Pierce kept ducking and bobbing his head as if something would fly at him out of the woodwork, and Jane, though she was doing a better job of dealing with it, looked as if she was about to vomit.

"This is normal!" Jake shouted at them. "It gets worse here in a moment," and smiled.

They glanced at him like he was out of his mind.

"Time!" Jane shouted, moving the body mold up and out of the way. The video monitors showed interference in the display as the sensitive equipment was jostled.

"Begin compressions!" Pierce yelled as he moved to the head of the chair and placed a mask and a resuscitation bag over Omar's nose and mouth and began breathing for him. Jane jumped on a stool and started CPR.

Peter saw the change in the display. "Are we going to get the data we need?" he asked Jake.

"It's not ideal, but it's picking up most of it."

On the monitors, Jake watched an obviously different NDE unfold. The light they had come to associate with the others was now a diffuse, blood red color and he could discern no one waiting to greet Omar in the afterlife. Omar looked around, panicked, as if something was going to jump up and grab him at any moment.

Then the displays went blank.

Jake glanced at the cooling system and saw that it was at 99%. The system was overheating rapidly.

"What's happening?" Peter shouted.

"The system is overheating! I have to shut it down!" Jake hit the abort button.

Nothing happened.

The video displays remained blank, but the discordant music continued to blare at them through the speakers. Jake hit the button over and over again, but the coolant levels remained at 99% and the noise actually seemed to grow louder.

"I can't shut it off!" Jake yelled.

Bodey was up now typing something one handed into one of the workstations and Jake went over to see what was happening. Bodey was attempting to stop the software and shut the system down from it, but it wouldn't let him access anything. The computer console was locked up.

"The main power grid!" Bodey yelled over the noise. "Kill the main power grid!"

Jake nodded once and ran toward the circuit breaker panel on the other side of the lab by the main doors. As he passed the chair, he heard a familiar ripping noise and could see the conduit between this plane and the other open up. Purple and red flashes of light burst out of thin air above Omar. He could smell ozone and the air crackled as he ran past.

Jane and Pierce had backed away, frightened, and Jake had to stop and go back to them.

"You need to keep trying!" Jake shouted. "It won't stop until you bring him back! Hurry!"

They glanced at each other and then slowly moved back, warily watching the growing rip in the air above the chair.

"Give the Narcan and Epinephrine now!" Pierce shouted as Jake ran to the electrical panel.

A wind started up inside the lab as he crossed the room. Reaching the panel, he yanked open the access door and started flipping breakers for the main computer system and power supply. Nothing happened.

Frantic now, Jake started flipping all the breakers to the off position and hope bloomed in his chest as the lights went out and the emergency lighting kicked in, but the horrible noise still droned on all around them. The wind picked up steam and the hole over the chair grew larger. He turned and saw Bodey yell something, but couldn't make it out.

Jake started back across the room so he could hear what Bodey was trying to tell him when one of the coolant supply lines in the ceiling ruptured and boiling hot water and steam gushed from the roof onto Morris and Johnson who were standing off to the side near the back of the lab.

Morris screamed and covered his face, but went down under the force of the pressurized steam. Johnson was able to jump to his left, but then the pipe itself tore free from its supports and fell on him, pinning him under its weight as hot water spilled from the break onto his trapped body.

Jake turned back to the panel and grabbed the main breaker's priming pump handle and began working it up and down so he could blow the breaker open. After five pumps, the panel was charged and he pressed the green button. The charge blew the contact open and all power to the building went out.

It made no difference.

The conduit was still open, the music blared, and the wind blew.

Another pipe ruptured on the other side of the lab and the hissing of the steam from both breaks added to the symphony of noise inside the lab.

Jake could see Pierce and Jane frantically working on Omar trying to ignore everything around them. Jane's hair whipped around her head as the maelstrom from the open conduit sucked dust, paper, and steam vapor into it.

Jake ran over and yelled, "I can't shut it down! It has a life of its own. We have to get him back. What can I do?"

"Take over bagging him while I push some drugs into his system. Squeeze this Ambu-bag every five compressions that Jane does. Hold the mask tight around his mouth and nose so it forms an airtight seal. Got it?"

Jake understood and took over for Pierce.

The room vibrated now from sound and pressure and then a loud explosion made him jump.

Jake knew the main cooling tank had just ruptured.

Pierce used a syringe and injected something into Omar's I.V. while watching the battery powered monitors they had hooked up to him.

After a few seconds Jane yelled, "V-Fib, We've got V-Fib!"

"I'll charge the defibrillator!" Pierce said, pulling a small pack out from under the cart and powering it up.

Jake looked up and saw Maddy over by the console holding on to the counter. Bodey was next to her trying to get her to go with him.

"Get her out of here!" Jake yelled at Bodey, but he wasn't sure if Bodey heard him over the sound.

Jake could feel the force of the vacuum pulling at his hair and clothes and he risked looking over his shoulder at the opening.

What he saw terrified him.

The opening was like a deep, bottomless, red void that pulled and called to him.

Once he looked into it, it held him and wouldn't let him go. The sounds of his lab coming down around him faded as he turned his whole body toward the opening. A humming thronged through his veins and he could feel heat pulsing forth onto his face as the blood red light pulsed inside the void.

Slowly, a murmuring of voices started in low and then grew to a steady hum. He could not distinguish individual words, but the meaning was clear. They were calling to him. Calling him, only he didn't want to go.

This was not the calm, soothing sounds he expected to hear, but a chorus of wanting, demanding, and needing. It grew in intensity, like the whining of children on a playground.

Not the happy sounds of laughing children, but the angry, whining, buzzing of spoiled adolescents denied their desires and then demanding them. A crowd of bullies, no, a stadium of them screamed now in his head, all demanding his attention at once. Then a voice louder than the clamor of the crowd called his name.

"Jake!"

He felt as if the voice was lifting him up off of his feet. He knew in his mind he needed to resist, but his strength had left him and his body felt foreign to him.

"Jake! Jake!"

He was floating, or at least it felt like he was. He could not feel the ground beneath his feet and the pulsing red light was all around him now, humming through his veins like blood. Beating to the rhythm of his heart.

Something faintly struck his cheek.

"Jake!"

The noise of the discordant music briefly invaded his mind. His face was struck again, harder, and the angry buzzing voices seemed to grow angrier but fainter.

"Hey asshole!"

His whole body shook and then he was back.

Peter was in his face yelling at him and Maddy was standing next to him holding onto the chair as wind whipped the hair around her face.

"Bag him!" Jake heard Pierce yell, "We're losing him again! Someone bag him!"

Jake looked around dazed and Peter handed him the resuscitating bag.

"You've got work to do! Come on!"

Jake grabbed the bag and started ventilating Omar again. He could feel the opening calling to him again, but he refused to turn around. It wasn't bad if he was looking away from it.

"I thought I was going to lose you!" Maddy shouted. "You looked drugged and it was sucking you in."

"Don't look into it," he said. "It almost had me."

"We need to shock him!" Pierce yelled above the wind and sound. "When I say 'clear,' step back away from him and don't touch the chair."

Jake nodded and bagged Omar again as Jane continued to compress his chest.

Pierce grabbed the paddles and placed them on Omar's chest and yelled "Clear!"

Jake jumped back, as did Jane, and Pierce fired the defibrillator.

Omar's body arched up and purple lightning erupted from the opening above their heads followed by a clap of thunder. The lightning shot out across the room and struck one of the battery powered emergency lights and blew it to pieces. Sparks flew from it as shards of the shattered glass shot outward spraying Bodey. He ducked but came up with small cuts on his face and arms.

Over the noise of the wind and discordant music came a throbbing and humming that vibrated the air.

"We still have V-Fib!" Jane shouted. "Hit him again!"

"Charging!" Pierce yelled.

A green light on the pack indicated it was ready and Pierce placed the paddles on Omar's chest again and yelled, "Clear!"

As the defibrillator discharged, Omar's body arched up again. A sound like a jet engine roared and the opening over him slammed shut with a thunderous clap as more purple lightning shot outward, striking Jane and Pierce in the chest. Peter was thrown back against the wall like a rag doll, and Jake and Maddy were thrown together against the console as a loud explosion rocked the ground underneath them.

Then, everything went blank.

66

January 19, 2010 – 9:32 p.m.

Orange Park, Florida

Jake woke to hissing.

As his eyes opened and came into focus, the sound of steam escaping from behind brought him back to the present. He was lying propped up against the console with one leg painfully folded underneath him.

After maneuvering his leg into a more comfortable position, the only other part of him that hurt was his head. He reached up and gingerly touched the crown of his scalp, wincing as pain shot through his head and down his neck. His fingers came away red.

He looked around trying to find Maddy but she was nowhere in sight.

A loud crash sounded behind him as something broke loose from the ceiling. He stood, shakily, and was shocked at the destruction inside his lab.

The only light came from a few emergency bulbs burning on battery power, but what he could see did not look good. The console was broken in two, probably from the impact of his own body. *Had Maddy been thrown against it also?* He couldn't remember.

Water was everywhere and steam still jetted from two ruptured pipes in the ceiling. The chair was lying on its side twenty feet from its original position and in its place a large gaping hole opened up in the cement floor. The edges appeared burnt and as he peered into it, steam escaped from somewhere down inside it. It was too dark to see the bottom.

Pierce and Jane were dead.

Large charred areas in the middle of their chests showed where the electrical current from the opening had shot into both of them.

Their eyes were gone.

Jake could see Morris and Johnson over against the wall and neither one of them moved. Maddy and Bodey were nowhere to be found.

Jake hoped they had escaped and he was about to exit the building to find them when he heard his name.

"Jake…"

Spinning around in a circle, trying to locate the voice, he missed Peter crumpled in a heap by a pile of debris near the electrical panel.

"Hey asshole…"

Jake spotted him and rushed over.

"You look like shit," Peter said.

Jake tried to grab Peter to help him up, but he pushed his hand away.

"No—leave me. I'm all in anyway."

Jake looked harder and could see his legs bent at an odd angle, but the realization set in when he saw the piece of metal sticking out of his stomach. Blood was soaked through his shirt and jacket.

"Oh, man…" Jake said.

Peter coughed and a trickle of blood ran down his chin.

"Listen," Peter said, "you've got to go after him."

"What? Who? No! I've got to get you to a hospital and I need to see if Maddy's all right."

"He took Maddy."

"Who?"

"Omar! He took her and left. You need to find him."

"Omar! I thought he was dead." Jake looked at the chair and noticed for the first time it was empty. "The last I saw, they hadn't got him back."

"He's back. And he's pissed. He took Morris's gun and Maddy hostage. He gave me this present before he left." Peter pointed to the piece of metal sticking out of him.

Jake shook his head. "I'm calling the police. They can handle this better."

"No! You can't involve them. They'll slow you down. They'll see this mess and start asking questions and then they'll detain you until they get the answers they want. After that, they still might keep you anyway. You have to do this yourself. You're the only one left alive who even knows he's here. I'd go with you, but I think my back is broken. I can't move my legs."

Jake looked him over and knew it to be true.

"How am I supposed to do this?" Jake said. "I don't even know where to start."

"The chip in his knee, remember? Take the laptop and chase him down."

Jake nodded, remembering. Then shook his head.

"I can't do this alone. I'm not like you. I'm not a killer. What do I do when I find him?"

Peter slapped him in the face, hard.

"What do you think you do? You kill him! Stop being a puss and do what needs to be done. He's got your girl! Now stop dicking around with me and get after him."

Jake looked hard at Peter. He knew he was right. No one else could do this.

"Take my gun," Peter said. "It's in my back pocket. You'll have to reach for it, I can't get it. Take the extra clips too, in my pocket here."

"Where's Bodey?"

"I don't know. He ran after them both, but I heard gunshots right after and I haven't seen him since."

Jake found Peter's cell phone as he was rummaging in his pockets for the extra rounds. He put it in Peter's hand.

"Call 911 when I leave," Jake said. "I've got to go."

Jake stood, but Peter grabbed his arm.

"For you, the best approach will be surprise. He doesn't know you can track him. Get him in a place where you can sneak up on him and shoot him point blank. That way you can't miss. He'll kill you in a gunfight."

Jake nodded.

"You can do this."

"I have to."

"Damn straight. Now get the hell out of here."

Jake turned and ran.

67

January 19, 2010 9:45 p.m.

Middleburg, Florida

Maddy's wrists were tied behind her and her mouth was gagged.

She was lying on the floor of a van heading God knew where with a terrorist screaming in Arabic into a cell phone. Tears sprang from her eyes thinking she would never see her mother, father, or Jake again. She wasn't even sure if Jake was still alive.

After the explosion that threw them into the console, she hadn't been able to wake Jake. He had been bleeding from his head and she knew he was alive at that point, but then Omar had grabbed her by her hair and dragged her out of the lab kicking and screaming. He had only paused long enough to take a gun and then stab Peter with a piece of scrap metal.

And poor Bodey. He had apparently chased after them and Omar had shot him in the parking lot. She had seen him go down, unmoving. She had no idea if he had survived.

Omar had searched the vehicles in the back until he found this van with the keys in it and a cell phone left on the center console. He threw her in and drove off quickly, then stopped a mile or so away to tie her up and gag her.

"You will be still and quiet, woman!" he had said. "If you cry or yell, I will cut out your tongue."

She knew he meant it, but she had seen something else in his eyes. Was it fear? He had said nothing to her since, but she could see he was very agitated and at one point it appeared he was crying, but she wasn't sure if she had imagined it.

He ended the conversation on the phone and cursed loudly.

He turned in his seat and looked back at her for an instant, and then he pulled over and got out. She could hear him walking around behind the van and then the door slid open. He grabbed her and turned her toward him.

"I must go to an island in the southern part of this state," he said. "It is called Sanibel. Do you know this place?"

She nodded slowly. He reached in and she flinched, but he only untied the gag and removed it.

"Do not cry out. Do you remember what I said?"

She nodded again.

"Good. Can you drive to this island?"

She nodded.

"You may speak, but softly." He looked at the ground, as if he were embarrassed. "I am injured and do not know the roads well. You will drive me to my destination and then I will set you free. If you do not do this, I will kill you now."

"Sounds like I don't have much of a choice. I will drive you."

He indicated that she should turn around and she rolled over facing the other way. He removed her bindings and she sat up, rubbing her wrists.

"How far is this island?" Omar asked.

"About five and a half hours from Orange Park. I do not know where we are now."

He suddenly looked very tired.

"Come," he said, beckoning her out of the van, "you will drive now while I rest. Does the area look familiar?"

As she stepped out, she looked around and nodded.

"Yes, we are in Middleburg. At least you went in the right direction. Sanibel is five hours from here. That is if traffic is good."

He nodded once and then indicated she was to go first. She slid into the driver's seat and adjusted herself. She started the engine and then turned the van south on SR21, accelerating.

"What is in Sanibel?" she asked.

"Please, do not talk. Just drive."

It was 9:34 on the dash clock. It was going to be a long night and she was already exhausted from the day. She hoped she would not fall asleep at the wheel. She turned once more to look at her captor and saw that his eyes were closed.

68

January 19, 2010 9:45 p.m.

Orange Park, Florida

Jake ran outside and looked for Bodey. He found him lying in between two cars in the side parking lot. He was alive but bleeding badly.

Jake wasn't sure if Peter would call 911 and even if he did, maybe no one would find Bodey hidden like this so he took out his own cell phone and made the call.

"911, what's your emergency?"

"Yes, my friend's been shot! He's in the side parking lot of the Encephalographic Systems building on Kingsley Avenue. He's lying in between two cars so tell them to look for him. Hurry!"

"You say he's been shot?"

"Yes, and he's bleeding badly."

"What's your name sir?"

"He's in the Encephalographic Systems side parking lot. You got that?"

"Yes. We've had multiple calls for the area and units are already on their way. I need your name and phone number sir."

Jake hung up.

Bodey looked bad. He had been hit in the stomach and upper right thigh. Blood was everywhere.

"Shot twice in one day," Bodey said. "Pretty good, huh? I should be able to get some redhead to pay attention to me now. I'll just show 'em my scars."

"Don't talk, man. Save your strength. You're going to be fine. The ambulance is on its way."

Jake could hear a siren in the distance.

"Bodey. I have to go. They're coming now and you're going to be ok. I can't get caught up in all of this. He has Maddy and I have to go after him."

"I know, dude. Go. I tried to stop him, but I suck."

"I know you tried," Jake said, smiling. "You have more balls then I do. I wish you were going with me."

Bodey doubled up on the pavement in pain and groaned. "Shit this hurts!"

"I'm sorry I got you into all this."

"Shut up and get the hell out of here. I'll be all right. Now go!"

Jake put his hand on his friend's arm and then got up and ran to his car.

"Shoot that bastard in the balls for me!" Bodey yelled after him.

Jake put the laptop in the passenger seat, started the car and exited the parking lot with the tires squealing.

He had one place to go before he followed Omar and Maddy.

69

January 20, 2010 12:26 a.m.

Tampa, Florida

Maddy drove in silence, her adrenaline and her thoughts keeping her awake for now.

Omar had fallen asleep but rested fitfully, mumbling in his sleep and sometimes crying out, only to wake briefly, sit bolt upright and then grab his shoulder in pain. Afterward, he would sit back again and doze off restlessly.

Sanibel. She couldn't imagine why he needed to be in sleepy Sanibel Island. *What could possibly be waiting for a terrorist in a small tourist destination off the coast of Fort Myers?*

Every time she pictured Qayum Omar on the beach in her childhood vacation spot, she could not associate his violent, destructive nature with the sea shell covered beaches and dolphins frolicking in the water. *Was there something sinister brewing just below the surface of the community?* She thought not. It was probably just out of the way. Somewhere he could hide without being spotted in some large city. Then again, he would probably blend in more in a city like Miami or Fort Lauderdale. Anonymity could be obtained a lot more easily in a crowd.

He was stirring awake and she was glad. She had to use the bathroom something fierce and could use some caffeine if she was to keep driving. They were outside of Tampa on I-75 and were making good time in the light traffic this late at night, but she could tell exhaustion was creeping up on her.

"Where are we?" His voice floated up out of the gloom, sounding too loud in the van after the ninety minutes of silence.

"Tampa," she said.

"How much farther?"

"A little more than two hours."

She could sense him nodding, but he did not say anything.

"I have to use the bathroom. Can we stop?"

"Yes."

"There is a rest stop two miles ahead. They have bathrooms and drinks."

"Will it be crowded?"

"Probably not this late at night, but more than likely, there will be some people there."

"No. Find an exit with a gas station or a place less populated."

"Fine," she said, squirming, her bladder protesting now that she was thinking about it.

They came to an exit ten miles later which had a number of truck stops and gas stations. He directed her to the loneliest one set back in the dark on the less traveled side of the off ramp.

He followed her to the unlocked restroom and waited outside. She would not allow him in, though he protested angrily. He finally relented, but when it was his turn, he made her stay in the bathroom with him, the gun resting on the sink within easy reach of his hand, as he stood over the toilet.

"Turn the water on!" he said, when he could not go.

She almost laughed at his embarrassment.

They got a couple of Cokes from a soda machine and then were back on the interstate heading south.

70

January 19, 2010 10:45 p.m.

Orange Park, Florida

Jake flinched as Mike McClaughlin yelled.

"I told you I didn't want my daughter involved in anything dangerous!" he said into Jake's face. "You promised nothing would happen to her!"

"Please, honey," Sara said, "this is not helping. Let him finish."

"You're right sir," Jake said, "and I take full responsibility for what has happened. But I need your help. I would never have allowed Maddy to be involved if I knew this was going to happen."

He paused, and then said softly, "I love her. I would rather die than have this happen and I'm willing to do that to get her back."

Sara put a hand on Mike's arm. Mike looked at Jake hard and must have seen something in his eyes, because he eased up and took a step back.

"All right, start talking."

"I'll try to be quick. He's got a two hour head start on me."

Jake explained the situation as briefly as he could while Mike and Sara listened closely. As the story unfolded, Mike's face grew worried and then set into a hard stare, wheels spinning.

"Well, we're going to need more than that pistol you have." Mike said. "Come on."

Mike led him into the garage and unlocked a storage room exposing a locker full of weapons and equipment.

"Whaddya' like? I prefer the shotgun myself," Mike said.

"Sir—uh—I don't know anything about guns. I don't even know where the safety is on this one. I trust your judgment."

Mike shook his head. "That Glock doesn't have a safety. You take the shotgun. It's pretty straight forward. I'll take the M16."

Mike grabbed extra ammo and a small satchel and threw them into the back of the Chevelle.

"We'll take the fast car. Any idea where he's taking her?"

"The tracking software shows them around Tampa on I-75 south. I'm not sure what his destination is."

"What tracking software?"

"He has a chip implanted in his leg that we can track via a satellite owned by the government."

"Does he know he has this chip?" Mike asked.

"No."

Mike smiled. "Good. Surprise is on our side and you're going to fill in the rest of the blanks while we drive."

"Yes sir."

Mike said goodbye to Sara and promised to be careful and bring her baby back.

"Don't call my cell," Mike told her. "You might give our position away right at the wrong moment. I'll call you with updates, ok?"

Jake could see the worry in Sara's eyes and swore to himself he would not be the cause of any more anguish for this family. He would find Maddy and get her to safety no matter what.

71

January 20, 2010 3:00 a.m.

Punta Gorda, Florida

Jake and Mike made good time and were on I-75 south passing the town of Punta Gorda.

The laptop showed Omar had stopped moving and was on an Island off the coast of Fort Myers. Jake was relieved that they at least had a destination.

"Sanibel Island," Mike said. "We go down there on vacation every year. Maddy knows it well. I wonder why they've stopped there?"

"Maybe he wanted her to take him to someplace she was familiar with."

"Could be, but I don't think that's it. What the hell could be in Sanibel that a terrorist would want or need?"

During the drive, Jake had filled in all the blanks for Mike. He seemed impressed and amazed at all that had happened to the group in the last twenty four hours.

"You must be exhausted," Mike had said. "Why don't you try and get a little sleep. You won't be doing anyone any good if you're a walking zombie."

So Jake slept for an hour or so and felt a little better. He couldn't seem to sleep any longer than that. He was too worried about Maddy.

He wanted Mike to push the car even harder, but Mike kept it at a reasonable 80 mph. He didn't want to risk being pulled over. Who knew if the authorities were looking for Jake after all that had happened at the lab.

They listened to the radio a bit and nothing was said about the explosions, but that didn't mean Jake was not a person of interest. Jake could only hope that Bodey and Peter, if they were still alive, covered for him.

As they approached their exit, Daniels Parkway, Jake asked what the plan would be.

"We'll get a good layout of the area and decide from there. The island has lots of condos and bungalows, so we'll plan our strategy based on what they're staying in. I'm hoping for a house or bungalow. It will make it much simpler."

Jake nodded and looked at the laptop again. The blinking red dot representing Omar was on the southern tip of the island, along the gulf coast side. Mike said they would cross the bay side over a causeway, cross the main north/south roadway, Periwinkle, to East Gulf drive, and try to determine where Omar and Maddy were along the road which hugged the coast.

The car couldn't seem to move fast enough.

72

January 20, 2010 3:31 a.m.

Sanibel, Florida

Omar's shoulder and head felt worse despite being attended to by the physician his contact in Miami arranged.

The man met them at the condo shortly after they arrived, disinfected the wounds, and stitched up the bullet hole in his upper deltoid.

He had refused pain pills from the man and regretted the decision. He had just wanted the so called doctor gone. The man reeked of alcohol and garlic, and kept leering at the girl.

When he and Maddy had arrived on the island, he had picked up a set of keys in a lock box at a local real estate office and driven straight to a condominium complex called *Ocean Breeze Bay*.

They were on the third floor near the ocean and this suited him well. The only possible entry was through the main door and that was good.

He told the girl she needed to stay with him for one more day and then he would set her free. He could see she was about to protest, but something changed in her eyes and she nodded. She was not ignorant and seemed resigned to her fate. Maybe he could find a way for her to live, but he doubted it.

She was sleeping on the couch now, snoring softly, one arm draped over her head, her hair spread out in an auburn fan beneath her, faintly glowing in the moonlight which was shining through the window. Her beauty did not escape him, but he could not concern himself with such things right now.

He kept reliving the events of the day and though he thought he had convinced himself it was all some elaborate hoax by the Americans to scare information out of him, he could not seem to get the visions out of his head.

The girl had wanted to talk during the drive, but he had refused at first. She kept at him saying she needed some type of stimulation to keep her awake, so he had relented. She was so innocent and naïve, questioning his heritage and family ties along with his beliefs. He could lie to her so easily at first, but he got the impression she knew when he was not truthful.

Eventually the conversation turned to the events of the day, like he knew it would. He did not want to go there, but she wouldn't let it go.

"I know you saw things you didn't want to," she said. "Were you surprised?"

"I do not know what you are talking about."

"We could see what was going on in your mind while they stopped your heart," she told him. "What I saw looked very bad. You seemed very scared."

"You are a foolish girl. These things cannot be. They simply drugged me and I was hallucinating or having a bad dream." But his words sounded weak coming from his mouth.

She shook her head and said softly, "You don't believe that. I can hear it in your voice."

He only stared out the window, thinking how horrible the dream had been.

"I know you have done many bad things in your life," she said, "but maybe you can still be forgiven. You can change your destiny. I know you think I am foolish and just a woman, but what you went through was real. We have seen these Near Death Experiences from many different people and yours was the first that scared me. What you saw is your fate, unless you change."

"You will drive now. I do not want to talk any longer."

She gave him one more look that was worse than anything she had said to him.

He could be angry at her for distracting him from his cause, and he could distrust her because she was an American woman and foolish in nature, but he could not understand why he was afraid. The pity he saw in her eyes made him forget about everything but what he saw hooked up to that awful machine. She knew it was real, and she felt sorry for him.

And this terrified him.

73

January 20, 2010 4:02 a.m.

Sanibel, Florida

Jake and Mike crossed over the bay to Sanibel Island and passed through the four way stop for Periwinkle Drive heading to East Gulf Drive.

The blip on the laptop's screen would periodically jump around, but as they got closer to the chip in Omar's leg, the target seemed to stabilize. He was just up ahead, about a block away.

"Turn right up here, Mike," Jake said.

Mike grunted and made the turn.

"Slow down," Jake said, "he's to the left here, up ahead."

They passed one condo complex on their left, which was the gulf side, as they headed back north along the coast, idling on the deserted road. To their right were houses which sat on canals giving owners of the homes access to the ocean. Another condo complex passed them on the left, then a set of tennis courts.

"He's in there," Jake said. "I think we need to backtrack to the entrance."

"Damn! I was hoping for a house," Mike swore. "And these are multi-story condos. Who knows what floor he might be on?"

"Hold on...," Jake said as Mike turned around at the next intersection and headed back to the entrance of *Ocean Breeze Bay*.

Jake clicked on a tab for the software which said, 'Elevation' and the display changed showing the height of the target in feet.

"I'll be damned. He's thirty two feet high. Do you think that will help?"

"Third floor—yeah that will help. Let's get him pinpointed."

As they pulled into the complex, Jake guided Mike to the northern most parking lot and then they had to turn toward the ocean and follow the lot to the back of the complex.

"Maybe we should stop here and park," Jake said. "This car is pretty loud. It looks like he's two buildings up."

"Right."

Mike pulled into an available spot and shut the engine down. Mike pocketed his pistol and Jake did the same with the Glock from Peter. They left the big guns in the car while they scouted the area out. Jake took the laptop with them.

They walked along a path which hugged the buildings, keeping to the shadows, and when they reached the second building, Jake ducked into a stairwell and opened the laptop. The screen seemed so bright in the dark of the night.

They were right on top of him.

Jake remembered something Peter had said about the accuracy being within so many feet but he couldn't remember if it was twenty five feet or five feet. Mike thought twenty five sounded more realistic so they had some deducing to do.

The red blip was to the right of their position, but the condo units were spaced every twenty feet or so. This gave them a choice of three possible units, but after seeing a for sale sign on the far right one, they eliminated it. There were lights on in the one closest to them and the one in the middle was dark.

"The dark one looks deserted," Mike said. "They have to be in the one with the lights."

"Hold on," Jake said, looking at the parking lot. "That van looks like one that Peter's group used. Let's see if the parking space has a number on it."

They walked into the open and got a closer look. 163.

Jake smiled at Mike and they looked up at the third floor. Unit 163 was the one that was dark.

"Good job," Mike said. "Let's hope he used his parking space."

All the other spots were occupied so Jake felt like their chances were good.

"Let's go around to the courtyard side," Mike said, "and see if there might be a way in besides the front door."

They slipped through the opening between buildings and entered a large courtyard which contained walkways on either side of the buildings. A fenced in pool sat in the middle of the manicured lawn.

The buildings of the condominium complex formed a large 'U' with the open end pressed up against the beach. Jake could hear the surf softly murmuring on the other side of the dunes. Nothing else moved or made a sound.

They counted the back screened porches until they came to the third one and Mike stepped back from the building assessing the situation.

Each unit had a porch, with walls on three sides, and a roof. The openings had waist-high aluminum railings and were covered from floor to ceiling with screen mesh. It would be possible to scale the porches from the outside as long as holes were cut or punched into the screen mesh, using the railings as footholds.

"This will work," Mike whispered. "He won't be expecting us from the backside. Let's get the guns."

Jake nodded and looked around in the gloom before he followed Mike back to the car. Only a few lights were on in windows throughout the complex.

The light globes spaced around the courtyard were painted black on the beach side to prevent the sea turtles from mistaking the glow for the moon. They provided only minimal lighting for the area. Hopefully it would be dim enough to keep their bodies from being backlit as they tried to enter from the porch. He turned and followed Mike back to the car.

Jake took the shotgun from Mike and looked it over, going through the instructions in his head which Mike had given him during the drive. He chambered a round, working the action, the noise sounding like a wrecking crew in the quiet of the night. Mike glared at him.

"Sorry," he whispered, as he loaded the fifth shell.

The gun was a Benelli M4 Tactical Autoloader and would fire rounds as fast as Jake could pull the trigger.

"Just point the gun in the general direction and pull the trigger. It kicks some so be ready," Mike had said. "Make sure Maddy is no where around."

Jake would be sure.

As he held the gun in his hands, he could see it shaking slightly in the dim light of the parking lot. He felt like he was going to throw up.

"If you're going to throw up, do it now," Mike said as if on cue.

"I'll be all right."

Mike nodded once. "Let's go."

Jake checked to make sure the Glock was snug in the small of his back, tucked into the waistband, and then turned and followed Mike to the courtyard.

Dawn was still about an hour away and the night remained as still and quiet as when they first arrived. All the vacationers were sound asleep, tired from a long day of fishing or golf. Most would be sleeping in, but Jake figured if they were successful he, Mike, and Maddy would be long gone before any would be waking up.

They stood at the bottom of the third unit and Mike took a large knife from a sheath on his leg and cut holes in the screen mesh for his hands and feet. He slung the M16 over his back and started climbing. The aluminum railing creaked a little with his weight, but settled down after a few seconds.

He reached up to the floor of the balcony on the second story and pulled himself up. The knife was in his mouth now, and he grabbed it and cut two more holes in the second floor's screen so he could get a decent grip on the railing.

When he was all the way up onto the second floor he waved Jake up.

Jake slung the shotgun over his back and started to climb. The going was not as easy as he thought and as he looked up to see Mike pulling himself up to the third floor balcony, his right hand slipped off the rail of the second story and he found himself hanging by one hand, his legs and free arm pin-wheeling trying to regain his balance and grip. The shotgun banged against the aluminum and then Jake got his other hand on the rail and braced himself.

The sound had been loud and both he and Mike froze in position and waited. After what seemed like an eternity, Mike signaled him up and he resumed his climb as he watched Mike disappear into the third floor balcony.

A hand reached out as Jake reached up for the third floor landing and Mike helped him the rest of the way up. He had to step over the waist high railing, through a hole Mike had cut into the screen, and then squeeze himself onto the porch between a table and chairs.

The condo remained dark with the shutters closed.

They had talked about how to enter the unit once they were on the balcony.

Jake nodded to Mike in the dark and watched him approach the sliding glass door on the right while he held the shotgun at the ready. Mike applied some pressure to the door and determined it was unlocked just as he suspected it would be. He turned to Jake and twirled his finger over his head. The ready signal to enter.

Jake crouched low and waited for Mike to open the door. No lights or movement from inside the condo. Jake hoped this was the right unit and at the same time wished it wasn't. He was terrified.

The door slid open silently and Mike rolled the sliding plantation shutters to the side and entered the dark condo. Jake could see nothing beyond the door. It was as if Mike had stepped into a black void and disappeared.

He waited.

One minute—two minutes—he didn't know what to do.

Mike was supposed to signal him in, but nothing happened. He listened with his whole body and could hear and see nothing. He shifted restlessly, torn. He would wait one more minute and then enter. *Come on, Mike—come on!*

The minute passed, so he stood slowly and moved to the door.

He peered in and could barely make out vague shapes of furniture but nothing more. He slipped in and panned his gun around the darkness and waited for his eyes to adjust. The room had some depth to it he could feel, but the unit was almost pitch black.

The lights came on and Jake was blinded.

"Drop the weapon!"

Jake raised his hand to shield his eyes.

"Now!"

"Do it," Mike said to his left.

Jake slowly lowered the shotgun to the floor and took in the room. Mike was to his left with his hands raised and Omar stood just inside the small kitchen at the front of the unit, with Maddy held in front of him. A pistol was pointed at Jake's head. Maddy was crying.

"You! Move next to the old man!"

Jake moved to his left and stood next to Mike.

He glanced over at him, but Mike was totally focused on Omar. He looked like a rubber band about to break. Jake could see Omar focused on this as he pointed the pistol at the two of them. Now he only had to cover one spot.

"Who are you?" Omar asked Mike.

Mike remained silent.

"Who are you?"

Silence from Mike.

"All right, I do not know you. But you," Omar said, looking at Jake, "I know."

Maddy looked horrible. She had dark circles under her eyes and her hair was disheveled as if she had just woken up. She was crying quietly and her eyes darted back and forth between Jake and her father.

"It's all right, Maddy," Jake said, with surprising strength in his voice. "Peter will be here soon."

"You are not a very good liar," Omar said. "Why are you here?"

"For her," Jake said, staring hard into the man's eyes.

Omar remained silent for a moment.

"Who is she to you?"

"Everything."

Jake could see Omar almost flinch. Something flashed briefly behind his eyes, and then it was gone.

"How did you find me?"

Jake hesitated, started to open his mouth, and then closed it when Mike shook his head.

Omar turned the gun on Maddy and pointed it at her head. She stiffened.

"How did you find me?" Omar asked again.

"There's a micro chip implanted in your leg," Jake said. "When they fixed your knee, they put it there. You can be tracked via satellite to within a few feet."

Omar nodded. "You are the scientist who put me in that horrible machine. I should kill you where you stand for such torture. Are you part of The Organization?"

"No."

"Then why did you do that to me and why are you here?"

"For her," Jake repeated.

"Why did you try and kill me and fill my head with those horrible hallucinations?"

"I didn't."

"Liar! You were operating the equipment! Why!"

"I did not want to do what they did to you. I protested, but they are like you. They, too, held a gun to her head."

This seemed to confuse Omar momentarily. He looked at the gun pointed at Maddy's head, and then turned it toward Jake and Mike again.

"What did that machine do to me?"

"The machine did nothing to you. It only records what's in your mind. They induced your death to give you a Near Death Experience."

"Why?"

"Because when you die, your life will flash before you."

"So…"

"The machine can record that and play it back. Your whole life—everything. They wanted what was in your head."

He nodded, understanding, and then he looked confused again.

"But why did you give me drugs to hallucinate? I saw horrible things."

Jake looked down and then back up again and locked eyes with Omar.

"You were not given any drugs to cause hallucinations. What you saw was what death will be to you."

Omar looked like he had been slapped. The gun wavered ever so slightly, and Mike started to move on Jake's left. Omar recovered and turned the gun on Mike, who stopped where he was.

"You are lying to me again," Omar said. "If she is so important to you, why do you lie?

"He's not lying," Maddy said, quietly. "You know this to be true."

"Silence woman!"

Maddy flinched and fresh tears began to fall.

"I am not lying," Jake said.

"I do not believe you!" Omar yelled, his eyes blazing. "You will not put me in that machine again! Ever!"

And Omar fired at Jake, hitting him in the chest.

Jake went down, the pressure of ten jackhammers slamming into his body.

74

January 20, 2010 4:34 a.m.

Sanibel, Florida

As Jake fell, he heard Maddy scream and watched in slow motion as she ducked, reflexively and dived for cover.

Then Mike was rolling to his gun as Omar fired point blank at him. Jake heard the shots as if through cotton.

He reached behind him and pulled the Glock from his waistband. It was like pulling his arm through thick syrup. He felt the gun would never come up.

Just as his gun swung up, he saw Omar's eyes shift to him and his pistol start to track back toward him. Shots fired again, and it was a second before Jake realized it was his own gun that had discharged. Omar spun and went down.

Then all hell broke loose.

Mike was up and grabbing the shotgun. He stepped over to Omar and pointed the barrel at his head, but Omar was practically dead already. Mike stepped on his wrist to keep him from using the pistol. Omar gasped as blood jetted from his neck. Jake's bullet had gone through his windpipe and carotid artery.

Suddenly the ground beneath them shook and a familiar tearing sound permeated the air. Jake was having a hard time remaining focused, but he could feel the wind begin to stir in the small condo.

"Oh no," Maddy said and she rushed to Jake. "Why is this happening?"

"Mike!" Jake tried to shout. "Get away from him! Now!" Jake started coughing uncontrollably and blood flew from between his lips.

A huge rip formed in the air, reaching from the floor to the ceiling. Red light pulsed from within it and Jake could see items from the room being sucked into it. Maddy's hair whipped around her head and the lights in the condo flickered.

The horrible musical chord he had heard back in the lab suddenly announced Omar's death and the windows shattered in the condo as it played its discordant notes. Mike ducked and threw himself toward Maddy.

Jake could hear voices again. The same angry voices he had heard looking into that awful red void. This time they seemed to mock him. They knew they had won and nothing was going to deny them. Jake heard screaming as it seemed Omar was lifted up from the floor. If he closed his eyes he could see thousands of arms grasp the terrorist and lift him into the void. When he opened his eyes, Omar was still lying on the floor, but he knew his energy no longer belonged to him.

The musical chord reached a volume Jake was sure would rupture his eardrums and then the conduit clapped shut, pillows and paper and dust vomited from the opening and silence settled into the room. Maddy cried.

The pain finally hit Jake and he started blacking out. He heard a ripping noise and the pain stopped.

He opened his eyes.

The light was blinding.

All around him, white light enveloped his body. As his eyes began to adjust, he heard music and Jake knew he was dying. The realization of this caused a moment of fear, but then the music grew louder and more beautiful and he felt calm—at peace.

He looked around and saw his body below him. Maddy was there, cradling him in her arms as Mike stood over them talking calmly into a cell phone. He could not hear what was being said.

He turned back to the light and saw a wondrous thing. Visions of his life passed in front of him. He wondered at the sights and thought he could watch them forever. As each scene passed, he relived it. Not just a memory, but an event he could see, hear, and feel. He realized now what Sara and Frank and all the others had felt.

His pathetic machine could not recreate this. It had been a poor substitute at best.

Time, he realized, had slowed and maybe even stopped. It was as if it didn't matter. When he looked down upon his dying body, time passed as it should, but when he looked back to watch his life review, it resumed as if it had been paused. He knew in the real world, the visions were flying by at incredible speeds, but here, it was paced. He needed to relive every single one.

He felt a presence next to him, turned, and watched a form materialize before him. He could hear his name and he recognized the voice. He began to cry.

Beth appeared in front of him, smiling radiantly and looking more beautiful than he ever remembered. She reached out to him, clasped his hand in hers and instantly felt her pass through him.

He gasped. It was as if she were part of him now. He could feel her soul and it was more beautiful than anything he had ever seen or felt. Tears flowed freely down his cheeks and he laughed with joy.

"Do you see?" Beth said.

"Oh, yes."

"You have been given a great gift, Jake," Beth said, "one which must never be abused. Only you can use it, and only with great care."

He couldn't think. Only feel.

He felt with his soul and all his being that this was true and right. That this place, with her, was the only place he was supposed to be.

"I've missed you so," he said, and she smiled so brightly his heart ached.

"You have wanted an answer for so long," she said. "Do you see now that it really was not important? You knew the answer in your heart all along."

And he did. He could hear Beth's voice clearly in his head now; *Jake—I love you. Be good to Madison and Lucas. Teri forgives you. I love you.*

And Teri was there beside Beth, smiling into his eyes, the warmth of her enveloping him along with Beth. She touched him and her whole life filled his as the universe opened to him.

Epilogue

The boy grabbed the doll from the girl, sand flying everywhere as she fought to keep it.

"You said I could have her!"

"No! She's mine!" Her four year old mind was in a panic. "You'll hurt her!"

"So—she's only a doll, anyway."

"You two, stop fighting and come in and eat!" their mother yelled.

"Mom! Lucas won't give me my doll!"

He flung it back at her, grabbing his truck instead and driving it through the sand as if nothing had happened.

"Lucas, Madison, do as your mother says. It's time to eat." Jake hated yelling at his kids, and usually made some kind of joke afterwards. "I'm going to eat all your pudding if you don't hurry up!"

Five year old Lucas Ryan Townsend and four year old Elizabeth Madison Townsend jumped up out of the sandbox in their backyard and laughed as they raced each other to the house. Jake bent to pick up his son and daughter and as they jumped into his arms, he grunted as pain shot through his chest.

"Daddy, are you ok?" Lucas said, looking very concerned.

"Oh yeah—I'm fine. Mommy just beat me up again."

Lucas and Madison giggled as he tickled them and set them down.

Maddy looked at him over the counter, and something passed between them. She smiled. She knew the old wound bothered him sometimes and was proud he bore it. He had come back for her.

"How 'bout a little sugar for Grandpa?" Mike McClaughlin said, and reached out for his grandkids. They laughed and jumped in his lap, hugging him. Sara smiled as she helped set the table. Jake's life was good.

* * *

After The Incident, as Jake liked to call it, Jake and Bodey had been discharged from their respective hospitals on the same day. Since Bodey was unable to fly home just yet, Sara and Mike welcomed the two into their home while they convalesced for a couple of weeks. Jake was just glad he had his friend with him.

When Jake had returned to the lab six weeks later, everything was as he had left it. Except for the bodies someone had removed. The media had been informed that an industrial accident had occurred, but no one had been injured. Since the exterior of the building remained intact and they had not been allowed inside, the interest eventually waned and they moved on to more captivating stories. Someone had covered their tracks very well. Jake never heard anything about The General, Morris, Johnson, Jane, or Pierce. He didn't even know if those were their real names.

In Sanibel, reports of an earthquake by a few residents had been dismissed as a hoax and soon forgotten.

Peter also vanished into thin air.

Jake had been almost certain he didn't make it, and when the police had finished their report of Bodey's shooting by some unknown mugger, nothing was ever mentioned about Peter or any of the other operatives Jake knew had been in the lab.

A year after The Incident, Jake received a postcard from Afghanistan. No return address, no writing, nothing. Just the card. Jake didn't know anyone in Afghanistan.

Teri was the only problem and Jake felt like her memory had been betrayed.

Someone had moved Teri's body to her apartment and set it up to look like she had been shot during a home invasion. Of course the police had no leads, only the fact they knew the body had been moved, but from where, they did not have a clue. Jake didn't make the funeral since he had still been in the hospital, but he knew Teri didn't mind. He had his own special connection with her that no one could take away.

Jake and Maddy eventually rebuilt the lab, and Bodey had helped get Andee up and running again. The only difference was they never used the disc. It had been a promise Jake had made to Beth, Teri, and himself and he never meant to break that promise.

Eventually a new Government organization came around like Jake knew they would and he took their money knowing full well he would never be able to give them what they wanted. At least not all of it. He also wanted to be sure no one else developed Andee beyond what he knew she could do. It was the only way to protect her.

Andee could still read minds and Jake and Maddy developed a system in which they could get the information from someone's head just by using a little psychology and some tact. This kept the government happy and Andee safe and under control. Jake was proud he was able to help thwart some pretty scary plans by some pretty awful people. It didn't even bother him that no one would ever know about them.

* * *

Frank opened the door and took an involuntary step backwards. "You!" Frank said.

"May I come in?"

"No. You'll just kill us when you get in here."

"You'd be dead already if that was my intention."

"What do you want?"

"Please—can we talk inside. I'd feel much more comfortable if our conversation was not overheard by every neighbor within shouting distance."

Frank hesitated. The man frightened him, but he'd been scared before. Eve, on the other hand, would be terrified.

"No. We'll talk around back."

Frank stepped outside, closed the door and walked around the side of the house to the backyard. He opened the gate and led the way around the pool to a small gazebo painted an off white and overgrown with vines. He sat down and pointed to the seat across from him.

"Now, what's this about?" Frank asked.

"She needs to hear this also."

"No."

"Fine. Maybe you will tell her later."

"I doubt it," Frank said.

Frank watched the man sitting across from him and couldn't understand why he hadn't killed them yet. He didn't look angry, as a matter of fact he looked happy. Almost at peace. Maybe it was just the way he handled his 'job.' A killer who enjoyed his work. I guess he would find out soon enough.

"I know why you're here," Frank said. "And I'm not afraid."

"You don't need to be. I've already explained I'm not here to harm you. Only to talk."

Frank hesitated. "Then talk."

"I know you killed a man."

Frank winced. "What? What did you say?"

"You heard me perfectly. I know you killed a man. Thirty five years ago."

"Now, why would you say such a thing?"

"Mr. Lucas, I saw it in your NDE."

"My NDE?"

"Yes. Your Near Death Experience. I saw it that day in the lab. The day they put you in limbo." Peter Smith paused. "I was there."

"You were there?"

"Yes. I wasn't paying much attention to what was going on, until they played back your experience. Then everything was clear."

"What was clear?"

"You were the killer. You stabbed him in the throat."

"What do you want?"

"I wanted to thank you," Peter said, smiling.

"Thank me for what?"

"That man was my father."

Frank went numb.

A rushing sound pulsed in his ears and his fingers tingled at the tips. He was worried another heart attack was coming on and he started breathing quickly, panicking.

"Take it easy," Peter said. "It's all right. You did me a favor. I was going to kill him anyway."

Frank could not believe his ears. This whole conversation was surreal. None of this made sense. Only one thought entered his mind.

"Why?" He had said it out loud.

"Why was I going to kill him?" Peter asked.

Frank could only nod.

"He killed my mother. That day. The day he raped Eve."

Frank flinched like he'd been slapped.

"Yes, I know that too."

Frank's mind whirled. *How could this be?*

"He beat my mother with a baseball bat. I watched him. She never screamed. Never made a sound. It was like she knew it was coming and there was nothing she could do about it. She was resigned to her fate and chose to go out the best way she could." Peter paused, staring off into the distance, remembering. "Then he came after me. I was five. Quick on my feet but not quick enough. All I remember was the bloody bat coming toward me, then nothing. Later, before they told me he was dead, I was thinking of ways to kill him. Pretty tough for a five year old to think about, but I hated him and I was going to make him pay. I never got the chance."

Peter was breathing hard now and Frank could see a vein pulsing in his temple.

It was quiet for a moment, the two of them sitting there in their own thoughts. Frank finally said, "I don't know what to say."

"You don't have to say anything," Peter told him. "The man was evil. Everything about him was wrong. He even smelled bad, like rotten meat."

Frank nodded, "I remember," he whispered.

"He did horrible things to my mother and me, and I'll never forgive him. Ever."

Frank looked into the eyes of his victim's son. The eyes he told Jake he had seen before. Dead eyes. Only now, they were something else. Not evil, yet not kind. Something in between, but something that *was alive*. This man had changed and Frank could see it.

The man he knew as Peter, stood, extended his hand and Frank reached up slowly to take it.

"Your secret's safe with me," Peter said. "I won't be back."

Frank nodded, letting his hand go.

"Thank you," Peter said. He turned and walked away. Frank never saw him again.

* * *

The dream was bad.

Jake was holding Beth in his arms as the life flowed out of her onto the cold, black pavement. The night was moonless, yet he could see in the gloomy light. Beth was mumbling and saying things he could not understand and he bent his head, trying so hard to hear, but the words slipped away, just out of reach.

A large, jarring, thump shook the air, and the ground trembled.

Jake looked around to see, but could find nothing. He noticed Beth had stopped murmuring and the air went still.

He was afraid to see her.

He made himself look down, and Beth was staring up at him. Her eyes were ringed red against her pale face and blood trickled, black, down her chin in the weird light.

She opened her mouth and said, "Jake—the balance."

He sat up in bed, sweat drenching his body, not sure of his surroundings until he noticed Maddy next to him, gasping for air and holding onto his arm.

"Oh no," she said.

Jake got up and crossed to the safe behind the picture of him and Maddy in St. Thomas.

Maddy joined him as he spun the dial. It made audible scratching noises as he tried to focus on the combination. It had been too long since he opened it last and he had to run the numbers twice. Pulling the lever down and swinging the safe's door open, he found he was holding his breath.

The disc was gone.

Or so he thought. Maddy pushed her hand inside, moved a few things around and came out with a CD jewel case containing the software upgrade for Andee. Jake took a breath and Maddy smiled.

"I guess it was just a good old fashioned dream," Jake said, turning back and crawling into his side of the bed.

"You mean nightmare," Maddy said. "Thank God it was only that."

Jake snuggled up to her as she crawled back into bed, the nightmare slowly fading as they often do. The only thing that seemed to itch at the back of Jake's mind, as sleep overtook him, was the fact that he and Maddy both had the dream together again.

He dismissed it as he slowly drifted off to sleep, thunder rumbling in the distance.

He slept soundly the rest of the night, where dreams, neither good nor bad, left him for other less weary, slumbering souls.

ABOUT THE AUTHOR

Richard C Hale has worn many hats in his lifetime including Greens
Keeper, Bartender, Musician, Respiratory Therapist, and veteran Air
Traffic Controller. You can usually find him controlling Air Traffic
over the skies of the Southeastern U.S. where he lives with his wife
and children.
Drop by his website and give him a shout. He'd love to hear from
you.
www.richardchaleauthor.com

7364049R00185

Printed in Great Britain
by Amazon.co.uk, Ltd.,
Marston Gate.